AN ACT OF WAR

by

MICHAEL K. McMAHAN

ISBN: 0615793339
ISBN 13: 9780615793337

Library of Congress Control Number: 2013905995
CreateSpace Independent Publishing Platform
North Charleston, South Carolina

Dedication

An Act of War *is dedicated to General (Retired) Barry R. McCaffrey and First Sergeant (Retired) Emerson E. Trainer, two of the bravest and finest men I know. They shaped my life when I was a young soldier and had a profound influence on me for all that followed.*

The book is also dedicated to the memory of General Creighton W. Abrams, Jr. (1914 -1974), a soldier of another time who served our country with honor and distinction. General Abrams was handed the difficult job of scaling down America's role in a losing war, a task he performed with great competence and dignity.

Prologue

Two Miles Southeast of the Parrot's Beak
Republic of South Vietnam
22 February 1969

SAT ON MY HELMET, QUIET AND STILL. Every muscle in my body ached or quivered like a marathon runner's legs on the last mile. For the past twenty-seven days my men and I had been bounced like the steel balls of a pinball machine from one firefight to the next, up and down the Cambodian border. My only pair of grimy jungle fatigues clung to my thighs and back like a wet bathing suit. My hands and arms were darkened and streaked by rich subtropical soil, and my fingernails were blackened crescents that a bayonet no longer cleaned. The eyes that stared back at me from the tiny mirror of my Army compass had shadows beneath them like the dark side of a half moon on a clear night in the Carolinas. I needed a shave as badly as I needed a haircut.

Still, like six other grunts in my platoon, I had raised my hand to volunteer for night ambush duty.

Volunteering for the night ambush squad was not the zealous act of an FNG. Even "fucking new guys" knew the risks of a night outside the company's defensive perimeter, where you could get your throat slit if you fell asleep, or your face blown off by a Claymore mine reversed by an unseen enemy. But night ambush squads, when they returned at dawn, got a day off at base camp, a clean towel and wash cloth, a small bar of soap, a steel pot full of clean water to wash up and shave, clean fatigues, a haircut, a hot meal, and sleep—sweet, sweet sleep.

As the only officer, I was in charge, but I knew better than to push these men or even myself. Pushing grizzled veterans like us was like pushing a wagon with a rope. Unlike the fresh, wide-eyed FNGs in their new fatigues and rucksacks filled with underwear, socks, and C-rations, we carried only the essentials—water, dehydrated meals, grenades, and ammo, lots of ammo. We knew too much. It was all crap to us now. We saw ourselves as pawns on the great chessboard of life. We no longer fought for country or honor. We fought to stay alive and to keep our buddies alive.

Death had laced its cold fingers into and through the fabric of our lives. We had carried too many young men out of the jungle, tied dog tags into too many boots, and zipped up too many body bags. We shared the distant stare of soldiers who were too often too close to the chilling crack of enemy small-arms fire. We knew that life and the loss of it were random. The tools of combat have no capacity for selection. Bullets, rockets, mortar rounds, and grenades are mindless objects. They have no conscience. If they hit you, they hit you. Fight long enough, and you will get hit. When your time is up, your time is up.

We were dead men walking long before the term was coined. We had breathed too much cordite and racked too many magazines of ammunition into our weapons. Our body bags were waiting. It was just a matter of time. The six other volunteers knew it. I knew it, too.

~~~

I called the men together about 1600 hours, 4:00 p.m. civilian time. I had broken down and scattered the parts of my .45-caliber pistol on a sandbag. I had an intimate relationship with this weapon. The old M1911 Colt .45, first put in service in 1911, had a relatively slow muzzle velocity. It fired a bullet the size of a man's thumb. Not meant for distant combat, it was an up-close-and-personal weapon, perfect for the close-in combat of Vietnam. It had replaced the .38-caliber pistols that Teddy Roosevelt found would not stop a charging enemy soldier in the Spanish-American War. The .45-caliber bullet did not slice into and through the enemy's body. It slammed into them with the force of a giant fist, pulverizing body tissue and knocking them down hard, like David's stone. I had qualified as "expert" with the .45, earning the best score in my officer's training class.

"Everybody clean their weapon today?" I asked—a question, not an order.

"Before we leave," Ferguson said.

The others nodded.

"Okay, let's leave in ninety minutes," I said. "It will take about an hour to get to the river." I tried to keep it friendly and low key. "No steel pots, just jungle hats. Everybody paint up good." *Paint* was the camouflage makeup worn on missions like this one. "See you in an hour and a half."

They all returned to their makeshift bunkers.

~~~

We snaked our way through the lush undergrowth of the jungle, each man about three meters in front of and behind the other, like tiny box-cars on a short train. Intel reports said that North Vietnamese regular army units, NVA for short, were moving men and supplies along a small stream that flowed from Cambodia into South Vietnam. I set up the ambush on a gentle slope overlooking a sharp turn in the narrow river. Positioning an M-60 machine gun up front, I put a man with a grenade launcher on each flank. The others lay on their bellies, M-16s ready to fire at anything that moved.

I set my field radio on silenced mode. I carried no weapon other than my freshly cleaned .45-caliber pistol. Contact with the enemy would find me calling in artillery and mortar fire. If the fighting got close enough that I needed an M-16, I could count on one or more lying on the ground nearby.

It was late February, and by 1830 hours it was dark in the thick jungle. Though we couldn't feel them, we knew that bloodsucking leeches were attaching themselves to our bodies. We would burn them off in the morning light when we returned to our unit. For now, it was just a matter of being perfectly still and quiet for twelve hours or until a target of opportunity emerged.

~~~

The full moon lit the river like a Las Vegas boulevard. We could hear the water's current and the occasional sounds of small nocturnal animals. Mosquitoes buzzed around us like miniature airplanes, looking for a place to strike. We kept them at bay with the repellent we reapplied throughout the night. We were experienced soldiers. We waited and watched. But no NVA moved on the river that night. It was a dry hole.

~~~

At 0630 hours, I broke up the ambush and quietly ordered the men to head in the direction of our unit. An hour would be needed to cover the short distance through the thick brush.

Sergeant Rick Dixon walked point, then Specialist Manny Hernandez behind Dixon. I followed Hernandez, the radio strapped to my back. The other four grunts, Bishop, Dawson, Alvarez, and Ferguson, brought up the rear.

The morning sun had just taken us out of the pre-dawn gloom when Dixon raised his fist, signaling us to freeze. Hernandez dropped quickly and silently to one knee. He raised his M-16 to his shoulder.

I pulled the Colt .45 from my shoulder holster, cocked it, and held it by my side, pointed at the ground. No one moved.

Dixon stood and waved us forward.

Hernandez advanced cautiously.

I had taken one slow step when I saw an enemy soldier in an NVA uniform and pith helmet just ten meters to my left. He pulled the string on a Chicom grenade and threw it toward the squad. The grenade fell four feet in front of Hernandez.

I turned and fired three times, catching the enemy soldier in the chest and driving him back and down into the thick jungle foliage.

Hernandez yelled, "Grenade!" at the same time I was firing.

The men all dived flat on their stomachs away from the grenade, but the grenade didn't explode. It was a dud.

After a minute that seemed like an hour, I stood in the waist-high elephant grass and advanced toward the enemy soldier's body. He lay on his back, his open eyes staring at nothing. Two of the three rounds I had fired caught him squarely in the center of the chest, killing him almost instantly.

I swung the field radio off my shoulders and motioned Hernandez over. I pointed him down a trail where he set up watch while I examined the body. It was obviously an NVA officer, probably the equivalent of a major in the US Army. Inside his jacket was a large map of the area with indications of NVA units not far from our position, mostly in Cambodia. I stuffed the map in one of the wide pockets of my jungle fatigues. I also found a wallet with money and pictures, including one that showed the dead officer standing behind a small boy with his arm around a young woman—a family photo.

I laid the wallet on the soldier's chest. That's when I saw the boy. He could not have been more than ten years old. He lay trembling in the underbrush, just a few feet from the body, his face streaked with tears.

I stripped a small pistol and two grenades from the officer's body. As I pulled the radio back on my shoulders, I picked up the fallen officer's pith helmet. It was practically new and had a red star in the middle front. I thought I could keep it as a souvenir and take it back to the States. I reorganized the men and motioned for Hernandez to recover.

We left the body on the trail, an act of professional courtesy among combatants. The dead soldier's comrades would find the body, then bury or cremate it. We headed back to camp without further incident.

~~~

An hour later, we stood naked in a circle and used lighted cigarettes to burn the leeches off our backs and legs as we waited for the mail and water choppers that would take us to base camp. Once I was cleared of the bloodsucking parasites, I pulled my filthy fatigues back on and reported to the company commander, Captain Walt Bradley. I gave Bradley the map I had recovered from the North Vietnamese officer's body. When I asked him if I could keep the pith helmet, he said I could.

Bradley was excited about the map and immediately called battalion HQ. He suggested that I be written up for a commendation, but I told him I had enough medals already, and all I wanted was to get to base camp for a day off. I said nothing about the boy.

~~~

As I was boarding the last helicopter to base camp, I saw Captain Bradley jogging in my direction, breathing hard and clearly upset.

"Why didn't you tell me about the boy?" Bradley screamed above the noise of the Huey.

I didn't respond.

"Ferguson said that Hernandez told him there was a small boy with the man you shot."

I nodded.

"You know, Sergeant McDaniels was killed by a twelve-year-old boy in Saigon."

"Can I go, sir?"

"You can go, but we need to talk about this when you get back. I'm sorry, but I have no choice but to write you up. You withheld vital information. Do you understand?"

I nodded and climbed into the chopper. Getting written up probably meant some type of disciplinary action, maybe an Article 15, and it would follow me the rest of my military career or until the bullet with my name on it found me. I was betting on the bullet. Career was the last thought on my mind in February 1969.

The man I had killed may have been the kid's father. That was bad enough. Compounding the injury by bringing the kid in, knowing he would end up in the hands of ARVN troops, was not anything I wanted on my conscience. The Army of the Republic of Vietnam was thoroughly corrupt, profoundly incompetent, and incredibly cruel. I would take the Article 15, no problem. Better to take the military punishment than to see a young boy turned over to the ARVN.

Chapter 1

"**I**'M NOT GOING TO SUGARCOAT THIS," Dr. Bill McClendon said. "I've been an ophthalmologist for thirty-five years, and I'm pretty sure what you're dealing with is some type of brain tumor. It's not your eyes. Not directly, anyway. I don't think it's a tumor attached to your optic nerve. Those are more common in children. But the headaches you describe, starting in the morning, waking you from sleep, and the blurred vision that sometimes follows… well, that sounds like some type of brain tumor to me."

"So, brain cancer?" I said.

"Not necessarily. Could be benign. If it's malignant, it certainly could be treatable. But you need to see a neurologist. I'd like to refer you to Dan Gunter. He's good, and he'll make seeing you a priority."

"You mean Phil Gunter's son, Danny?" I sat forward in my seat.

"Yes. Dan is an exceptional neurologist, highly respected."

"I can't believe he's old enough to be a doctor, much less a neurologist. I remember him as a skinny little kid who played football with my son, Brad."

"Well, he's grown up now and very accomplished." McClendon seemed irritated. "We're lucky to have him here in Darden. I'm sure he could have gone to a much larger community—anywhere he wanted, really."

"I didn't mean anything by it." I shrugged nonchalantly. "He just seems awful young to be fiddling around with people's brains, especially mine."

McClendon laughed. "Well, hell, the doctors look young because we're getting older. Fact of life. Can you see Dan next week? I've already called. He wants you to get an MRI on your spine and brain before you come in. I've got that set for Monday, and you would see him on Tuesday."

"You're serious about this, aren't you?"

"Look, my friend, this is serious." He put down the papers he was holding, removed his reading glasses, and looked directly at me. "The sooner you find out what's wrong, the sooner you can decide what to do about it."

"Bill, you're a good friend, a longtime friend. I trust you completely. But I'll tell you one damn thing. I'm not going to put myself or my family through what we went through with Claire. She was young and wanted to see more of our children's lives. She wanted to hold her grandchildren, and thank God, she did get to hold both of our granddaughters, but the boys came a little too late. She went through ten years of chemotherapy, hope and disappointment, up and down… mostly down. I drove her to the hospital when Jackie was born. Claire was bald and weighed eighty pounds. It was near the end for her. She didn't even wear a wig. She held Jackie and little Megan, who was just eighteen months old. I have a picture of it I carry in my wallet. She died two days later." Tears ran down my cheeks. "I'm not doing that, Bill. I'm not putting my kids through that, any of it. If it's my time to go, I'll go. No problem. But I won't do chemo. End of story."

McClendon nodded. "I understand. But at least find out what's wrong. Then you can decide on treatment, or not. Your decision. Be at the hospital diagnostic center at 7:00 a.m. on Monday morning. You need to fill this prescription and follow these directions prior to the procedure." He handed me a small piece of paper and a one-page letter telling me what to do, and where and when to arrive for the procedure.

As I left the office, memories of Claire and her suffering filled my mind.

~~~

Sergeant First Class Brad Kelly scanned the nearby hills with his binoculars. He stood behind a shallow bunker with two grunts lying on their bellies like young brothers in invisible twin beds. The stocks on their M4 carbines were extended, sights trained on the flat, dusty landscape that faded into hills and rose to jagged mountains in eastern Afghanistan. They were just three miles west of Pakistan. Night brought mortar and rocket fire from the nearby hills. Brad was preparing his defensive artillery targets so he could respond quickly and accurately to the enemy's nightly barrage.

His sister, Jen, had e-mailed him about the children, eight-year-old twin boys and two girls, thirteen and fourteen. The boys had been an accident, as she often said. But the tragic irony of it was a wound on her heart that could never fully heal. The father of her children was killed six months before the boys were born, crushed in his car by a drunk in a pickup truck. Her children idolized their Uncle Brad. He spent as much time with them as he could between deployments.

Brad's short-timer's calendar was down to weeks and days now, with black marks blotting out the fifteen months of his third hardship tour—one in Iraq and now two in the dusty hellhole that was Afghanistan.

"Firestorm four niner, give me one Willie Pete, up one hundred on fire target three, over," Brad called into his field radio.

A minute later, the white phosphorous round exploded in a puff of white smoke one hundred meters above the designated target.

"Firestorm four niner, give me one round of Hotel Echo on fire target three, over." He asked for a high explosive round on the ground on the now-confirmed target.

Brad continued locking in his targets. Once he was confident he had the areas covered well in the event of an attack of any kind, he relaxed and knelt in the bunker.

"Keep your eyes peeled on this area, guys," he said to the young privates. "If they come at us tonight, it'll be through that dry creek bed in front of your position."

"You trying to keep us awake, Sarge?" one of the men asked.

"Absolutely," Brad said before standing and walking back to the HQ bunker on the remote outpost.

Captain Tom Martin greeted Brad as he entered a large bunker in the center of the camp. "You got a call from Division. Your replacement is here tomorrow. When do you rotate?"

"One four and a wake-up." Fifteen days, in Army lingo.

"So you'll have a few days with him before you pack up and get out of here?"

"Just a few days," Brad said. "I can't wait to get home."

"I understand. Me, too. I'm two months behind you."

Martin had followed his father and grandfather to West Point. His father was one of only thirty-five active-duty four-star generals in the Army. At six feet tall and 180 pounds, he was shorter and slimmer than Brad. He had sharp facial features and buzz-cut blond hair. He and Brad had developed a close friendship over the past four months as they managed a two-platoon operation on the edge of America's presence in this province. Both men had seen more than their fair share of action here and in their prior duty in-country.

"I've finished my input on your efficiency report," Martin said. "I want you to read it before I submit it to First Sergeant Oliver for the final draft."

"First time I've ever been offered the opportunity to review my own efficiency report. Can I write one on you?"

Martin smiled. "I wish you could. I'd prefer you to some asshole at Battalion who has spent one tour in the Green Zone in Iraq and a second in an air-conditioned trailer in Kabul." He handed Brad the report. "So, is this it for you, or do you take it to twenty or thirty years and retirement?"

"I don't know, Tom. I joined the Army after trying to squeeze four years of college into six years. I was still a couple courses short of graduating when I dropped out. My mom died in 1997 after a ten-year bout with breast cancer. I sort of lost my way those last few years when she was so sick. I would just get in my car and drive home and spend a few days with her. Now I'm glad I did that. The sense of purpose I gained in the Army helped get me straight again. I enjoyed the training--basic and advanced infantry, paratrooper, and Ranger schools. I re-upped on 9/11 and have done three hardship tours. Being single, I thought it wouldn't be so bad, but I'm burned out right now. I may just take some time off and come back, but maybe not."

"You know you're probably walking away from a thirty-thousand-dollar re-up bonus."

"I know. But I've saved virtually everything I've made for the last twelve years. How could I spend it? I can go to work in my father's old business, a tool and die company. They make precision parts for medical devices, automotive, and oil rigs. It's a pretty big operation."

"Your father started it in the eighties?"

"Yes, but he's retired. Sold out to my uncle and some private equity firm. I don't think I could last there too long with him in charge." Brad stared across the interior of the bunker as he thought about his relationship with his father. "Don't get me wrong. I love him and I respect him, but we've had our differences. I was close to my mother, but my father, not as close. He taught me how to run a lathe when I was a kid. Probably illegal as hell. Worried my mom. I made money in high school making arrows for bow hunters. The machines are all computerized now, but I'm sure I can do whatever is needed."

"Remind me about your father."

"He's okay, but old school. Doesn't understand why I'm career. He was an Army officer, six years active in the sixties. Got out a captain. I know that much. My mom told me, not him. He never talked about any of it.

He hates the Army, doesn't trust the government. The Vietnam thing was tough on a lot of vets like him." Brad spoke as he dismantled his rifle and prepared to clean it. "My mom died a couple of years before I joined the Army. He was devastated about her and mad as hell at me. Stayed drunk four or five years, but sobered up after Jen's husband was killed. Jeremy was a good guy. He was T-boned by a drunk driver six months before the twins were born. Dad was there for her. Bought her a house just a few miles from his farm. Jeremy worked for Scotts, the lawn care company, and they got a pretty good amount of insurance, plus Social Security. She works some as a physical therapist, but with four kids, she has her hands full. Dad helps her a lot, I know. I want to be there more for her and the kids."

Brad clicked the last part of his clean M4 carbine back in place just as the first mortar round hit the hard Afghan dirt outside the bunker. Both men tumbled to the ground. It was a close, flat crack that sent deadly shrapnel several meters in all directions. More rounds followed. Each one was like a small earthquake. Next came the unmistakable sound of Russian-made Kalashnikovs firing on the perimeter, lighting up return fire from M4 carbines and M249 SAWs.

"Oh, shit," Brad muttered. He tightened his Kevlar breastplate, pulled his helmet on, and darted out to meet the Taliban forces pouring through the nearby hills.

Chapter 2

AS I NEARED MY CABIN on a country road that was lined with tall pines, I could see puffs of smoke rising from the chimney. Each puff looked like a wayward spirit on their way home after a long night spent tormenting the living. Since it was the middle of July, smoke climbing into the blue morning sky meant only one thing: Florence Johnson had decided to knock the chill off in the den and kitchen before cooking breakfast. By three o'clock in the afternoon, the temperature would reach nearly one hundred degrees, and she would be perfectly comfortable doing housework with no air conditioning.

My stomach growled as I stopped the truck a few feet from the blacktop, leaned over, and opened the passenger side door. Ralph jumped in for the short ride home, offering his characteristic yellow Lab smile.

I parked in the drive-through carport and walked to the barn to put some food and water out for Ralph. The dog lapped the water, but ignored the food and followed me back to the cabin.

"Where you been?" Florence said as I opened the front door for Ralph and myself. "Not out drinking all night, I hope."

"Good morning, Florence. It's good to see you, too."

"Answer my question, if you want me to put some more eggs and bacon on this stove." She stood in the middle of the kitchen with her thick hands on her hips, like a tired linebacker staring at the opposing team's quarterback. She wore a checkered apron over her size-sixteen blue smock. Her coarse white hair, clipped close to her head, glowed against skin the color and texture of old coffee grounds. Her big white teeth sparkled as she smiled through what was supposed to be a look of intimidation.

"I worked at the Boys and Girls Club last night, then went straight for a doctor's appointment. Is it hot in here, or is it me?"

"I'm just knocking the chill off. I'll put out the fire in a little while," she said. "Why you need to stay at the Boys and Girls Club overnight?"

"Summer program chaperone. My job is to watch the boys and prevent them from infiltrating the sleeping quarters of the girls. You know I haven't had a drink in a very long time. I'm not going back there, Florence. I promise."

"Well, that's good." She patted me on the shoulder and turned back to the stove. "Was that at the Kelly Center?"

"The Claire Kelly Center," I said.

"Go get cleaned up for breakfast, and we'll eat together. Ralph already ate."

"I figured as much." I smiled. "Thank you, Florence. I'll shower quickly." Ralph followed me to my bedroom.

~~~

Florence set two plates covered with eggs and bacon on the kitchen table. She also filled two large mugs with black coffee. I sat down and started to eat, but she stopped me with a hard stare. Then she bowed her head and said a short prayer.

Afterward, she picked up her fork and narrowed her eyes at me. "Don't you say grace anymore?"

"No. I guess I sort of got away from that." I refused to blink.

"But you help Josh at the Boys and Girls Club?" She finally smiled.

"Yes."

"And do you go to services on Sundays?"

"No. I guess I sort of got away from that, also," I said. "Most Sundays Ralph and I go fishing, or I sleep in a lounge chair in front of baseball games."

"Well, I suppose there is still some good in you, Travis Kelly, but you ain't perfect by a long stretch, that's for sure." She took a big bite of eggs.

"I thought you were coming tomorrow. Why are you here so early in the morning?"

"I came early to finish early, and yes, I was supposed to come tomorrow. My sister in Atlanta needs me to come down there and help her. She's taking chemo, and her daughter is out of town for a week at some kind of computer seminar in New Orleans, of all places. What was that doctor's appointment about?"

"Just routine. Tell me about your sister. Is that Alma? Where's her cancer?"

"Yes, Alma. She's five years older than me. Breast." She stopped speaking abruptly.

I put my fork down. "Sorry."

"It's okay, Travis. At least she's nearly seventy-five. It ain't like it was with Claire at fifty. That's too young to go home."

I had lost my appetite, but I drank the coffee and talked with Florence about her sister's prognosis.

~~~

Brad sat exhausted in the shade of a water trailer. The two-hour firefight had ended with three of his men KIA and twelve wounded, one seriously. Captain Tom Martin had taken a bullet through the lower part of his left arm and had been evacuated with the other wounded.

The brigade commander, Colonel Marsh Peeler, had personally brought in a reinforcement company. Brad watched as he spoke with the company commander and another young officer on the perimeter. Peeler looked in Brad's direction and said something to the young officer, then walked toward the water trailer.

Brad dragged himself up on unsteady legs as the colonel approached. Peeler was a square-jawed man in his late forties and solidly built—the poster child of a career Army officer. His balding head was neatly shaved, and his dark brown eyes burned with intensity.

"As you were, Sarge," he said as he approached Brad.

Brad remained standing but steadied himself with his right hand on the water trailer. He was a good six inches taller than the colonel.

Colonel Peeler put his hand on Brad's left shoulder and said, "Let's sit and talk, son."

Brad sat beside him in the shade of the trailer.

"How is Captain Martin?" Brad asked.

"It looked pretty bad. Left wrist. Just pray he doesn't lose that hand. If not, he'll be in for multiple surgeries I'm afraid—some serious rehab, but he'll probably make it okay."

Brad nodded but said nothing.

"I was a major when we invaded Iraq," Peeler said. He squinted when he spoke, as though he were pulling up a grainy black-and-white movie in his mind. "It was my first time in close combat. I was XO of a tank unit and got in several pretty good scrapes. I remember how exhausted I was after those firefights. Couldn't eat for days. Hell, couldn't sleep for days." He handed Brad a bottle of cold water.

"Thanks." Brad drank half the bottle without stopping.

"I remember how thirsty I was after getting shot at," Peeler said.

Brad nodded and took another drink.

"First Sergeant Oliver says this isn't your first rodeo."

Brad nodded again. "He's from Texas," he said, trying to smile.

"I'm writing you up for a Silver Star, your third, according to the first sergeant. My adjutant has talked to just about every one of your men. They say you would have been overrun had you not done what you did."

"It wasn't enough for the three and maybe four we lost," Brad said.

"You did your best, and based on what I see, your best is pretty damn good." He held out his hand, and the men shook. Then he stood and walked back to the perimeter.

~~~

Ralph and I were in the barn rebuilding a carburetor for an old tractor. It was mid-afternoon. Ralph sat at my feet in a supervisory capacity. I had built the barn a year after Claire died—the year I sold the business, before I built the cabin. It was more of a workshop than a barn, but I did have a tractor for mowing the grass on the property. The four-bedroom, three-bath cabin sat on the shore of a four-acre, spring-fed lake in Darden, North Carolina. The lake emptied into a creek that flowed into the South Bend River, which bordered the farm on three sides. I had supervised a crew of six Hispanic men who helped me build the cabin over a period of two years, using sturdy logs harvested from the three-hundred-acre property. I had lived in the barn for eighteen of those twenty-four months. Rejecting the idea of renting the property, I kept it available for Brad between tours. He had never taken advantage of it.

Ralph ran outside and barked as though he had treed a squirrel. I followed and watched a black sedan drive to the front of the cabin. The driver's door opened, and a tall, gray-haired man unwound from the vehicle. I had developed a headache and my vision was clouded, so I couldn't see him well.

"Lieutenant Kelly?" the man said as I approached the car.

"'Kelly' is right, but I got out a captain about thirty-five years ago."

"Sorry, sir. I'm Manny Hernandez. We served together in the 7th Cav in '69." He was a couple of inches over six feet tall, thin, with brown eyes and a shock of gray hair. He wore dark blue slacks, a white shirt, and a red-and-white striped tie, loosened at his neck. His suit jacket hung from a hook in the back of the car. A shoulder holster held a large pistol snugly beneath his left arm.

"Manny," I said, quickening my pace to shake hands vigorously with my old Army friend. "My goodness, it *is* you. My eyes aren't what they used to be."

Hernandez smiled broadly. "Yes, sir. It's me. You look exactly the same."

"Right," I said, my voice dripping with sarcasm. "You look good, Manny, but I would never have recognized you with the gray hair. You seem taller."

"Not taller, but maybe thinner. In spite of the heat and conditions, I still weighed more in Vietnam than I do now. I've been on a pretty bland diet for years due to high cholesterol. Your hair is still brown, not a trace of gray." He grinned.

"Only my hairdresser knows for sure. How about a cold glass of iced tea?"

We walked through the front door. Florence was waiting with a curious look on her face. I seldom had visitors. Actually, I had never had a visitor that I could recall.

"Florence, this is an old Army buddy, Manny Hernandez. Manny, this is a childhood friend, Florence Johnson. She's sort of like a first sergeant."

"Nice to meet you, ma'am," Manny said.

"And you, Mr. Hernandez. Can I get you something cold to drink?"

I said, "I'll get it, Florence. Any lemons cut?"

"Yes, and I just made a fresh pitcher of sweet ice tea. I'll get back to my work." She walked toward the upstairs bedrooms as I poured two glasses of tea with lemon.

"It's hot in the Carolinas," I said. "I assume you retired from the Army."

"Yes, sir. I made E-8 and retired about ten years ago." He took a sip of tea as we settled into chairs around the kitchen table.

"Manny, please cut the 'sir' stuff. I've been a civilian for more than thirty years. I'm just a retired small-business owner and part-time farmer. And call me Travis. That's what my friends call me, and you'll always be my friend."

"Yes, sir—I mean, okay, uh, Travis." He smiled and took a big drink of tea.

"How did you find me, and what brings you here?" I asked.

"Finding you was pretty easy. They gave me an address, and Mapquest got me here, though I got confused and made a wrong turn. You always said you would go back home after the Army. This is a small town. I just started asking if anyone knew Travis P. Kelly, and of course, everybody did. I'd like to say I just wanted to find you and see how you're doing, but I'm actually here on official business."

"Official business? I thought you were retired."

"I retired from the Army and got a job with Homeland Security just after 9/11. One of my old sergeant majors called me and made me an offer I couldn't refuse."

"Homeland Security? Fighting terrorists?"

"No fighting." He took a big gulp of tea. "At least, not so far. Just administrative and investigative type work. I've had to learn a lot, but I like it and the pay is good, especially on top of my Army retirement."

"Okay, so what brings you here?"

"Do you remember Captain Walt Bradley?"

I nodded. "Sure, I named my son, Brad, after him. We've stayed in touch. I just sent him an e-mail a month ago, and we spoke on the phone last week. He's helping me find somebody in Vietnam. You remember that boy?"

"Yes, sir. And I will never forgive myself for getting you in trouble about that."

I dismissed this with a wave of my hand. "It's okay. Long time ago. Anyway, I was trying to find that boy, now maybe a fifty-year-old man, if he's alive. I know it would be like finding a needle in a haystack, but I read an article about a Vietnamese man who claimed to be the grandson of Ho Chi Minh. In the story he talked about how his father was killed on a trail near Cambodia in 1969. He claimed that he was with his father when he was killed by an American soldier. I e-mailed the story to Walt, and we talked on the phone last week. Is that what this is about?"

"I don't know. I just know I was sent here to take you back to DC."

"DC? Today?"

"Yes, today."

"That's an eight-hour drive. I don't think I want to jump in a car and drive to DC in this heat."

"It won't be a car," he said.

Just then, I heard the powerful engines of a large helicopter in the distance. The helicopter, a Blackhawk, I thought, landed in a field in front of my cabin. I looked out at the big helicopter and back at Manny. "What's this about, Manny?"

"It's about General Bradley. He's dead."

Chapter 3

BRAD WAS IN GERMANY, near the Wiesbaden Army Airfield, on his way home. He stood under a warm shower, the third he had taken in the last twelve hours. He bowed his head so his six-foot-four-inch frame could absorb as much of the water as possible. Rivulets of water bounced off his suntanned skin like small-arms fire off an Abrams tank. He shampooed his short hair, then spread soap on a washcloth and scrubbed his arms, chest, and shoulders. He had not experienced the luxury of a modern bathroom since his last leave eight months earlier.

As he closed his eyes, however, he saw six men carrying three body bags to a waiting helicopter. Phillips, McDowell, and Esposito, none more than twenty-two years old, killed just over one week ago in his last firefight in Afghanistan. McDowell said he was engaged to his high school sweetheart. Phillips and Esposito had been on the firebase just three weeks.

"Damn," he said out loud.

His Army BDU—battle dress uniform—was starched, pressed, and laid out on his bed. When traveling, he preferred wearing BDUs to a Class A uniform, the Army's dress attire with shirt and tie, and a jacket with ribbons and citations. He dressed and checked himself in the mirror. In spite of the stress and toll of multiple combat deployments, he still took great pride in the uniform and the service. In addition to his sergeant first class rank insignia, his uniform also displayed his Combat Infantryman Badge, Airborne wings, and a Ranger insignia on his left shoulder, more than enough evidence of his commitment to his country, as well as his honor and bravery. He picked up his hat, slung his duffel bag over his shoulder, and turned to the door of the mid-level German hotel.

A bearded cab driver of Middle Eastern descent pulled to the front of the hotel. He met Brad at the back of the cab to take his duffel, and Brad told him he was going to the international airport. The driver nodded and got in the driver's seat as Brad slid in the back.

He squirmed in the small German taxi, trying to get comfortable.

Soon the driver spoke in broken English. "You American soldier?" he asked, glancing in the rear view mirror.

"Yes."

"From war in Iraq?"

"Afghanistan," Brad responded without emotion.

"Very bad," the driver said. "Too much killing in name of Allah. Not good. Allah not want killing."

"I agree," Brad said.

No more words were exchanged as Brad sat quietly, his mind caught up in disturbing thoughts. His gut told him something was wrong at home. Where was Jen? They had never been disconnected for such a long time during his deployments. He would often find multiple messages and photos on his computer after long combat patrols. If something was wrong with Jen or the children, why had his father not been in touch? Brad could not get these thoughts out of his head.

When the cab stopped in front of the terminal, Brad carefully counted out the fare and added a couple of euros.

The driver nodded and said, "Thanks. Peace with you."

Brad smiled. "And also with you."

~~~

Manny had left one of his men at my farm to drive his sedan back to DC. Our flight in the big helicopter took nearly three hours due to a strong northeast wind. The Blackhawk eventually landed at an abandoned airstrip in Virginia, and we had barely disembarked when it took off again into the northern Virginia sky. We walked together toward three black SUVs with darkened windows that sat silently near the runway like dark giants waiting in ambush.

A short, stocky man in a jacket and jeans emerged from the middle vehicle. "Mr. Kelly, would you please approach this vehicle and put both hands on the hood?"

I stopped walking and looked at Manny.

"Sorry, Travis, everybody's on high alert."

The officer ran his hands up and down my body and nodded that I was okay, but stopped me before I could step into the vehicle's open door.

"Sir, though I have searched you and found nothing, I have to ask you if you have any weapons of any kind."

"No," I said.

The officer stepped aside and allowed me to slide into the back seat of the SUV.

Manny, who had confiscated my cell phone at my farm, placed it back in my hand and walked to the trailing vehicle.

The seats in the rear of the large black Suburban had been rearranged in club style, facing each other. The engine was running, and the air conditioning cooled the humid Virginia air. An attractive woman with pale skin and blond hair tied back in a ponytail sat across from me. She looked to be in her mid-thirties. She closed the door after I got inside.

"Mr. Kelly, I am Deputy Director Stephens with the Department of Homeland Security," she said. "May I have your cell phone?"

I nodded and handed it to her. The vehicle started moving, and we were quickly traveling at a high rate of speed.

"You should buckle up," she said as she strapped her seatbelt in place.

I did the same. "What's all this with the cell phone?" I asked as I settled back into the comfortable seat.

"We have to ensure that you are not communicating with anyone. Can I ask what you've been doing for the past twenty-four hours?"

I looked at her without speaking. She wasn't very tall, maybe five-three, but she looked strong, with solid arms and a runner's physical confidence. She wore black pants and socks, black lace-up shoes with thick rubber soles, and a dark brown blouse with a thin black jacket over a Kevlar vest that was surely hot and uncomfortable, even in the air conditioning. Her blue eyes never left my face as she waited for an answer.

"Could I see a badge or some identification?" I asked. "I know Manny, and I know—or knew—Walt Bradley."

She nodded without smiling and reached inside her jacket. She pulled out a black wallet, flipped it open, and showed me a thick metal badge with her ID on the opposite side. It looked official.

I nodded.

She flipped the wallet shut and put it back in her jacket.

"Do I need an attorney?" I asked, my frustration showing.

"I don't know. Do you?"

"Look," I said. My face felt hot and flushed. "All I know is that an old friend from more than thirty years ago showed up at my house this afternoon, told me that my former company commander in Vietnam had been assassinated and ordered me, I say again, ordered me, aboard a helicopter which flew us to a deserted airport, where I was searched and put in the back of this vehicle. I understand about the need for precautions after an undersecretary of Homeland Security has been murdered, but I don't understand how this relates to me."

"Assassinated, as you first said, not murdered. Will you answer my question and tell me what you have been doing for the past twenty-four hours?"

"Well, let's go backward. Manny got to my house about four hours ago. We talked and got on that Blackhawk, and here I am. So that leaves twenty hours. From nine this morning to one this afternoon, I've been on my farm doing chores. I had a one-hour doctor's appointment this morning at eight, and just prior to that, I spent the night at the local Boys and Girls Club, keeping the boys and girls in separate quarters."

She was taking notes on a small pad. "Can anyone corroborate any of this?"

"Florence Williams, a good friend who helps me with housework and cooking; my ophthalmologist, Dr. Bill McClendon; and my friend Josh Bingham at the Boys and Girls Club. Their numbers are all in my phone, which you have. Do I need a lawyer?"

Stephens didn't answer, but flipped open my cell phone, scrolled through the numbers, and dialed Florence. They talked for a while, and Florence confirmed my story.

Stephens looked back at me. "Okay, sorry, but I had to confirm. You know that Undersecretary Bradley is dead." Dark emotion crept into her eyes, but she managed to push it down. "He was assassinated on the front steps of his home about 0700 hours this morning. Would have been impossible for you to have killed him. But we had to check."

I nodded.

"I was General Bradley's chief of staff. We sent for you." She paused. "I sent for you because we need to solve this puzzle."

"I haven't seen Bradley since 1969, probably May of '69," I said. "I've had very little contact with him until a couple of weeks ago. But we had stayed in touch, and I knew about his appointment to Homeland Security. Recently I read an article on the Internet about a Vietnamese industrialist, and I forwarded it to Walt."

"He must have been looking into this." She picked up a thick file from the seat beside her. "He had this with him when he was killed. It was stuffed underneath his Kevlar vest." She turned it around so I could read it. In bold letters at the top, it read, *Kelly, Travis P.*

"He was wearing a vest?"

"Yes, and he was armed. He must have been threatened in some way. He was taking precautions, but he was shot in the head from behind as he stepped out of his house. They searched the house, we think for this file. His wife—" she paused. "They killed his wife on the stairs. We think she heard them." The emotion returned briefly.

She gestured to the file. "This contains about every detail of your life. I read through it this morning. High school, college—everything. You volunteered for the Army and went to Officers Candidate School. Served in the 82nd Airborne at Fort Bragg, then Vietnam. Your first company commander was killed and replaced by Barry McCaffrey, who later became a four-star general and served in the Clinton Administration. You were later transferred to another company and served under Bradley. You did something of note off the record, not sure what, but it is noted in your official Army file. You earned about every commendation they gave out in Vietnam—Distinguished Service Cross, Silver Star, Bronze Star with V, two Purple Hearts, Air Medal, and on and on. Unbelievable. You went to college and grad school after the military. Your wife died in 1997. It's all in here. Bank accounts, investments, family details, grandchildren... Why would Walt have this, and why was he hiding it? Was he delivering it to someone? It doesn't make sense. Who would kill him for this file, if that's what happened? Is this just coincidence?"

I reached for the file, but she didn't offer it.

A sudden explosion shook the road on which we were riding, interrupting my thoughts. I looked through the windshield and saw that the lead SUV was on fire.

"RPG!" our driver said as he swerved off the road.

We bounced forward. I could see that we were heading toward a line of trees. Then we hit something solid and came to a violent stop. The airbag deployed in the front seat.

I was disoriented, but heard Stephens speak in a weak voice: "Get out."

My heart thudded in my chest as I unsnapped my seat belt. I reached across to do the same for Stephens, but she pushed my hand aside and did it herself. We climbed out, and I tried the driver's door; it was locked. I got back into the vehicle to unlock the door from the inside. The driver was groggy and his face was bleeding, but he began moving as I unhooked his seat belt. I pushed him out of the car. He stumbled blindly and sank to the ground. As I propped him against the vehicle, he pulled a nine-millimeter pistol out of his jacket and handed it to me. It was a Glock 17.

"Doesn't have a safety," he said. "Seventeen rounds in the clip."

I ran my right thumb over the place where the safety would be on my old .45.

"Ready to fire," he added. "Just crank one into the chamber."

Somewhere on the other side of the SUV, shots rang out.

"AK-47s," I said to Stephens and the driver as I cranked a round into the Glock.

Chapter 4

BRAD SETTLED INTO HIS SEAT on the Airbus 380. Though he had called, e-mailed, and sent numerous text messages, he still had received no reply from Jen. It wasn't like her. He was concerned. Perhaps he should call his father. That was usually his last resort.

A British Airways flight attendant approached him and stood in the aisle next to his seat. "Sir, there's a passenger who wants to exchange seats with you for the flight to Atlanta." She smiled down at him.

"I'm sorry," Brad said. "I really need the aisle."

"Quite right that you should. It's just that he saw how tall you are, and he wants to give you a seat with even more leg room, in business class. I think he's a former associate."

A small man in dress slacks and a golf shirt walked up behind her.

"Sergeant Kelly?" the man said. "I'm John Jeffries. I was Colonel Peeler's adjutant. We met briefly a couple of weeks ago."

Brad stood. He towered over the flight attendant and Jeffries, who looked to be about five feet eight inches tall.

"Yes, sir," Brad said. "Lieutenant Jeffries, right?"

"Mr. Jeffries. My four-year ROTC commitment was up a couple of weeks ago. I'm a civilian now. Please call me John. You're Brad, right?"

"Yes, sir. Brad."

"Look, Brad, get your stuff and take my seat, please. You're twice my size. I'll be fine right here." He turned to the people who were looking on as Brad gathered his gear from the overhead compartment. "This man is a real hero, folks. Not many like him. None that I know. Three combat tours. Three Silver Stars."

An older couple seated immediately behind Brad started clapping. Then others clapped as Brad followed the flight attendant toward business class. Some were standing and saying, "Thank you." He was relieved to find his seat and settle down.

"Can I bring you anything at all, sir?" the flight attendant asked.

"No. Just some quiet," Brad said. He shut his eyes and leaned back in his seat.

~~~

Deputy Director Stephens knelt at the front of the SUV while I knelt at the back, with the vehicle providing cover between us and the road.

A man dressed in camouflage shirt and pants came running down a drainage ditch in our direction. His weapon was on full automatic. He fired wildly toward our vehicle, hitting nothing and no one.

I waited until he was thirty feet away, then I stood and knocked him down with two shots from the nine millimeter. As I ran toward him, he raised the AK. I fired two more shots into his chest. I put the pistol in my belt behind my back, picked up the Kalashnikov, and switched the firing mode selector switch to single shot.

Two more figures appeared on the road above us, also firing wildly. I aimed carefully with the AK, shot one, and then the other. They fell backward onto the asphalt.

Stephens helped the driver stand. He wiped the blood off of his face with his sleeve and seemed to regain his vision.

I ran back to them and handed the driver the Glock.

"Let's get away from this vehicle," Stephens said. "Try to flank them."

We turned in unison and ran into the trees. Soon we found a wide trail that looked like a road for farm vehicles. Stephens ran fast, followed by the big driver, who seemed to pick up speed with each step. I tried to keep pace, but fell behind the farther we ran.

Soon they slowed and allowed me to catch up.

"They're following us." I pointed up the trail toward a clearing. "Take cover on that hill opposite the clearing. The sun will be at your back."

They immediately ran in that direction and slid down out of sight in the area I had pointed out.

I stumbled down an embankment from the trail toward a small creek and circled back toward the road. Along the way, I grabbed a handful of wet dirt and rubbed it on my face and hands, then took up a position lying on my stomach slightly below the trail. I ejected the clip from the AK to count the remaining rounds. There were ten. I reinserted the clip, and waited quietly in the lush vegetation about fifteen feet off and below the trail.

A few minutes later, I heard men approaching. They were loud and undisciplined, like buddies heading out on the town, not soldiers on a mission. I counted four voices. I low-crawled up the embankment behind them and saw that there were five of them—too many to handle. I could kill three, maybe four with luck. No way could I kill five. I had to let them walk into the ambush and hope Stephens and the driver could knock down one or two.

~~~

Nguyen Li Minh sat in the air-conditioned comfort of a rented sedan. A thick file lay open on his lap. He had watched the firefight from a distance and made an assessment that Kelly would survive. It was time to cut his losses.

"Airport," he said to his driver, and the vehicle immediately lunged forward. He called the pilot of his private jet. "We are going to Darden, North Carolina, near Charlotte. We will need two cars. Let me speak with Trang."

Minh's cousin, Quan Trang, answered.

Minh spoke in Vietnamese. "*Bạn và Trần sẽ đi với tôi. Chúng tôi sẽ đưa con gái của ông và bốn đứa con trở lại với đất nước của chúng tôi.*"

"*Được rồi,*" Trang said before hanging up.

A man of few words, Minh thought as his vehicle drove toward a private airport in Maryland. *We'll take Kelly's daughter and precious grandchildren back to my country and wait for him to come get them.*

He dialed another number. "Stand down and get out as soon as possible," he said to the leader of the ambush party. "I've got the file."

Chapter 5

WATCHED FROM THE COVER OF the forest as one of the five men answered his phone. He said nothing, but held up his hand and motioned that the men should reverse course. They walked back in the direction of the paved road.

A few minutes later, the two Homeland Security officers and I regrouped and quietly followed the ambush party. As we neared the blacktop, we heard engines starting up and vehicles driving away.

"Sounds like they're leaving," Stephens said. "Do you think they left anybody behind?"

"I don't think so," I said. "These men aren't pros."

"They looked like street thugs—Asians with new uniforms, but also dreadlocks and tattoos," the driver said. "And they were young." He looked at me. "I'm Tony Anello, sir. Thank you for pulling me out back there. Are you CIA or special ops?"

"No, I'm a civilian, but I've done this before. I guess it's like riding a bike. But this was too easy. These men had no idea how to carry out this kind of operation."

Stephens pulled out her cell phone and punched in a number. "I'll get backup out here ASAP." She turned to me. "I need to ask you to give me your weapon, Mr. Kelly. As a sworn law enforcement officer, I can't let a civilian carry a loaded assault rifle without authorization."

Anello looked at her and at me. "Ma'am, don't you think it would be okay for him to keep the AK until backup arrives?"

She hesitated. "Okay, but as soon as backup arrives, I need you to turn over your weapon to me."

I smiled. "Yes, ma'am."

Manny and three other men approached us near the first SUV. The vehicle was smoking like a doused fire at a campground. Manny reported that they had been pinned down by a sniper and unable to get away from the cover of their SUV. They saw the ambush party collect their dead and flee the scene in two black Hummers.

All the men in the lead vehicle were dead. They had been injured in the explosion and then shot at close range.

Manny, Anello, and I pulled the bodies out, putting some distance between them and the SUV in case of a gasoline explosion.

The first backup to arrive was local law enforcement. Three county sheriff's vehicles skidded in with sirens blaring. One of the sheriff's deputies grabbed a fire extinguisher and ran to the lead vehicle to tamp down the fire.

Engaging the safety on the AK, I handed it to Deputy Director Stephens, who was still talking on her cell phone. She smiled and laid it on the ground beside her.

Anello and I returned to the SUV we'd been riding in, and I scanned the back seat for the file. It was gone. In its place was a small note card with the numbers 22369 and 11.530982/106.463013 written on it. My cell phone was lying on the floor of the vehicle. I picked up the phone and put it in my pocket, but didn't touch the note card. When we caught Stephens's attention, we motioned for her to join us outside the vehicle.

"What is it?" she asked as she ended her call.

More vehicles were arriving, black sedans with darkened windows.

"The file. It's gone, I think. Look at this." I pointed to the card.

"Don't touch anything. Just wait outside. That's FBI. Let me talk to them." She walked over to one of the sedans as two young men were getting out. A minute later, they were carefully picking up the card with a handkerchief and depositing it in a clear plastic bag.

"What does it mean?" I asked Stephens.

"I don't know, but I'm betting we'll find out soon."

~~~

Stephens and I sat in the back of a sedan traveling at a high rate of speed on a rural Virginia road. We were quiet and still as though sitting at a funeral service. The sedan would take us to an FBI office near DC. After we had driven a few miles, I noticed that she was looking at me. She held her right hand in front of her, and it was shaking. I held out my right hand and showed her that mine was shaking, too. She smiled.

"Comes with the territory," I said softly. "Shaken, not stirred. Live bullets and steely nerves are a myth. If you don't mind my saying so, you were incredibly brave back there. Very professional."

"I got men killed," she said. "And my guts are trembling inside. I think I'm going to puke any minute. You seemed so calm."

"I was wired then, and I'm not calm now, as you can see. My guts are trembling, too. I won't eat for two days."

She took a deep breath. "How did you know exactly what to do? How did you act with so much composure with bullets flying everywhere?"

"I had some good training when I was a young man and great role models, men like Barry McCaffrey, Walt Bradley, and my first sergeant in Vietnam, Emerson Trainer. You just have to understand what the adrenaline is doing to your body, use it to your advantage, and decide, 'I may be killed, but I'll be killed doing my job. I'll fight well to save the lives of my comrades.' It's using your mind to control your body. That's all I know about it." I smiled. "Plus, I'm a lot older than you, and I probably have less to live for." I thought about Claire and my undiagnosed brain tumor.

"Thank you, Mr. Kelly," she said, her big blue eyes looking up at me through long lashes. "But honestly, other than this job, I don't have a lot to live for, sadly."

"You can start calling me Travis any time you like."

"Okay, Travis. Please call me Erin." She smiled. "You know you still have mud all over your face?"

I touched my forehead. "Oh, I forgot. That's an old Airborne Ranger trick, blend in with the environment."

"It's okay. You can wash up when we get to the FBI office."

We rode the rest of the way in silence.

~~~

In the bathroom of a nondescript four-story office building in Alexandria, Virginia, I removed my shirt and washed the mud off my face and arms. I studied the face and body reflected in the mirror. My eyes looked tired. Claire said she could always tell when I wasn't sleeping. "You've got those tired eyes," she would say. Her illness lasted years. I lay awake many nights listening to her breathing and praying it wouldn't stop.

As the mud coursed down the drain, I cupped more water in my hands and ran them through my short hair. I had never let my hair grow more than an inch or two. Some men look good with long hair, but I was not one of them.

Claire's friends sometimes said that I looked like Dan Rather. She would smile and say, "I think Dan Rather looks a little like Travis, but not nearly as good-looking." It always got a laugh. The mirror simply reflected a tired old man who had been through a hell of a firefight.

I studied my arms and shoulders. For a man on the low end of his sixties, my body was still in pretty good shape. No flab. No gut. No washboard abs, but my stomach was flat and hard. My arms and shoulders were not as robust as when I graduated jump school at the age of twenty, but I still exercised vigorously virtually every day. I could still bench press my body weight plus a few more pounds and had no problem with chin-ups or running six miles several days every week.

I put my shirt back on, looked in the mirror one more time, and returned to the conference room where Erin and two FBI agents were waiting.

"Water?" Erin said as I walked into the room.

I nodded and took the bottle of water from her, twisted off the plastic cap, and drank a long swallow.

"This is my second," she said, holding up her own bottle. "You look better."

"Please have a seat, Mr. Kelly. I'm Special Agent Bill Zeller. My partner is Special Agent Armando Guerra." He pronounced it "Gerra."

I nodded. "May I ask you something?" I said as I settled into a comfortable chair.

"Sure."

"Are all the agents in the FBI 'special'? It seems like on TV, they're always 'special agents' like you."

Zeller smiled. "It's a designation that relates more to the assignment than to rank. We're 'special agents assigned to Homeland Security.' Ari and I are certainly not 'special.'"

Guerra didn't join in the banter. He was all business and sat stoically as we talked.

"Mr. Kelly," Special Agent Zeller said, "have you ever been convicted of a felony?"

The question took me by surprise. "Why do you ask?"

Erin spoke up, gesturing to me. "This man just risked his life to save me and my crew. I'm not too concerned about his background, under the circumstances."

"But we're trying to figure out what is happening here, ma'am. Will you answer the question, Mr. Kelly?"

"Yes," I said.

"Yes, you will answer the question, or yes, you have been convicted of a felony?"

"Yes, I am a convicted felon." I looked at Erin and couldn't tell if she was surprised, disappointed, or confused.

Chapter 6

FLORENCE JOHNSON OPENED THE FRONT door of Travis Kelly's cabin at nine o'clock in the evening. She had driven toward Atlanta as far as Greenville, South Carolina, when she realized she had left her purse and, more importantly, her insulin kit on the kitchen table at the cabin. She found the purse, dug out the insulin kit, and sat down to check her blood sugar level. She gave herself three units of insulin and then decided, rather than driving back to her house and disturbing her daughter and the grandchildren, she would sleep a few hours in the downstairs bedroom and leave for Atlanta at about four o'clock in the morning. That would put her there in time to have breakfast with her sister.

Ralph greeted her as she returned to her car to get her small suitcase.

~~~

Nguyen Li Minh walked toward the three rental sedans that waited outside of the general aviation terminal near the Charlotte Douglas International Airport. He looked at his watch. It was ten o'clock, warm, and humid, not unlike his home country. He wiped his flat forehead with a handkerchief and got into the front seat of the lead vehicle beside Quan Trang, who would drive. The other six men had divided up in the following sedans.

"*Chúng ta đang đi đâu?*" Trang asked.

Responding in Vietnamese, Minh gave directions for the interstate and west to Darden County. He told Trang to drive carefully and observe the posted speed limits.

Trang nodded and did as told. The other vehicles followed.

Minh had programmed his iPhone first for directions to the home of Travis Kelly and then to that of Kelly's daughter, Jennifer Phillips. There was something he wanted to find at Kelly's home, something that Kelly had stolen in 1969. Then he would find and take something of even greater value to Kelly. He smiled.

~~~

"And when was this that you committed this felony?" Guerra asked. He was not, in appearance at least, the prototypical FBI agent. His face was round and marked by a losing battle with childhood acne. He had thin lips and slits for eyes. The white shirt he wore strained to hide his flabby bulk. Nothing hid his sneer.

"About eight years ago," I said, finding myself speaking to Zeller and avoiding eye contact with Guerra. "When my wife died in 1997 and my son, Brad, joined the Army, then re-upped after 9/11, I gradually migrated from a moderate drinker to an outright drunk. One night, in a bar near my home, I was pretty wasted when a young biker poked me in the back and started calling me 'hero.' I let it go a couple of times, but the third time he did it, I grabbed his wrist, twisted his arm behind his back, and slammed his face into the bar. Somebody called 911. I was walking out of the bar when a highway patrolman drove into the parking lot. I sat on the hood of my truck to wait.

"When the paramedics rolled the kid out, the patrolman came over to me and asked if I had broken the kid's nose and dislocated his right shoulder. I said I didn't know. A sheriff's deputy drove up. I got in my truck, rolled up the windows, and locked the doors. The officers ordered me out of the truck, and I refused. They broke the passenger's side window, unlocked the door, forced me out, and placed me under arrest.

"At the trial, everybody in the bar testified on my behalf, but I was convicted for resisting arrest and given thirty days in the county jail. I guess that qualifies as a felony, but I met a man there named Joshua Bingham, who had also been arrested for DSSWI."

"What's DSSWI?" Zeller asked. Unlike Guerra, Zeller looked as though he had walked off an FBI recruiting poster. Tall and slim, impeccably dressed, he resembled a young George Clooney, absent the prematurely gray hair.

"Doing Something Stupid While Intoxicated," I answered. "Bingham and I became friends and sobered up together. It turned out to be a good thing for me, but maybe not so good for the biker, unless he learned that you shouldn't go around poking old men in the back when they're about three sheets to the wind."

"You never killed anybody?" a sour Guerra asked.

"Other than today, yes," I said.

"When and where?" Guerra said.

"Vietnam, 1968 and 1969. Why are you asking these questions?"

Zeller spoke. His voice was smooth and deep. "Sir, the FBI was alerted through Homeland Security and the State Department that an e-mail message arrived in the DC offices of HS and State, stating that you have been indicted for murdering a citizen of the Socialist Republic of Vietnam and that steps are being taken to bring you to justice. We're not sure what those steps are, since we have no extradition treaty with Vietnam. Other than today or in combat, have you ever killed anybody, intentionally or unintentionally?"

"Indicted?" I said.

Guerra responded, "Yes, indicted by the highest court in the Socialist Republic of Vietnam, the Supreme People's Court. Have you killed a citizen of Vietnam?"

"When?" I said.

"Ever," Guerra said. "Have you ever killed anybody?"

"Yes, in 1968 and 1969, and a couple hours ago, I shot three Asian men who were trying to kill me and others. They could have been citizens of Vietnam. How would I know?"

"Do these numbers mean anything to you?" Zeller pointed at the card inside the clear plastic bag with the numbers 22369 and 11.530982/106.463013 written on it.

"No," I said. "Could be a code. What has five numbers? Not a telephone number or a social security number."

"A zip code, or how about a date of birth?" Erin said. "Mine is five nineteen seventy-two." She repeated it, one digit at a time: "Five-one-nine-seven-two."

A cell phone rang.

Erin and the two FBI agents pulled their phones from their belts like cowboys drawing pistols in a gunfight. Then they all realized the sound was coming from my direction. I pulled my old flip phone out of my pants pocket.

"Should I answer it?" I asked.

Zeller nodded.

I flipped it open and said, "Hello?"

Guerra held up a sheet of paper that said, *Put it on speaker.*

I pushed a button on the side of the phone that engaged the speaker and waited.

"So you survived the ambush, Mr. Kelly. I assumed you would."

The voice on the other end was strong and sounded like it belonged to a middle-aged man. There was a distinct Asian accent.

Zeller produced a portable recorder from his briefcase. He turned it on and held it close to the phone, recording the conversation.

"Who is this?" I asked.

"An old acquaintance. I'm on my way to your home to recover some property you stole many years ago, when you murdered my father. Then I plan to visit your daughter and your four grandchildren."

I looked at the others, not sure how to respond. "How do you know me?" I asked. "What are your intentions with my family?"

"I remember you well, Mr. Kelly. Very well. I won't hurt your family, but I know if I have them, you will come to me."

"I'll come to you without you involving my family. Just tell me where you are, and I'll come to you."

"Not so fast. I'll get back to you."

The phone went dead. I immediately punched the numbers to speed-dial my daughter, Jen.

"Hello," she said on the fifth ring.

"Jen?"

"Yes, Dad, where are you? Florence said you had been called out of town."

"Never mind that now. Are you at home with all four children?" I tried not to reveal the panic in my voice.

"Yes. What's wrong?" Now she sounded nervous. Her motherly instincts were kicking in.

"Make sure your doors are locked. We're sending law enforcement over." I tried to speak calmly, but I'm sure I sounded worried.

Her voice thickened, as if she were crying. "Dad, you're scaring me. What's going on?"

"I'm sorry, honey. Look, some crazy person has threatened me, and he might use you and the kids to get to me. But he's miles away, I'm sure. I'm going to ask the police to come over and provide protection. Just keep the doors locked."

"This sounds serious?" Jen's voice rose higher. "Where are you?"

"In DC. I'll get home as soon as I can. Lock all the doors and check the windows. I don't think he'll hurt anybody. He's after me."

"Who is he?" She sounded a little calmer.

"I don't know. It has something to do with my time in Vietnam. Keep a phone in your hands and wait for law enforcement. I'm going to hang up to keep your line clear."

"Okay."

"Don't worry, honey. I'll get there as soon as possible. I won't let anybody hurt you or the kids." I knew it might be a promise I couldn't keep.

"I know," Jen said.

We hung up our phones.

Erin was already engaged, sending FBI from the Charlotte, North Carolina, office. "Address?" she asked me.

I gave her Jen's address.

"They'll get to her house in less than an hour," Erin said.

"I need to get home," I said to nobody in particular.

"It's after ten," Zeller said. "We can get somebody to fly you home in the morning."

"No. I'm going tonight."

"It's an eight-hour drive," Erin said.

"There's an airport nearby," I said. "Just west of here. I know it well. The owner of the FBO is a good friend of mine. I can call him and rent a plane from him. I can be home in two hours."

"Travis, let us handle this," Erin said. "We can protect your family."

"Am I under arrest?" I asked.

"No," Zeller said.

"Good. I'm leaving. I'll take a cab." I headed for the door of the conference room.

"Wait," Zeller said. "We'll drive you."

"And I'm going with you," Erin said.

~~~

It was about eleven o'clock on a hot, muggy night when we arrived at Manassas Regional Airport. Tank Willis met us on the tarmac. I had known Tank, the owner of the Fixed Base Operation at Manassas, for thirty years. He and several of his employees had even come to Claire's funeral. Six foot five and heavyset, he had gotten his name from his size.

He shook my hand and said, "I can rent you November 767 Charlie Alpha right here on the line, Trav. How long will you need it?"

"I'm not sure," I said. "Ms. Stephens is with the Department of Homeland Security. This is sort of official business. Maybe a week."

"Why didn't you fly up in your plane?" the big man asked.

"It's a long story. When I return the plane, I'll tell you, but we need to get going as soon as possible. Do I still have an account?"

"Of course. Here's the key. There are two headsets already hooked up. It's got a G1000, like your plane. It's full of fuel, though I know you'll do a preflight routine."

"Thanks, Tank. This is great."

Erin climbed into the front passenger's seat while I completed the preflight checklist. Soon we were bouncing down a taxiway, turning onto the runway, and climbing into the night sky.

Chapter 7

FLORENCE AWOKE WITH A START. She sat up on the side of the bed, pulled on a thin robe, and slipped her feet into her bedroom slippers. She stood, stretched, and ambled toward the den.

"Travis, is that you?" she asked in the direction of the upper floor of the cabin.

A small Asian man walked out of the nearest bedroom and started down the stairs toward her. He held some kind of hard hat with a red star on the front of it.

"Who are you?" Florence asked. "What are you doing here?"

"Sorry to disturb you," he said. "My name is Nguyen Li Minh. I thought no one was home. Mr. Kelly has been keeping this pith helmet for me, and I came by to pick it up." He descended the stairs rapidly, closing in on Florence.

"Well, you will just have to leave it here until he returns, I'm afraid. I can't let you take something from his home unless I know he approves." She stood her ground.

Minh pulled a knife from his pocket and snapped the four-inch blade into place.

Florence took one step back.

Minh dropped the pith helmet and pushed her against the wall, pinning her there with his left forearm. Florence instinctively put her left arm across her stomach as he jabbed at her with the knife. She felt the sharp blade penetrate her forearm, slicing through the soft tissue and muscles between the radius and ulna, and barely penetrating her abdomen. She screamed, slid toward the floor, and curled into a fetal position.

Florence moaned slightly when Minh pulled the knife from her arm and stomach, but she remained curled in a tight ball, her eyes closed. Blood flowed freely from her wounds, pooling on the hardwood floor. She kept her eyes closed, praying that the man would think she was dead or dying. She did not move as he picked up the pith helmet, stepped over her, and walked through the front door of the cabin.

~~~

I leveled the Cessna at 7,500 feet. I had not taken the time to file an instrument flight plan and was flying VFR, visual flight rules. The moon was full, and there was a ten-knot tailwind that would die down by the time we reached the Carolinas. When I had the plane in trim at about 125 knots, I engaged the autopilot and relaxed.

"The wind that slowed the Blackhawk on our way to Virginia has abated somewhat," I said to Erin. "What's left is now a ten-knot tailwind pushing us south. We're doing about 135 knots true speed. We'll be there in just over two hours. If the moon remains bright and the skies clear, I'm going to land at my farm."

"You have a runway on your farm?" Erin asked.

"Not really a runway, but a straight, level road. I'm sure I can put down there. I'd be more confident in daylight, but I think I can get us in there safely, even at night. Depends on how bright the moon is. Right now, it would be fine."

"Is there no other place to land?" Erin sounded apprehensive.

"I need to get to my truck. Plus, I'd like to get my gun. I have a con-cealed carry permit," I added. Suddenly I felt a headache coming on. I tried to push it back.

"I thought you had a felony conviction. How did you get a permit?" She seemed skeptical.

"I'm pretty close with local law enforcement. In fact, my nephew is a county cop." Closing my eyes for a few seconds, I reached up with my right hand and pinched my nose.

We flew several minutes in silence.

"Do you have any idea who this is?" Erin finally said.

"Yes," I said. "I know exactly who it is."

"Why didn't you say something back there?"

"I just figured it out. The number 22369 is not a date of birth. It's a date of death."

"February 23, 1969?" Erin said.

"Right. I was in Vietnam. I'm pretty sure that was the day I shot and killed a young NVA officer. There was a boy with him who could have been his son. I let the boy go."

"How would he know it was you? Why now, after all these years?"

"I don't know, but it fits. The man I contacted Walt Bradley about, his name was Nguyen Li Minh. That was a few weeks ago. I read a story about him. He said his father was killed on the Ho Chi Minh Trail by an American officer. He claimed it was murder. He said he was ten years old at the time. It fits. The place where I killed the officer wasn't actually on the Ho Chi Minh Trail, but nearby. I got in trouble because I didn't retain the boy who was with him. I let him go. In his mind, I murdered his father."

"But this was during the war," Erin said. "It wasn't murder."

"I shot him, and he died. That's probably all he needs to know. I killed a lot of people in Vietnam, I'm sure of that, but this incident has followed me all my life. I've never forgotten about that little boy, crying and trem-bling with fear. Minh claims to be the grandson of Ho Chi Minh. I don't know if that's true or not. But he is now a very wealthy businessman in Vietnam, which means he's a high-ranking member of the Communist Party. When I read the article, I thought it could be him. The age was right. So I contacted Walt and asked him how I could find out. He apparently did some research on it, and I guess it got him killed."

"And Mia."

"Yeah," I said, and we flew on in silence.

Finally Erin asked, "What about the other numbers?"

"Coordinates," I said. "Latitude and longitude in degrees, minutes, and seconds. I wrote it down and put it in my pocket, but I'm pretty sure it's a specific site on a map. See the GPS coordinates display panel in front of you?" I pointed to the electronic map on the dash of the plane. "I could program in those coordinates, and the plane would fly right to it. Of course, we'd need a little extra fuel."

"So it was the date and location that you killed his father?"

"Yes, if he's the son of the soldier I killed that day."

"Will my cell phone work up here?" Erin asked.

"Sometimes."

She dialed a number. I couldn't hear her speaking over the engine noise and with my headset on, but I could tell she was carrying on an animated conversation. She hung up and put her headset back on.

"What?" I asked.

"I called the Charlotte FBI office to get a report. They said they sent two agents. It should have taken no more than twenty minutes, but they haven't heard from them. I asked if they had followed up with local law enforcement, but they hadn't. I chewed some ass."

I handed her my phone. "Look, see if you can get a signal with my phone and dial seventeen. That's one of Brad's high school friends. His name is Michael Simmons. He's a county police detective. Jen is also good friends with his wife, Annemarie. Let me speak with him, if you can get him on the line."

After a minute or so, she handed the phone to me and nodded. I held it tightly to my ear, keeping one ear in the headset for air traffic control.

I spoke loudly. "Michael, will you send somebody to Jen's home? She may be in danger. I'm flying home right now. I'm about an hour away."

"What is this about, Mr. Kelly?"

"I don't have time to explain. But somebody has threatened me, and they say they're going to use Jen and my grandchildren to get to me. Can you get somebody over there?"

"I'll go myself. I'm on the way."

"Thanks, Michael."

I put my headset back on. "Michael and Brad played football together in high school. They're still close. He and his wife, Annemarie, live just up the road from Jen. He's big, like Tank Willis, about six-five and two hundred thirty pounds of muscle, even at age forty. I should have called him first." I pinched my nose hard again and closed my eyes, fighting the headache.

"Are you all right?" Erin asked. She hugged her arms across her chest.

"Just a headache. Are you cold?"

"A little."

I reached over on her side of the plane and turned the heat on. "This will warm you up fast. Let me know if you get too warm."

"Thanks," she said. "How long have you been flying?"

"I flew some in the Army at Fort Bragg, Pope Air Force Base, actually, before I went to Vietnam. Then I got my private pilot's license, maybe twenty years ago. I own a Cessna like this one, just a bit larger. I've got about two thousand hours."

"Good," she said. "Ever crash?"

"No. I'm pretty careful. No problems so far." I smiled. "Tell me about yourself. How did you get into this line of work?"

"I went to West Point and was a military officer for ten years, the last four in the Pentagon working for General Bradley. He was a three star. We worked for the Joint Chiefs. After he retired and got the undersecretary job, he asked me to come over. I'm technically still in the Army, but sort of have dual status. I'm a major, soon to be a lieutenant colonel, but working for a civilian agency. There are several like me."

"What was West Point like as a woman?"

"What do you mean?" She seemed offended.

"I'm sorry, I didn't mean anything. It's just, well, we didn't have women, other than nurses, when I was in the Army. I can't believe the men I served with would have done so well with women around, especially in combat."

"Women aren't supposed to serve in combat, but it happens." She paused.

"West Point wasn't so bad. It was worse when I was assigned to a unit as a young second lieutenant. Some of the NCOs and the other junior officers were shits, if you really want to know. But I just toughed it out and did my job. I got excellent efficiency reports and moved on and up. When I got to the Pentagon, it was much better, very professional. General Bradley was my mentor, and he sort of took me under his wing. I can't believe he's dead." She finally allowed herself to cry, and I kept quiet. "Mia, that was his wife," she said through light sobs. "Mia was like a mother to me. She was so gentle and kind. I'd love to get my hands on the bastard who shot her." Her anger brought her out of her grief.

~~~

About an hour later, I pointed to the multifunctional display panel and showed Erin how we were flying toward the GPS coordinates for my farm. "We'll be there in fifteen minutes," I said.

Once we were over the farm, I turned on the landing light, lowered the flaps, slowed the plane, and lost altitude. At eighteen hundred feet on the altimeter, actually one thousand feet above the ground, I circled the farm in a typical landing pattern, downwind, base to final with the flaps down and the power nearly off. I kept my right hand on the throttle to avoid a stall, maintaining a speed of about sixty miles per hour. At about three hundred feet above the ground, I lined up on a straight, level dirt road.

Erin took a deep breath and closed her eyes.

"We're doing just fine," I said, concentrating on the task at hand. I kept the nose up as the plane lost altitude. The stall horn beeped as the landing gear touched the road. We bounced a little over the rough sur-face.

I kept the nose gear up as long as I could, essentially allowing the plane stop itself. It was a perfect soft-field landing. My flight instructor would have been proud.

"Okay," I said, as I stripped off my headset. "I'm going to taxi as far as I can, then we'll have to walk."

I rolled the small plane up the road until I could no longer see clear-ance for both wings. I applied the brakes, killed the avionics, turned off the landing light, and turned the ignition key to stop the engine. "Let's go," I said, and stepped out onto the dirt road.

Chapter 8

IT WAS NEARLY MIDNIGHT. JEN stood beside one of Brad's best friends, Michael Simmons, in the den of her home. Two FBI agents in dark suits waited politely near the front door. They had assured her that they could handle the situation and that local law enforcement was not necessary. She wasn't completely convinced.

"Do you want me to stay?" Michael asked.

She looked at the two agents. "Do you mind if I have some private time with my friend?"

"No, ma'am. We understand. We'll just wait on the front porch."

They walked out of the front door and closed it behind them.

"I'm scared, Michael. Not so much for me, but for the children," Jen said. Her lower lip trembled just slightly. "You know Dad. He would not have called me unless this was a serious threat."

"Look, why don't I just stay upstairs with you and the kids, and we can leave these FBI men down here? Or, better still, why don't you pack up and come over to our house? We've got plenty of room, and Annemarie would be delighted to have you over."

"I . . ." She hesitated. "No, I think we'll be okay. Will you keep your cell phone on and next to your bed? You're just five minutes away. If anything happens, I'll call you."

"Are you sure?"

"Yes. It's probably nothing, and two FBI agents ought to be enough if it is. I'll call you at the slightest disturbance."

"Okay."

Jen hugged him like the good friend he was. "Thanks for coming."

He nodded and left.

~~~

I hurried up the dirt road alongside Erin. The full moon was still cooperating. It lit the road and surrounding fields like a big spotlight in the sky.

"You'd better get that nine millimeter out in case we have a welcoming party," I said.

She nodded, pulled the Glock from the shoulder holster, and cranked a round into the firing chamber. She held the pistol in her right hand, pointed at the ground. Her arm was straight and her trigger finger rested outside the trigger guard, angled toward the front of the weapon.

As we neared the house, I realized that Ralph had not come out to greet us. There were no lights on inside the cabin.

I led Erin to the back door, unlocked it, and walked slowly inside. I held up my hand, signaling her to proceed slowly through the kitchen. "You wait here," I whispered.

I walked quietly in the dark through the kitchen and up the stairs to a bedroom where I kept a pistol in a locked case. I turned on a lamp and was reaching high on a shelf for the gun box when I sensed that someone had been there. Then I realized that the pith helmet was missing from the closet. "Damn," I said aloud.

I worked the combination for the gun box, then removed the .45 and two empty magazines. I didn't keep the magazines loaded because the springs wore out over time, something I had learned firsthand in Vietnam. I opened a box of ammunition and poured a handful of bullets into my palm. I quickly thumbed seven rounds into each clip, slammed one of them into the butt of the pistol, and cranked one round into the firing chamber. With the safety engaged, I stuffed the Colt in my belt behind my back and put the second clip in a front pocket of my pants. I ran downstairs and told Erin, "He's been here."

"How do you know?"

Without responding, I ran out the front door and immediately saw Florence's car.

"What?" I said in shock, before turning back toward the house. I switched on the lights inside the den.

Erin stayed with me, step by step. "What is it?"

"My friend, Florence. Her car shouldn't be here." I saw wet bloodstains on the floor outside the downstairs bedroom. "Florence!" I screamed. I began to search the house, turning on lights, and found her in a downstairs bathroom.

"Is that you, Travis?" she asked from the floor, where she sat holding a large butcher knife in her right hand. Her left forearm was wrapped in a bloody towel and pressed against her stomach.

"Florence," I said. "You're hurt."

She was still bleeding, but not badly. "He stabbed me. I played dead."

"We need to get you to the hospital," I said. "Come on."

I helped her stand. As we walked toward the front of the house, I explained that Officer Stephens and I were on our way to Jen's house because we thought someone, probably the man who had attacked her, was on his way there.

"He said his name was Win Lee Men," she said. "I think I fainted. I need to check my blood sugar. Not sure how long ago it was. Maybe an hour."

"Yes, that's him," I said as we walked with my hand on her back.

"Look, Travis, you go on. I can drive myself to the hospital. I was mostly hiding in the bathroom in case he came back. I'm hurt, but I can drive. You need to get to Jen's house." She picked up her purse and dug out her car keys.

"I think you're right, Florence," I said. After she had checked her blood sugar, I helped her into her car.

I pointed to my truck. Erin and I ran quickly toward it.

As I got in on the driver's side, I saw Ralph's dead body near the carport. "Damn him," I said. "I'm going to kill this son of a bitch, I promise." I started the engine and spun out of the carport onto the drive.

When we got to the highway, I turned right toward Jen's house. In my rearview mirror, I saw Florence turning left, in the direction of the hospital.

~~~

I pushed the truck up over eighty miles per hour. "There was a pith helmet I brought home as a souvenir from Vietnam. It's missing. He must have gone to my house to get it. He surprised Florence there. What was she doing there? She could have been killed." I slammed my hand into the steering wheel, then reached into my pocket and handed my phone to Erin. "Dial 'pound one.' That's Jen."

Erin dialed the phone and handed it back to me.

I put it to my ear. "Come on, Jen, be there."

No answer.

I held the phone out and punched pound two, Jen's cell phone.

No answer there, either.

I decided to stop calling and concentrate on my driving, since Jen's home was less than three miles away.

When I got to her drive, I turned in and gunned the truck toward the dark house. I slammed on the brakes behind a dark sedan. I put the truck in park, pulled the old forty-five from my belt, released the safety, and ran toward the house.

Erin was right behind me with her nine millimeter out and ready. She ran hard, catching me before I got to the front porch.

The front door stood open. I raised my left hand to stop Erin. "Go around to the back," I whispered. "Be careful. Don't come in until I call you."

I slowed and walked carefully across the porch. I braced my back against the wall, then swung around and into the den with the Colt .45

pointed into the room. A streetlight illuminated the front of the house. I took short, cautious steps into the entry hall.

Two bodies in dark suits lay on the den floor. *FBI, not killed here,* I reasoned, due to the neat manner in which the bodies were laid out. *Must have been dragged in.*

I searched the lower level and was about to run up to the second floor when the phone in my pocket rang.

"Hello," I said.

"Mr. Kelly, well, you may know by now that I have your family. So sorry about your housekeeper and your dog. Collateral damage, I am afraid. Say hello to your father, Jennifer."

"Dad, it's a trap," Jen said, and the phone went dead.

Automatic weapons' fire rang out in back of the house, followed by several shots from a nine millimeter pistol. Erin was returning fire.

I ran out the front door and around the house in the opposite direction that Erin had gone. As I reached the back yard, I saw two men advancing toward the house with automatic pistols, MAC-10s, blazing.

I ran straight toward them. I knew that the MAC-10 was horribly inaccurate. If they hit me, it would be by accident. I fired twice, missing both times.

The men turned toward me and raised their weapons.

I took a deep breath, steadied the pistol, and fired two quick rounds. The closest man went down like a target at a county fair. I dived to the ground and rolled to my left, feeling bullets splashing the ground around me as I rolled. Stopping on my stomach, I took a deep breath and fired two quick shots at the second man. One shot hit the gunman in the leg. He staggered to one knee, recovered, and started to raise his weapon. I stood deliberately and walked straight toward him, firing the last round in my clip into his chest. The gunman fell backward with the automatic pistol firing toward the sky.

"Erin," I said as I turned toward the house.

She was crawling toward the porch.

I ran to her. As I turned her over, she pointed the nine millimeter at me, but I brushed it aside. I could see blood on her upper torso seeping from beneath the Kevlar vest. I tore open her blouse and loosened the clasps that held the vest in place. She had two wounds. One bullet had penetrated her chest wall and a second, though stopped by the tough Kevlar, had left a large hematoma the size of a man's fist on her chest. No blood from the second wound, but it had probably broken a few ribs. I pulled off my shirt and folded it into a compress, then lifted her back to look for an exit wound. There was none, which was both good and bad. The vest had stopped one bullet and slowed the other, but a bullet had penetrated her body.

"Glad you were wearing the vest," I said to her.

She nodded.

The vest had saved her life. She was bleeding from the wound in her upper left torso, but not too badly. The non-penetrating wound on her right side probably caused the most pain. I didn't touch it. Nothing I could do. On the other hand, I knew exactly what to do with the penetrating wound. I had been trained and had, unfortunately, done it many times before. First, stop the bleeding. Second, check the breathing pathways for obstructions. Third, call for help.

I laid her flat on her back and pressed down on the compress I had made from my shirt. She winced. I checked her mouth and saw that she was breathing fine. She was obviously in severe pain. I took out my cell phone with my free hand and dialed 911. As a volunteer fireman, I knew all the emergency operators. The fire station was less than a mile from Jen's home.

"Nine-one-one, what is your emergency?"

I recognized Sheila Rhyne's voice. "Sheila, it's Travis Kelly. I'm at Jen's house. A federal officer is down, shot, behind the house. Send paramedics ASAP."

"My god, Travis, is Jen okay?" she asked.

"No time to talk. Send paramedics ASAP!" I hung up the phone.

Erin was beginning to fade. Her eyes fluttered.

Shock, I thought. "Stay with me, honey," I said.

She opened her eyes. "Okay, sweetheart."

I pressed harder on the compress, trying to slow the bleeding.

She moaned.

"Pain is good," I said. "As long as you can feel it, you're still with me."

"Fuck you," she said.

"Just talk to me, Erin. Think of something pleasant. Tell me about your parents."

Sirens blared in the distance, getting louder as they neared Jen's house.

"Parents divorced," she said through shallow breaths.

"Boyfriend, brothers, sisters?" I said, trying to keep her talking and conscious.

"Sister. Sarah, in Richmond. Niece, two years old. Samantha."

"When did you see them last?"

She didn't answer.

"Erin, honey, stay with me now. Please stay with me."

She opened her eyes just as the paramedics rounded the corner of the house.

They went straight to work. They put a sterile compress on the wound and started an IV. I helped them get Erin onto a stretcher and into an ambulance. They put an oxygen mask on her and wrapped her in blankets, and I climbed into the vehicle with her and held her hand.

"Erin, if you can hear me, I'm going to call a high school friend who's a thoracic surgeon. He's the best in this area. He'll meet you at the emergency room. I can't go with you, though. I have to find Jen and my grandchildren."

She never opened her eyes.

Chapter 9

PULLED OUT MY CELL PHONE and called my high school friend, Dr. Mark Beam.

The phone rang seven times. When he answered, I said, "Mark, it's Travis."

"Travis, what time is it?"

"One or two, not sure. Listen, I just put a federal officer in an ambulance. Shot twice in the upper torso. One shot didn't penetrate her chest wall but may have done internal damage. She was wearing a Kevlar vest. The other shot penetrated her upper chest area, but I don't think it's too deep. They were subsonic .45-caliber rounds from MAC-10s at close range. She'll be at the hospital in five minutes."

"I'll be there in six," Mark said and hung up.

I stood in Jen's backyard for a minute, not sure what to do next. I decided to search the bodies of the men I had killed to see if there were any clues. As I was looking through one man's pockets, the other man's cell phone rang. I found and engaged the phone.

"Trang?" the voice said.

"Trang is dead," I said.

"Ah, Mr. Kelly, you are indeed a very resourceful person, a worthy foe."

"I'm not your foe. Where is my family?"

"With me and quite safe. Do as I instruct, and they will remain so."

"Okay, asshole, instruct," I said, nearly crushing the phone with my hand.

"No need for vulgarity, Mr. Kelly. We are quite possibly flying over Kentucky, I think, at this very minute. We are returning to the scene of the crime, so to speak."

I glanced up at the night sky. "Look," I said, "you want *me*. Just turn around, and go back to the Charlotte airport. I will wait for you there. Leave my family in the General Aviation terminal, and I'll go with you."

"No deal. Too many dead bodies lying around. Too much explaining to do. I am returning to my country. We are flying to Ho Chi Minh City without delay. We are in a new Gulfstream 650. We have an eight-thousand-mile range and can fly at nearly six hundred miles per hour. You can find your daughter, your four grandchildren, and me where you killed my father, over forty years ago. Your family will be well cared for. As you say, it is you I want. Please don't delay."

The phone went dead.

"Son of a bitch," I said. I tried to redial the number, but it was blocked. I didn't know what to do. But I knew I would follow my family to Vietnam, somehow. I ran back to my truck just as I heard sirens in the distance, probably county police on the way to Jen's house. Not too enthusiastic about engaging in a police investigation, I quickly drove away from Jen's house on my way back home.

I parked in the carport. My headlights illuminated Ralph's dead body. "Damn," I said. The dog had been shot in the head.

I scooped him up, carried him toward the barn, and buried him quickly in the soft dirt of a nearby pasture. "Sorry, Ralph," I said with the last shovel of dirt. We had been constant companions for the past ten years.

Back in the house, I took a quick shower to wash away the dirt and blood that covered my hands, arms, and torso. I threw the socks, underwear, and khaki trousers I had been wearing into a trash bag for disposal and dressed in another pair of khakis—my "uniform," as Claire used to say—along with a green golf shirt and a pair of work boots. I fired up my laptop computer and pulled up the British Airways website. It showed one available flight to Saigon that originated in Atlanta and had connections in London and Singapore. Though I would normally drive to Atlanta, I could save a few hours by catching an early-morning flight from Charlotte.

It was the best I could do.

~~~

Jen sat facing her four children in a soft leather seat on a luxurious business jet as it flew north and west. *Perhaps we're over Canada now,* she thought. As she scanned the children's faces, her love and determination to protect them nearly overwhelmed her.

"Okay, this is how it is," she said, keeping her voice even and calm. "We can be strong. We can look out for each other. We can make it through this, whatever this is." She nodded at them. "Megan, as the oldest, I need you to take over for me when I'm not around, if that happens. Can you do that?"

Megan nodded. She held one of the twins' hands.

"Jackie, you're next in command. You help your sister. I need both of you girls looking out for the boys and for each other."

LB spoke up. "But . . ."

Jen nodded to him. His name was Lawrence Bradley Phillips, but she called him "LB" so he wouldn't get nicknamed "Larry." Larry was the derisive name the New York Mets called Chipper Jones when he came to bat in the Mets' stadium. She loved Chipper Jones, but didn't want her child to be called Larry.

"Joe and I are eight years old," he said. "We can be strong, too."

Joe nodded in agreement.

"You will *all* have to be strong," Jen said. "I'm very proud of all of you. Now I'm going to talk to this man. You stay together right here."

Jen stood and walked toward the front of the cabin, where Minh sat with a middle-aged woman who appeared to be his secretary. Two small

Asian men sat in the back of the plane, watching Jen and the children. She didn't like the way they looked—hard and vile.

Minh stood as she approached. "Please have a seat," he said, gesturing to the empty seat in front of him.

"I prefer to stand," Jen said and crossed her arms. She was taller than Minh. She stared intently into his eyes. "There are two things you need to know if you are true to your word and mean us no harm."

"I assure you, it's true. I am a family man with a wife and two children. You will not be harmed."

"One of my sons—his name is Lawrence, but we call him 'LB'—is Type 1 diabetic. I grabbed his medical kit before we left, but we will need to resupply his insulin and testing strips. I have to check his blood six or eight times each day, and he gets four to six shots of insulin per day."

Minh nodded. "I will alert my doctor as soon as we arrive. You will be staying in a guesthouse beside my home. The doctors in the Socialist Republic of Vietnam are very attentive, not money-hungry businessmen like the doctors in your country."

"I'm sure they are," Jen said. "But this is very important. Life or death, do you understand?"

"Yes, I understand. There is no problem."

She turned and started to return to the children.

Minh touched her shoulder, and she turned back to him.

"You said there were two things," he said, smiling politely.

"Yes." She struggled to contain her anger, which boiled inside her at the sight of this man. "I need to tell you that my father is going to kill you. Though he has successfully kept it bottled up as long as I have known him, I always knew that below the surface, he was capable of extreme violence. My mother knew it, too, though I'm not so sure about my brother. It's there, however, and I can guarantee you that he *will* kill you. If you turn this plane around now and leave us at the Charlotte airport, I will ask him to have mercy on you. If not, you're going to die. That's a fact." She returned to her children with her heart pounding in her chest.

Chapter 10

OPENED A SMALL SAFE IN the closet of the master bedroom of my cabin. My head was throbbing with each heartbeat. The muscles in my neck and shoulders were tense and taut. Concerned that the county police would pull up in my drive at any minute and I would become thoroughly entangled in a complicated investigation, I moved with a sense of urgency. I had no idea what was going on in Virginia, if anything.

Like many naïve people in the late 1990s, I had accumulated thousands of dollars in cash just prior to what was then called "Y2K," shorthand for "Year 2000." This was the date that all the world's computers were expected to crash because no one had programmed them to function beyond December 31, 1999. Though I was still dealing, emotionally, with Claire's illness and death at the time, I slowly built up a stockpile of twelve thousand dollars in US currency and stored it in a small safe in the closet of the master bedroom in my home. I had not thought about the money for years, but now I reasoned that it could serve an important purpose.

First, I retrieved my passport from a small drawer in the safe and stuffed it in the back pocket of my khakis. Then I spread the cash out on the floor of the closet. I took a few minutes to divide the money into stacks of bills of larger and smaller denominations. To my surprise, I was able to make a relatively small bundle of eight thousand dollars using hundreds and fifties. I put the rest of the money back in the safe and carried the cash to the bed.

I would not create a record of my travel plans. I had memorized all the flight schedules and would simply show up at the counter and pay cash. In our post-9/11 world, paying in cash and carrying little or no luggage would subject me to more scrutiny by the TSA, but I would deal with that when it happened. I pulled out a rain jacket with lots of pockets that I had bought on a trip to Dublin. I broke down the cash and put it in six different pockets that closed with Velcro. I pulled the jacket on over my golf shirt, zipped it up, and left the house.

It was four o'clock in the morning. With luck, I could check on Florence and Erin and still be in Atlanta in just over four hours.

At the hospital, I found the office for the triage nurse immediately to the left of the emergency room lobby. The nurse on duty was Meredith Thompson. She was about twenty years younger than me, but we knew each other well. A few years after Claire had died and after I'd regained some sobriety, I ran into her in the grocery store. She'd told me that her rotten husband had left for the final time and she had changed the locks on the doors. And, by the way, if I needed anyone to spend time with, she had an extra key. But I never called.

I knocked on her open door. "Meredith?"

She looked up from a file and smiled. A good sign, I thought.

"Travis?" She broke into a laugh. "Too late. I got married six months ago."

I tried to smile, but I was too tired and concerned about Jen and my grandchildren. "Congratulations," I said. "Listen, Meredith, Florence Johnson came in here a few hours ago with a stab wound. How is she?"

"She's fine. Took a lot of stitches. They let her recuperate for a couple of hours and then let her go home."

"That's good. Also, a federal officer was brought in here, maybe an hour ago, with gunshot wounds to the upper chest. Mark was going to operate on her, I assume."

"Mark did operate on the federal officer. Do you know her?" Meredith's brow wrinkled in confusion. "Was this also related to Florence? What's going on?"

"It's complicated. I don't have time now to get into it. The agent is named Erin Stephens. Is she okay? Can I see her?"

"She's still in post-op, but I think she came through pretty well. Third floor. Elevator through those swinging doors."

"Thanks, Meredith."

I pushed through the doors and caught the elevator to the third floor. The nurse on duty in post-op looked unfamiliar, and I was about to introduce myself when Dr. Mark Beam walked up behind her, still wearing surgical scrubs.

"Travis," Mark said. He looked tired.

"How's the federal agent doing?" I asked.

"She's fine. Come on back." He turned to the nurse. "It's okay. He's family."

I wasn't sure whether he meant his family or Erin's, but I followed him back to a small room.

Erin was still sedated and had a breathing tube down her throat. She looked pale and small beneath a cotton sheet.

"The penetrating wound wasn't too bad or too deep. You were right about the non-penetrating wound. It busted her up pretty good—bruised ribs and some internal bleeding. I had to open her up, and she needed a unit of blood. But overall, she's fine. No permanent or serious damage. She'll be okay in a few days, but she won't be chasing bad guys for a while, I think. How long have you known her?"

"Since yesterday."

"Well, you've made an impression on her. She was calling for you before we got her fully under. I thought you were close."

"In a way, we *are* close, sort of like Army buddies. We've been through a lot in one day. Listen, Mark, I've got to leave the country. Will you tell her that I came by to check on her and that I had to follow Minh to Vietnam? She'll know what that means. I'll call somebody in her DC office and let them know where she is."

"Who are these men you're following to Vietnam? What is this about, Travis?"

"M-I-N-H. It's his name. In 1969, during the Vietnam War, I killed a young officer. His son has come looking for me. That's what this is about. He's gone back to Vietnam. Now I'm going looking for him." I didn't tell him about Jen and my grandchildren.

"Shouldn't you let the authorities take care of this?"

"I'm working with them. It's complicated. When it's over, I'll tell you the whole story. Thanks for coming in and taking care of her. She's a good person. I'm glad she's going to be okay."

"That's my job."

We shook hands, and I left the hospital.

~~~

It was a twenty-minute drive from Darden County General Hospital to the Charlotte Douglas International Airport. I decided to take the interstate partway and then Highway 74. I had plenty of time before the 6:00 a.m. flight to Atlanta, but I needed to buy a ticket and get through security. I accelerated down the on-ramp and pushed my truck up to about seventy miles per hour. In ten minutes, I turned off the interstate and onto a road that led to Highway 74. I got through three traffic lights without stopping, turned left onto the highway, and drove across the Catawba River bridge.

A heavy fog hung over the copper-colored water like white smoke over a doused fire. I was thinking about fishing with Brad and Jen when a black SUV with flashing blue-and-white lights closed in fast on my truck. I thought it was county police. I slowed, but before I could stop, a black sedan passed the SUV, pulled up beside me, and forced me off the road.

I wrestled the truck to a stop and was about to get out when a swarm of men with guns drawn ran toward me from both sides.

"Get out of the vehicle and keep your hands above your head," a large man ordered as he approached the driver's side of the truck.

I put the truck in park, opened the door slowly, and got out. Before I had closed the door, two men were on me, pushing me to the pavement and twisting my arms behind my back. I was in handcuffs and being dragged to my feet again before I could think about what was happening. I was pushed roughly across the hood of the truck and thoroughly searched. One of the officers removed my cell phone and wallet and turned me around.

"What is this about?" I asked as I gasped for breath.

"Are you Travis Paul Kelly?" a big man in a dark suit asked.

"Yes, and who the hell are you?"

"Special Agent Marcus Wahl, FBI, Charlotte Bureau." He held up a badge and identification wallet. "Mr. Kelly, you are under arrest for the murders of FBI agents Cedric Marshall and Timothy Swenson." Wahl read the Miranda rights that I remembered from my run-in with the law a few years back . "Do you understand these rights?"

Before I could answer, the men dragged me to the black sedan and deposited me in the back seat.

As we were driving east toward downtown Charlotte, I said, "Yes."

The agent in the front passenger's seat turned to look at me. "What did you say?" he asked.

"I said, 'Yes.' The big asshole asked me if I understood my rights. He didn't let me answer. The answer is yes. I understand my rights."

"Okay, you are on record as understanding your rights. Now keep your mouth shut."

I did.

~~~

Within ten minutes, we arrived at a tall building on Trade Street in uptown Charlotte, North Carolina. The car pulled into an underground parking deck. From my position in the back seat of the vehicle, I couldn't see all the security measures, but it took several minutes before they settled into a parking space. The driver stopped the car and killed the engine. The agent in the passenger's seat assisted me from the back seat and pushed me toward the building's underground entrance. I stumbled over the curb and fell to my knees on the hard pavement. The agent pulled me up roughly and led me to a bank of elevators.

When we arrived on the twenty-fourth floor, I was taken to a small room in the interior of the building and placed at the head of a small oblong table. I sat alone for a few minutes until Special Agent Wahl arrived. He had removed his jacket, and there was no pistol in his shoulder holster. I assumed this was so I couldn't wrestle it away from him. But Wahl was at least six foot four and clearly a devoted weightlifter. Besides, he was more than twenty years younger than me, and my hands were handcuffed behind my back. His pistol would have been perfectly safe.

"You've been read your rights. Do you want to cooperate and answer questions now, or wait for an attorney?"

I hesitated as I thought about this for a few seconds. "If you assholes had exercised a modicum of professionalism in arresting me, I might be inclined to be cooperative. But under the circumstances, I think I'll exercise my rights and ask for an attorney to be present during the interrogation."

Wahl smiled. "I don't think I have ever heard the words 'asshole' and 'modicum' used in the same sentence by anyone in this room. Okay, here's a phone. Do you have a lawyer?"

"Not the kind I may need. Can I call a friend who's a real estate lawyer and ask for a referral?"

"You can." He removed the handcuffs. "Call away. Dial nine."

"Uh, can I have my cell phone back?"

"Why is that?"

"My friend's number is on speed dial. I can't remember the number."

Before Wahl could stand to leave the room, the door opened and another agent brought in the cell phone. I then realized that they were listening and probably watching from outside the room.

"Get the number and use the in-house phone," Wahl said.

I pressed a number on my cell phone and read it, then dialed the phone on the table. In a few rings I got my friend and attorney, Horace Walton, at his home. "Horace, this is Travis."

"Travis, kind of early. But, hell, I've been up since four. Prostate problems. Can't sleep for pissing. Sometimes can't piss at all, which is worse. Are you okay?"

"Yeah, sorry to call you at home so early. Sorry about the prostate. But, no, I'm not so good. Actually, I've been arrested for murder."

"What?" Walton said, his voice rising. "Murder? Are you serious?"

"I am. Right now I'm sitting in a conference room in Charlotte with FBI agents. I need a lawyer."

"I'm a real estate lawyer. You need a criminal defense attorney."

"I know. I'm calling for a referral."

"So the feds have arrested you?"

"Yes, the FBI."

"Okay, and I assume they're listening to this conversation, since I'm not your attorney in this matter."

"Probably."

"Okay, let me think. In Charlotte, Joel Henderson with Polk, Davis, and Henderson. He's tried many high-profile federal cases. He's the best."

He paused. I could hear him leafing through some papers. He gave me a telephone number which I wrote down and repeated back to him.

"Right," he said. "Joel Henderson. Call him. In the meantime, I can come over and sit with you."

"No, it's all right. I'll call Henderson. When I can, I'll get back to you. Thanks, Horace."

Chapter 11

I HAD WAITED ALONE IN THE conference room for two hours. My head was throbbing and my vision was blurred. Without notice, a short, fat man in a gray pinstriped suit burst through the door. He wore thick, round glasses and a conservative red tie, and he carried a leather briefcase which, though new, was made to look old. His nearly bald head still boasted a few wisps of hair, which he had combed left-to-right.

"Mr. Kelly, I'm Joel Henderson," he said with a voice like a foghorn.

I stood to greet him. "Thank you for coming."

He pushed his glasses up on the bridge of his nose and sat down. "This is an engagement letter which I require my clients to read and sign." He pushed a piece of paper across the table to me. "If you will do so, then I am your attorney."

I read the letter carefully. It said that I would use the services of Polk, Davis, and Henderson exclusively in this legal matter; that I warranted that I would always be truthful with my attorneys; and that I would promptly pay any and all fees. There would be a $25,000 retainer to be wired today and an additional $150,000 if we went to court. I signed the document and pushed it back across the table to him.

"Okay, tell me what's happened," Henderson said, again adjusting his glasses.

"I think this room is bugged," I said.

"Not now. They won't jeopardize their case by violating client-attorney privilege."

"Fine. This is going to take some time."

"You have contracted for twenty-five hours at a thousand dollars per hour, so let's get to it."

I told him the whole story, starting with killing the young North Vietnamese officer in Vietnam in 1969. Henderson used a small recorder, but also took extensive notes on a yellow legal pad. When I stopped talking, he started asking questions.

"So the federal officers in Virginia, were they FBI or Homeland Security?"

"Homeland Security, then later FBI. They sent the FBI to my daughter's home."

"And the FBI agents were dead when you arrived?" Henderson asked as he continued to write on his legal pad like a law student taking notes.

"Yes. Lying on the floor in my daughter's den."

"Okay. And this Homeland Security officer, Officer Stephens, she can corroborate everything that happened at your daughter's house? She saw the dead FBI agents?"

"No. She was behind the house when I entered it. When I heard gunfire, I ran from the house and ended up shooting the two Vietnamese men. I assume they were Vietnamese."

"When can she talk?" Henderson asked. "And your friend Florence?"

"Maybe later today, I think." I ran my fingers through my short hair as though feeling for the brain tumor that I assumed lay beneath my scalp. "Florence could talk right now, I'm sure."

"Okay. Have you been mistreated?"

"Well, considering that these guys think I killed a couple of their buddies, I'd say not too bad."

"Explain," he said. He removed his glasses and cleaned them with a handkerchief.

"Well, they pushed me around a little. I've got a few bruises."

"Okay. This is what's about to happen. They're going to put you in a holding cell, in isolation. I'm going to chew their asses for the prior rough treatment, so you'll probably be treated pretty well from here on, but don't expect any chocolates on your pillow. If I can't get the charges dropped, there may be an arraignment in federal court, but prior to this, they will have to disclose to me any evidence they have against you. I'm guessing it's pretty thin. In the meantime, perhaps Officer Stephens and Florence will be able to make statements on your behalf." He put his glasses back on and pushed them up his nose.

"How long will this take? I've got to get to Vietnam. My daughter and grandchildren are in jeopardy."

"I'm going to them right now with this information regarding the kidnapping of your family. The FBI and State Department will have to take over this matter. They'll get your family back." His chubby face was flushed, as though he had spent too much time in the summer sun.

"What if they don't believe what I've told them about my family? And this guy seems well connected. A private jet. Access to high levels of our government. What assurances do I have that our government will go after my family?"

"I think they will. But right now, you're here, and there isn't much we can do about this until the arraignment, or until we can get Officer Stephens's deposition and I can talk to Florence. Best case is I get you out of here late this afternoon or early evening. Maybe tomorrow morning. I'm sorry. But I'll do my best."

~~~

They kept me in solitary confinement in some type of holding cell, which was fine with me. I had spent a few weeks in jail before and knew more than I would like to have known about the general population of local jail cells. The meals were fine, and I had access to a television. But my mind was on Jen and my grandchildren. Although my head still ached, the worst pain had subsided. My vision had cleared, but I couldn't concentrate on anything. I used the time to plan the mission to Vietnam to recover my family.

I needed sleep. I tried, but it came in fits and starts. It was a long night.

At ten o'clock the next morning, Joel Henderson arrived at my cell, escorted by a uniformed officer. The door was left open as Henderson settled in.

"They have dropped all charges," Henderson said as he flopped his wide body onto a straight chair. "You're free to go with me."

"When?" I said as I stood from my bunk.

"Right now. I've processed all the paperwork. Officer Stephens and Florence provided detailed depositions on your behalf. Stephens said the Department of Homeland Security was working back channels to find your family in Vietnam, and you should contact them as soon as possible." Henderson stood. "Are you ready to go?"

"Sure," I said. "I need my things."

Henderson handed me a large manila envelope. I opened it and found my wallet, cell phone, and the keys to my truck.

"I had a backpack with some clothes and a rain slicker with some money in it, plus my passport."

"Here's a cashier's check for all the money you had in your possession at the time of the arrest." He handed me a check for eight thousand dollars. "They're keeping your passport, and as a condition of your release, you're not allowed to leave the country."

"What do you mean, 'as a condition of my release'? I thought I was free."

"You *are* free, but they don't want you going overseas, especially to Vietnam, and meddling in international affairs. The government is working on finding your daughter and grandchildren, and you are not to interfere with their investigation in any way."

"Like hell I won't," I said.

"Look, Travis, just get out of jail first. I'll work for you on these other matters. Take it one step at a time."

I paused for a few seconds to organize my thoughts, a little longer to let my temper cool like a boiling pot taken off a flame. I took a deep breath. "Okay, you're right. Let's go."

I walked with Henderson through two sets of steel doors. My truck was parked in a side lot, with my backpack on the front seat. Joel opened the driver's door, and I climbed in.

"I had my secretary program all my contact numbers into your cell phone," he said. "Call me anytime if you have any further problems. Officer Stephens said to tell you that she will be in Darden County General Hospital a few more days. Then she's going to rehab at her sister's home near Richmond. She'll call you and help you keep track of the investigation relating to your family."

We shook hands through the open window of the truck.

I said, "Thanks, Joel. I'll call you if I need you. Send me your bill, and I'll get you paid."

"No need. The money you had wired to my law firm will more than cover my time on your case. You're due a refund. It's been a pleasure."

I nodded, started the truck, and drove away, prioritizing my next few moves. First I needed to find Bo Jarvis, a man I thought I'd seen for the last time eight years earlier.

~~~

During my drinking days, I had spent a lot of time with people who lived off the record. These were invisible people with no reportable income, completely off the grid. They did not file income tax returns. They weren't around when census takers or utility service men knocked on their doors. They lived on cash, not always obtained in legally acceptable occupations. I knew where and how to find one of these people who I knew could help me, and I could be there in less than thirty minutes.

My first stop would be at Coop's Nest. There was a time in the not-too-distant past when you couldn't buy beer in North Carolina, so there were several small bars like Coop's in South Carolina, just across the state line.

A half hour later, I was parking my truck in a gravel lot and walking into a small concrete block building with *Coop's Nest* written on it in large, green letters.

"My god," Billy Cooper said as I walked into the dark room. "Look what the wind blowed in. Did you fall off the wagon?"

"Not yet," I said as I straddled a stool at the bar.

Billy Cooper had been called "Coop" most of his adult life. He was forty, but looked older. His skin was brittle and brown like an Egyptian mummy's. A cigarette dangled from his lower lip. His red hair was curly as if he had a perm, and his head danced above his pencil neck like a balloon on a string. He wasn't a handsome man, but he was always smiling.

"Say, do you have any aspirin or Tylenol?"

"Sure. I'm a bartender." He handed a bottle of Extra-Strength Tylenol across the bar.

I removed three pills and swallowed them.

"Water?"

"No, I'm fine. I'm looking for Bo Jarvis. Know where I might find him?"

"Uh, not my business, but Big Bo Jarvis ain't the kind of person who really lives anywhere or likes to have people looking for him, if you know what I mean." He pulled the cigarette from his lip, looked at it, pinched it between his thumb and forefinger, put it back to his mouth, and sucked out the last drag. He tossed it on the floor and crushed out the remaining glow with the toe of his boot.

"I need to speak to him. It's important."

"Well, there's a trailer park about four miles south of here on 160. Go south to the flashing caution light, take a right, and go about a hundred yards. If you see a '91 lowrider, red with yellow trim, then he might be in a nearby trailer with a girl or playing cards. I'd knock and announce myself at the door, if I was you."

I put a twenty-dollar bill on the bar. "Thanks, Coop."

"Travis, keep your money." He pushed it back and smiled. "Or, give it to Josh at the Boys and Girls Club for me and tell him I miss his black ass."

I picked up the twenty and shoved it in my pocket. "I'll do that. I promise."

~~~

I found the trailer park and Jarvis's bike. Our last conversation years ago had not been pleasant, so I knocked on the door with some trepidation. Before I could announce who I was, a gruff voice from inside said, "Who the hell is it?"

"Travis Kelly," I said.

The door opened. Jarvis was barefoot, in tattered jeans and wearing a biker's vest with no shirt. Although I stood an inch or two taller, he was a large man with broad shoulders and thick hands and wrists. Tattoos covered every inch of skin on his massive arms and chest. He held a beer in one hand and a Smith & Wesson .357 Magnum in the other.

"Son of a bitch, if it ain't the Mexican lover hisself, in the flesh. I heard you stopped drinking and got religion." He put the pistol in his belt and ran his right hand through his long, graying black hair.

"Stopped drinking, but still short on religion," I said. "I need your help, Bo."

"So I'm Bo now that you need my help," he said and spat in the yard. "Last time we talked, I was a rotten bastard for taking advantage of illegal immigrants. Now you need my help, and I'm Bo."

"Listen," I said firmly, "the last time we talked, I had been drinking all day, and I have no idea what we talked about. But right now, I need your help. My daughter and grandchildren have been kidnapped, and I've got to get them back."

Jarvis opened the door wider and stepped back. "Okay. Come in and tell me how I can help."

Chapter 12

BRAD HAD FORGOTTEN THE OPULENCE and frenetic pace of American air terminals. He watched hordes of people swarming around the Hartsfield-Jackson Atlanta International Airport, pushing to and fro in front of larger-than-life posters of beautiful women wearing little and smiling wryly about perfume, watches, or gadgets that made them mysterious and seductive. Arriving and departing passengers packed themselves into underground railcars like agitated bees in a hive with too little honey and zoomed from one terminal to the next. Since he had checked his duffel bag in Germany, Brad followed the signs to international baggage claim.

He avoided eye contact with the other passengers on his flight as he waited quietly in a corner for his duffel bag to emerge through a small hole in the wall. An older man, stooped, frail, and certainly north of eighty, quietly walked up to him. He offered his bony hand. His skin was translucent and streaked with large blue veins. His face had the texture of a dried gourd, but with more wrinkles.

"Thank you for your service, son," he said. "I was in the 82nd on D-Day and jumped into Normandy behind Utah Beach. But it was only one tour for me, just over two years, about a year of real fighting. Took longer to get there and get back than the actual war. Didn't have to keep going back into the thick of it, like you boys do now."

"Thank you for your service, sir," Brad replied. "Without you and the people before me, there wouldn't be any country to serve."

The old man nodded and walked with the aid of a cane to a short woman at least twenty years younger. He kissed her on the cheek. She put her arm through his elbow as they walked toward customs with their bags trailing them on hidden wheels.

Brad retrieved his duffel bag and threw it over his shoulder. With his left hand, he pulled out his cell phone and dialed Jen again. The call went straight to voicemail. "Damn," he said.

He had decided to rent a car and drive to North Carolina. If the Atlanta traffic did not jam him up, he could be home in less than three hours. He strode quickly to the lines leading to customs.

~~~

I stepped into Bo Jarvis's trailer and pulled the metal door closed, keeping the warm air out and the slightly cooler air in. A very young girl in jeans and a halter top slept soundly beneath a dirty blanket on an even dirtier sofa. Her blond hair was stringy and in desperate need of shampoo. She was thinner than a runway model.

Jarvis sat at a round, Formica-covered table and pointed to an empty chair. "Want a beer?" he asked.

"No thanks. Listen, Bo, I need some documents, and they have to be good, very good."

"What kind of documents?"

"Driver's license and passport. I think my daughter and grandchildren are overseas. I can't get a passport because of a felony conviction a few years back," I lied.

"Resisting arrest," Jarvis said. He smiled through bad teeth.

"Right."

"I was there when it happened. Where's your family? Who took 'em?"

"It's complicated. Probably better for both of us if I don't tell you much about it."

"Yeah, you're right." Jarvis had been in and out of prison since he was eighteen years old and knew the advantage of plausible deniability. "Sure, I can get you a driver's license and a passport. It takes twenty-four hours and two thousand dollars cash—half now, the rest when docs are delivered. I need a picture, date of birth, name, address, etcetera."

"Here's my current driver's license. Can you use that picture for both?"

He nodded. "For the license. Maybe for the passport."

"You got a piece of paper and a pen?"

Nodding again, he stood and disappeared down a cluttered hall.

While he was away, I looked at the girl more closely. She was probably late teens or her early twenties, at least twenty years younger than Jarvis. I wanted to wake her and send her home to her parents.

Jarvis returned with the pen and paper, and I wrote down the information he needed:

Marvin Evans
9/23/46
305 Baltimore Avenue
Cramer Village, NC 28036
Green eyes, Brown hair, Caucasian
6 feet 1 inch tall, 210 pounds

I slid the paper across the table to Jarvis.

"You'll need a middle name," he said.

"Peter," I said. "Marvin Peter Evans."

"I'll need half the money up front. You may want a social security number, too."

"Okay. Makes sense. Can you follow me to the bank?"

"Okay, but the social security number will cost you another five hundred."

"No problem. I'll have to go to Carolina Commerce Bank in Darden County to cash a check before I can get you the money."

"Okay. Let's take a better picture for the passport, just in case. Then we can go."

Jarvis had a makeshift photography studio in a bedroom. We took the picture and returned to the front room in the trailer. He pulled black biker's boots on his bare feet and stood.

Outside, I got in my truck and pulled out of the driveway with Jarvis following on his Harley. As I drove, I thought about Marvin Evans. Marvin had been my platoon sergeant in Vietnam. The men called him Pepper, which got abbreviated to Pep. He was a hell of a soldier. He wouldn't have minded that I used his name. He hadn't needed it since 2300 hours on 10 May 1969. That's when Pep died defending LZ Phyllis.

~~~

Billie Blake was the opposite of the girl on Bo Jarvis's sofa. She was clean, chubby, and engaged. She asked me three times if I really wanted to cash an eight-thousand-dollar check and walk out of the bank with that much money. I assured her that I did, but she still felt obligated to consult with the branch manager before completing the transaction. She spoke into the intercom, "Mr. Campbell, can I cash an eight-thousand-dollar cashier's check for Travis Kelly?"

I leaned over the teller counter. "I'm going on a long trip, and there won't be any automatic teller machines," I explained to my friend and fellow Vietnam veteran, Ed Campbell. Campbell told Billie it was okay and he would sign for it.

"That's a lot of cash," Billie said. "I guess you want hundreds?"

"Yes, if you have it. Just give me eighty one-hundred-dollar bills," I said. "Also, Billie, if you have a small bag, I would appreciate it."

She walked back to Ed's office and came back with a small cloth bag.

I watched her count the money several times. She divided it into eight stacks of ten bills. I nodded to confirm her accuracy. Finally I was able to leave the bank.

"Thanks, Billie," I said as I walked toward the door.

"You're welcome, Travis. Be careful."

"I will."

In the parking lot, I nodded to Jarvis and pointed to a fast food restaurant on the other side of New Hope Road. Jarvis gave me a thumbs-up and cranked his bike. I drove across the road in my truck.

I ordered iced tea. Jarvis didn't want anything. We sat in a booth. There were no other customers in the dining area.

"Here's thirteen hundred," I said, counting out thirteen Benjamins. "If you can get it done in twelve hours instead of twenty-four, I'll double your fee. Five thousand instead of twenty-five hundred."

Jarvis folded the money and stuffed it in the pocket of his jeans. "I'll do my best, but I doubt it. You know I'd like to make the extra scratch, but this is delicate work, and it has to be done right. Plus, it takes twenty-four hours to get a clean social security number and tie it to the names on the passport and driver's license."

"Just thought I'd ask." I wrote my cell phone number on a napkin and handed it to him. "Call me when it's ready."

He stood and headed for the door. "I'll call you. Probably about this time in the morning. We could meet back here."

"Okay." I watched him leave and climb on his Harley as I sat drinking my tea and thinking about my next move. I pulled out my cell phone, called the hospital, and asked for the room of Erin Stephens.

"Hello," Erin answered. Her voice was weak and scratchy.

"Erin, it's Travis."

"Did you get out of jail?"

"Yes, I guess thanks to you. So, thanks."

"You're welcome." She spoke just above a whisper. "I like your attorney, and that's difficult for me, since I usually align more closely with the prosecution."

"I think he's a good egg," I said. "How are you doing?"

"Pretty sore. Fighting to stay off the pain meds. Mostly losing the battle. Hurts when I breathe. Your friend has been by. He's a good doctor."

"Yes, I think he is." I paused. "Do you have a contact for me at Homeland Security so I can try to find out what's happening with my family?"

"I do. Where are you now?"

"Just leaving Charlotte," I lied.

"Do you have access to e-mail?"

"Yes, I guess. Why?"

"I'll e-mail you the contact information for the person in DC you need to speak to. His name is Sherman Duffy. We call him Duff."

"Better than Sherman, I guess." I heard her laugh and then groan as the pain must have flared. "Sorry. I think I can get on a computer soon. I'll come by to see you later," I lied again.

"Okay, please do," she said.

~~~

Brad pulled off the road in front of Jen's house, a two-story frame with gray siding. He had made the three-hour drive from Atlanta in two hours and forty-five minutes. His heart rate shot up when he saw the yellow crime scene tape encircling the lawn and the police and sheriff's vehicles that lined the road. Still in his BDUs, he got out of the car. He straightened and spotted his good friend and county police detective, Michael Simmons, standing near the house. He called Michael's name.

The detective turned and approached him, ducking under the yellow tape. His expression was somber.

"What's going on?" Brad gestured toward the house.

"It's a long story, and I'm not sure I really understand it fully."

"Where are Jen and the children?" Brad asked, looking back at the house. "Are they okay?"

Michael shook his head. He was somber. "We just don't know. I'll tell you everything I do know." He hardly took a breath. "Your dad called me night before last and asked me to come over to Jen's house. He said somebody was threatening him, and he thought they might use Jen and the children to try to get to him. I came over and stayed about an hour. Two FBI agents came by, and Jen thought it would be okay for me to go home.

"The next morning, the two FBI agents were found dead in Jen's den. Two Asian men were lying dead behind the house. A Homeland Security officer was wounded in the backyard, and Jen and the children were missing. Still are."

Brad stared at his friend in shock. "What about my father?"

"It gets more complicated. The FBI arrested your father for the murder of the FBI agents. He was cleared, of course, and was released this morning, but I don't know where he is right now. Florence Johnson was attacked at your father's farmhouse. I spoke with her. She's fine and is at her home."

"Damn. I can't believe all this." Brad waved his arm in a circle toward the house.

"Dr. Beam did surgery on the Homeland Security officer. She's in Darden County General Hospital."

Brad raised his brow. "She?"

"Yes. It was a female officer. Pretty high up, I understand."

"This is unbelievable." Brad shook his head. "I've got to get in touch with my father."

"Have you tried to call him?" Michael asked.

"No. That's always my last resort." Brad pulled out his cell phone, dialed the number, and waited.

Chapter 13

JEN AND HER FOUR CHILDREN sat in the back seat of a large Mercedes sedan as it cruised down a narrow road that seemed to hug Vietnam's eastern coastline. She couldn't relax, despite the comfortable and opulent interior of the expensive vehicle. The rear leather seats were designed to seat three adult passengers, which meant that she and the children were unable to use the seat belts properly. She braced Joe on her lap. Megan did the same with LB. Jackie sat between them in the middle seat.

Looking out the window, Jen longed for the familiar North Carolina countryside. The landscape of Vietnam was verdant and lush. It was a beautiful country. But the humidity and heat were nearly unbearable. In the short walk from the jet to the car, she had felt as though she were walking through a steam bath at the YMCA.

She watched Minh as he sat in the front seat. He was engaged in an animated telephone conversation in what she assumed to be Vietnamese. The strange language was becoming all too familiar to her in these frightening circumstances.

Describing the limo driver as a large man would have been a gross understatement. Jen estimated his height to be just over six feet and his weight at well over two hundred pounds, maybe two-fifty, most of it solid muscle. Her first impression of him was that he was African American. As she studied him more carefully, however, she realized that he was of mixed heritage, maybe the son an African American soldier of the war and a Vietnamese mother. He did not speak to Minh or to anyone, for that matter. At the airport, he had opened Minh's door and closed it. He stood and watched as Jen and the children were herded into the back seat of the limo by the two bodyguards, she assumed, who had been on the plane. Seated beside the big driver, Minh looked like a child waiting to sit on Santa's lap.

She realized that Minh had hung up his phone.

"Where are you taking us?" Jen demanded.

"As I said on the plane, to a guest house beside my residence. I was just arranging a meal." He turned to look at her. "Do you and your children enjoy fish?"

"Fish is fine," Jen said, irritated by the pretense that they were guests rather than prisoners. "Did you remember that I will soon need to resupply insulin and testing strips for LB?"

"Yes. I sent an e-mail to my family physician from the plane. I'm guessing the necessary supplies will have already been delivered."

"I will need to speak with the doctor to ensure the doses are the same as in the US," Jen said. "Does he speak English?"

"No. But I can interpret."

Jen persisted. "I would prefer speaking with a doctor who speaks English. I don't want to give him four units of insulin when I think I'm giving him three, and I need to know what type of insulin is provided." She spoke with confidence, looking directly at Minh.

"I know a doctor who speaks English well. I'll call him, and you can speak with him, but you will need to be careful in conducting the conversation. I am treating you and your children as guests, but that circumstance can change at my discretion. Do you understand?" He spoke evenly and returned her steady gaze.

Jen did not reply, as they rode on in silence.

~~~

I drove my truck aimlessly with no destination in mind. I was burning gas and killing time. I dialed Florence's cell phone.

She answered after several rings. "Hello?"

"Florence, this is Travis. How are you doing?"

I pulled the truck into a parking lot ringed by empty stores killed by the Great Recession. The truck bounced across the cracked pavement toward the shade of a large oak, where I turned off the engine and rolled the windows down.

"I'm at my home now and doing just fine," she said loudly. "Still a little shaken. That little rat tried to kill me, Travis. If I hadn't pretended to be dead, my family might be planning my funeral right now. What's this all about? How are Jen and your grandkids?"

"I'm just glad you're okay. Jen and the kids have been abducted."

Florence gasped.

"I'm pretty sure he's taken them to Vietnam," I said. I opened the door of the truck and got out to ensure better telephone reception.

"Vietnam? Why would he do that? How do you know for sure he did?"

"It's complicated. I'll tell you all about it when it's over. Right now, I'm just glad you're okay. I'm going over to Vietnam to get my family back. But don't say anything about that if you're asked."

"Shouldn't the CIA or the Army or somebody from the government handle this for you?" Her voice was heavy with concern. "How are you going to get to them?"

"Yeah, the government should, but the government should do a lot of things it doesn't do, and it shouldn't be doing a lot of things it is doing. I haven't relied much on the government up to this point in my life, and this is certainly not the time I'm going to start." I heard the anger creeping into my voice. "This rat, as you call him, has Jen and my grandchildren, and I'm going to go and get them back. End of story." I saw that I was getting another call. "Florence, I'll have to call you back," I said as I accepted the incoming call. "Brad," I said eagerly into the phone.

"Yes, it's me. Look, Dad, I'm at Jen's house. What in hell is going on?"

"So you're back. Glad about that, but it's a bad situation here. 'Hell' is a good word for it. I don't want to come there. And I don't want to talk about it on the phone. Do you remember the Wired Coffee House, near the lake?"

"Sure."

"Meet me there in fifteen minutes."

"Okay."

~~~

I sat at a high table in the back of the coffee house, sipping black coffee. I saw Brad park and unwind from a small sedan, probably a rental. He still wore his Army uniform. We weren't permitted to wear combat fatigues away from post when I served in the 1960s. I guess they thought the hippies would throw flowers at us.

I stood as Brad stepped into the establishment, and he spotted me. He stopped at the cash register and ordered a coffee from a young girl wearing a green apron. A message was embroidered in bold white letters on the apron:

Ask me for help! I'm wired!
The Wired Coffee House

She smiled and told Brad she would bring the coffee to his table.

"Welcome home," I said as Brad approached. I offered to shake hands, and he accepted.

"Thanks."

The young girl brought his coffee and placed it on the table. "Aren't you Brad Kelly?"

"I am."

"I thought so. I'm Addie Jenkins. I'll tell my mother I saw you."

Brad smiled. "Your mother?"

"Yes, her maiden name was Brandy Thompson. She was a cheerleader when you played football at Darden High. She showed me your picture in the paper last week when you got that medal."

"Sure, I remember Brandy. Very pretty and smart. Your look just like her."

The girl grinned and walked back to the counter.

Brad looked at me. "I guess I'm getting old, Dad."

"So am I," I said.

For a moment we sipped our coffee in silence. Then Brad leaned back. His face looked tired. "So what's going on here? Where are Jen and the kids?"

"It's complicated and a very long story, but you need to hear it all."

"I'm listening." He was curt.

"Okay, here goes. It started in Vietnam in 1969, two three February six nine, to be exact." I used the clear staccato language he understood well for dates and time. I told him the story of killing the young Vietnamese officer, the boy I had refused to detain, and everything that had happened in the last two days. When I finished speaking, I took a long drink of my coffee and sat with my hands folded on the table.

Brad was shaking his head. "Damn. I can't believe this. So your plan is just to take your forged passport and travel to Vietnam and bring them home?"

"Yes. I'm going to get them," I said with confidence. "Do you have a better idea?"

"Well, yes. Get on the phone with the FBI and get the full force of the US government raining down on this asshole immediately." His face reddening, he crushed his coffee cup and threw it toward a trash can. He missed and stood to drop it in the can.

"This would be the FBI that just arrested me, detained me for twenty-four hours, and withheld my passport," I said as Brad sat back down. "They've been very helpful."

Brad leaned forward, his elbows on the table. "Look, Dad, they have resources. They can put boots on the ground long before you can even get to Vietnam. Plus, they can bring in the State Department, the CIA, and the government of Vietnam. You need to work with the authorities on this."

"Like hell I do. I'm driving to Atlanta as soon as I get my documents. I'm buying a ticket and flying to Vietnam. I'm going to get Jen and the kids and get them out of the country. Then I'm going to kill this son of a bitch. *That's* what I'm going to do."

Brad looked at me for a long time without saying anything. His dark blue eyes were intense. "Okay," he said finally. "You go, but I'm going to the authorities. I'm going to work through the system. I'll start with the Homeland Security officer at Darden County General. What's her name?"

"Erin Stephens," I said. "Don't tell them I'm on my way to Vietnam as Marvin Evans. They told me not to leave the country."

Brad's eyebrows rose. "I'm sure Officer Stephens is going to want to know where you are and what you're doing."

"Tell her you don't know. Just give me twenty-four hours. I get my passport in the morning, and I'll be in Vietnam within twenty-four hours after that. I'm guessing I can get Jen and the kids out just hours after I arrive. Minh wants me, not my family. I'm planning on doing a straight-up swap."

"And you think this man, who assassinated an undersecretary of Homeland Security and his wife, and killed other US federal officers, is just going to let Jen and the kids go and take you instead?"

"I will remind him that, had I not done what I did for him forty years ago, he would have died a few hours, or at most, a few days, after I killed his father. But it wouldn't have been a simple bullet. It would have been slow and painful, at the hands of the ARVN. He has lived the past forty years because of me. That's a fact."

"Well, good luck with that." His tone was skeptical. "I'm going to engage every governmental resource I can to get Jen and the children home." He stood and looked down at me. "You do what you want. I won't out your cover. But that's all I'm willing to do."

I looked up at him but remained seated. Even in his sleep-deprived state, he was a remarkably good-looking man. He had inherited some of my features—the heavy eyebrows, strong jaw line, and a five o'clock shadow, even at ten in the morning. But to me, he looked like Claire, with his lightly tanned complexion, sandy hair somewhere between brown and blond, and eyes the color of the sea from thirty thousand feet. He had broad, muscular shoulders and strong hands. I loved him dearly. I had always known that he loved his mother more than he loved me, but that was okay.

"You don't get it, son. I guess you never will. The government doesn't give a rat's ass about us. They never have, and they never will. We're just their ATM. They extort money from us in the form of taxes, give it to the people who they think will vote for them, and ram their fists down our throats. I'm not waiting for the government to do anything for me. I'm going to get my family back. End of story."

Brad said nothing more. He simply turned and walked out of the coffee shop.

After he left, I asked the proprietor of the shop to loan me a computer. I recovered the contact information for Sherman Duffy from an e-mail that Erin had sent me and checked the flights from Atlanta to Vietnam. I would probably end up flying west through Japan instead of east through London and Singapore, but that was fine. Until I could get my documents, I would check into a cheap motel and try to sleep as much as possible. But first, I would go to one of the big-box stores and purchase a tablet computer, some prepaid credit cards, and a throw-away cell phone. I removed the batteries from the cell phone in my pocket. I would store the phone in the glove compartment of my truck and use it only when necessary or to get numbers and addresses prior to leaving for the Atlanta airport. I assumed some government agency somewhere was tasked with tracking my movements.

I tossed my empty coffee cup and nodded to Addie Jenkins on my way out the door.

~~~

Brad checked into the Hampton Inn near Darden County General Hospital. After he had showered and shaved, he lay flat on his back on the hotel bed and closed his eyes. The Army had taught him the benefit of sleep and how to get it even when his mind was racing and all hell was raining down around him. He slowed his breathing, and within a minute, he was asleep.

It was mid-afternoon when he awoke. He slid out of bed and used the iron and ironing board from the closet to press his Class A uniform, including his shirt and tie. He dressed and left the hotel for the hospital.

~~~

Brad knocked at the open door of the room assigned to Erin Stephens.

An attractive blond woman about his age, he thought, maybe a little younger, sat upright in a hospital bed. Two fat pillows were behind her back. She seemed to be typing a text message into her phone.

"Ms. Stephens?" he asked.

"Yes," Erin said. She pulled the sheet up over her thin hospital gown.

"My name is Brad Kelly. I think you know my father."

"I do, if you mean Travis Kelly. Please come in."

Brad approached on the left side of her hospital bed. He held his beret in his hand and stood towering over her. "How are you doing?"

"I'm fine, I think. Got shot a couple of times and had some surgery. Your father saved my life. Do you know where he is? I've called him on his cell, and I was just sending him a text message." She brushed her hair away from her forehead.

"I really don't know his whereabouts right now, but I spoke with him this morning. I just got in from a tour in Afghanistan. Dad told me the whole story. Unbelievable. Do you know anything about my sister, my nieces and nephews?"

"That's what I've been trying to get in touch with Travis about. My associates at Homeland Security and my contacts in the FBI tell me that they have confirmed that Nguyen Li Minh could not have ambushed my vehicles yesterday, nor could he have kidnapped your sister and her children."

"Why not?"

"Because Minh is participating in a Communist Party convention in Hanoi. He's been there the past four days. They sent pictures of him at the convention, dated and time-stamped. I've seen the pictures. I never saw Minh here, and neither did Travis. I've seen his picture on the Internet, and it is definitely him at the convention, if you can believe the Vietnamese officials. Somebody killed Undersecretary Bradley and his wife, ambushed me and my crew, killed two FBI agents, shot me twice in the chest, and abducted Jen and the children. But it apparently was not Nguyen Li Minh."

Chapter 14

INTERSTATE 85 CONNECTED ALABAMA TO VIRGINIA, slicing through Georgia and the Carolinas. Although it was a boon to commerce for cities and towns along its route, especially between Atlanta and Charlotte, like all the interstate highways, it had drained the life out of towns fifteen or more miles off its path. I preferred the pre-interstate roads when I wasn't flying my own plane, but I had no time to enjoy the past now.

I plowed past the signs for Clemson University near the exit for Anderson, South Carolina. Warm summer air rolled through the truck like a strong sea breeze. I liked the wind in my face. I preferred open windows to artificially cooled air. The truck's tires hummed as they chewed up the hard, white concrete. In better times I would be listening to Nora Jones or my old Johnny Cash CDs. But these were not better times. No distractions were permitted. I was deep in thought about getting to Minh. My gut told me that he had lied about taking Jen and the children to the place where I had killed Minh's father. But when I arrived in Vietnam, I would go there first, just in case because I did not like the thought of my family in the jungle.

I had awakened early from a restless sleep in a strange bed in a cheap motel in Fort Mill, South Carolina. My head hurt and my vision was blurred. As promised, Bo Jarvis had delivered the passport and driver's license at about nine o'clock in the morning. It was now nearly noon. My head still throbbed. I pulled a protein bar and some Tylenol from a knapsack, swallowed both quickly, and washed them down with a bottle of water. I was trying to get to the Atlanta airport as soon as possible without speeding.

Though the speedometer indicated that I was spot on the posted seventy-mile-per-hour speed limit, cars and trucks were overtaking and passing me as though I were riding an old mule. Still, I resisted the temptation to speed. I didn't know how Marvin Evans would feel about getting a speeding ticket forty years after he had been killed on Landing Zone Phyllis. Nor was I certain how well my new documents would interface with law enforcement. Plus I didn't want to spend enough time with a highway patrolman to expose my occasional blurred vision.

I thought about Marvin Evans. All the men in my platoon called him Pep, short for Pepper. Marvin was a twenty-three-year-old sergeant first class. This would not be possible in today's Army. Following basic and advanced infantry training, Pep had attended NCO school and had become a non-commissioned officer. Like me, he was airborne and had graduated from Ranger school. Graduating first in his class, he was awarded staff sergeant's stripes. A year later he was an SFC. Rank came fast during the Vietnam era. Replacements were needed for the dozens of young officers and NCOs who were getting killed and wounded every week.

Unlike Marvin, who was a college graduate, I didn't attend college when I graduated from high school. During my senior year I had taken some courses at the community college and had been offered an academic scholarship to a big state university when I graduated. Most of my high school classmates joined the Marines or Air Force the day after graduation, thus avoiding the draft. I smiled at the memory. The pull of the military and the opportunity to marry Claire sooner, rather than later, combined to push me to volunteer as soon as I turned eighteen. I had a nearly perfect score on the Army's entrance exam and was directed to Officers Candidate School.

Claire quit her job and followed me to Fort Benning. We got married on post, and she lived in a cheap apartment while I finished OCS, jump school, and Ranger training. A year later she was nine months pregnant, and I had orders for Vietnam.

In August 1968, I was assigned as an infantry platoon leader in the First Air Cavalry Division at Quang Tri in the north-central coastal region of South Vietnam. The first person to greet me when I stepped off the Huey that delivered me to Quang Tri was Marvin Evans, also newly assigned as platoon sergeant. Evans grabbed my backpack, slung it over his shoulder, and escorted me to the CO's bunker.

The men called us Salt and Pepper, although they generally called me Lieutenant to my face—maybe something else behind my back. The life expectancy for platoon leaders in Vietnam, young lieutenants like me, was about that of a Monarch butterfly. If we didn't get killed in the first ninety days, we might make it six to nine months. Few made it for the full twelve-month tour. How long we lasted depended on how many firefights we ran into and whether or not we got fragged by a disgruntled soldier we had assigned to walk point. Whether it was enemy or friendly fire, however, Pep had my back.

There were just three other black troopers in the platoon. Taking orders from a black platoon sergeant didn't sit well with some of the enlisted men from the Deep South. Two weeks after I took over the platoon, a squad leader from Texas told me he wouldn't work for a black platoon sergeant.

"I've got ten years, and I'm on my second tour," Staff Sergeant Gil Meacham from El Paso, Texas, told me when we were alone. "No disrespect meant, Lieutenant, but I can work with a ninety-day wonder like you okay. I figure the Army knows officer material, and you're taking a lot of risk doing what you do. But I'll be damned if I'm going to work for a twenty-three-year-old platoon sergeant nigger who's going to get me and my squad killed."

I took a step closer to Meacham, grabbed a handful of his shirt, and pulled him to his toes. "Sergeant Meacham, I read your efficiency reports going back six years. On your first tour over here, you spent most of the time in Saigon getting drunk and screwing prostitutes. You've been busted twice for insubordination. How you made it back to E-6 is a mystery to me. But here you are. You're a squad leader in my platoon, and you will work under the direction of Sergeant First Class Evans. If I hear you use that word to describe him ever again, I will bust you down to PFC and get you transferred to another company where you can walk point until Charlie blows your guts out or your tour ends. You understand?"

Meacham was silent for a minute. Then he nodded.

Two weeks later, he got popped in the right leg by a Chicom grenade. Pep ran through machine gun fire to drag him off the battlefield and carried him on his back a half mile to an evacuation point. Two minutes later, and he would have bled out. The medics stopped the bleeding, wrapped the leg, and started an IV. Before they put him on medevac, he asked to speak with Pep and me.

His voice was weak. He smiled through the morphine-induced haze. "Pep," he said, "you saved my life, man. I want you to know that I'm coming back, if they'll let me. It's been an honor to serve with you." He looked at me as two men lifted the stretcher to put him on the chopper. "And with you, sir," he said. "If you'll have me back."

Pep patted him on the shoulder. "I'm betting you make it back, Gil. Lieutenant Kelly and I both will be glad to have you."

I nodded as they took him away.

Meacham made it back. He did a good job, and he cried like a baby when Pep was killed on LZ Phyllis. A lot of men cried that day. I was one of them.

~~~

There were three bedrooms in the guest house next to Minh's seaside mansion. Jen had disassembled and moved all the beds into the largest room so that she and all four children were together. She was relieved that they had been treated well, but she knew full well that they were prisoners. Leaving the house was forbidden without escort. She was not allowed to take her children to the beach, though they could hear the sounds of children playing in the nearby surf.

When someone knocked on the door, she met them outside and would not allow them in, if possible. She tried to keep the children calm and didn't want them to see her fear. She allowed herself to cry softly only when they slept.

As the five of them sat eating breakfast on the fourth full day of their captivity, she heard a strong knock. She opened the door and stood resolutely in the opening. The black driver stood on the porch. He pointed toward the main house and stepped aside. It was then that she realized he could not speak. He was mute.

"I don't want to leave my children alone," she said in a quiet, calm voice, trying her best not to be intimidated by his size and presence. "Do you understand English?"

He nodded affirmatively.

Jen held out her hand and said, "My name is Jen Phillips."

He declined to accept her hand, but nodded. He gestured again toward the house.

"If I go to the house"—she looked in that direction and ran her hand through her short black hair—"will my children be okay?"

The big man looked over her shoulder toward the children, who were gathered around the breakfast table. He reached inside the pocket of his pants and withdrew a key. He placed it in the lock of the door and demonstrated that it was the key to the deadbolt lock. He gave her the key.

She closed and locked the door, then offered to return the key to him.

He shook his head, indicating that she should keep the key.

She understood and nodded. "Thank you," she said as she walked with him toward the main residence. She slipped the key into the front pocket of her jeans.

The driver opened the door to the main house. Minh greeted her as she entered. "Jen, I want you to meet my wife and family."

An attractive Vietnamese woman stood behind him, flanked by two teens, a boy and a girl.

"This is my wife, Tran Thi Lam, my son, Nguyen Tran Due, and my daughter, Nguyen Lien Kim."

Jen nodded to them politely, but said nothing.

"I want you to know that they are fully aware of what is going on with you and your family." Minh smiled, his small, dark eyes opened as wide as possible. "They know that we are essentially waiting for your father, and that at that time, you and your children will be transferred to the United States consulate here in Ho Chi Minh City."

"So they know that we were taken against our will and that you have tried to kill my father?" She stared at him without blinking.

"They don't speak English, so please be careful in your demeanor. I am trying to make this as normal as possible for you and, as you can see, I am a family man and I want no harm to come to you or to your children. My dispute is solely with your father. If you'll let me, I will make this as painless as possible."

Jen forced a smile. She nodded again toward Minh's wife and children. "Thank you for your hospitality," she said, then turned and walked back toward the front door.

The driver appeared and escorted her back to the guest house. She opened the door with the key. He opened his huge palm, indicating that she should return the key.

Jen placed the key in his catcher's-mitt sized hand. "Thank you."

He nodded.

Jen entered the house and heard the door lock behind her.

Chapter 15

Brad pulled into the circular drive in front of Darden County General Hospital and parked his freshly-washed Jeep Wrangler at the curb. He got out of the vehicle just as a nurse's assistant rolled a patient in a wheelchair through one of the front doors of the hospital. Brad walked around the back of the Wrangler and opened the passenger door.

Erin Stephens stood from the wheelchair and hugged a large African American woman. "Thank you, Tonya. Good luck with your baby," she said. She turned to Brad. "I didn't want to ride in the wheelchair, but it's hospital policy. Good morning. You look nice in your new civies." She handed him a metal briefcase with a combination lock. "My Glock and some other items are in this case. Regulations require that I carry it at all times. Will you slip it on the floorboard behind my seat?"

Brad nodded. He wore khaki slacks and a black golf shirt with brown loafers. It felt good to be out of uniform. He thought Erin was very attractive in her blouse and pants, but he didn't complement her. "How do you feel?"

"I'm fine. Still sore, but improving. Glad to be out of the hospital."

She climbed slowly into Brad's Jeep, and he closed the door. She put the seatbelt on and adjusted it so it was below the wounds on her chest.

Brad got into the Jeep and started the engine, adjusting the air conditioning. "Let me know if you're too cold or warm." He placed the briefcase behind her seat.

"So we're going to fly to Virginia?"

"Yes. I spoke with Tank Willis. He wants his Cessna back, if possible. I flew it from the farm over to the local airport this morning, filled it with one hundred low lead, cleaned it up, and did a full preflight inspection to ensure there's no damage from the soft field landing and takeoff. We'll fly from there up to Manassas."

"How long have you been flying?" she asked as Brad guided the truck out of the parking lot.

"Dad started me when I was fifteen, but I couldn't get my license until I was sixteen." Brad thought about some of the few happy times he had spent with his father. "I flew a lot up until I joined the Army, and mostly on leave since then. I love it and stay as current as possible. I mostly fly simple planes like the Cessna, but I do have a current instrument rating. I can fly single-engine or twins, but I wouldn't fly a complex twin right now without a good co-pilot or instructor pilot in the right seat. Even in the last ten years, I've been able to get in fifty to a hundred hours per year. I'm a fair weather pilot right now, and today is a fair-weather-flying day." He crossed the interstate on a four-lane highway that led to the local airport. "It's less than two miles. Do you need anything or want to stop for a snack?"

"No, I'm fine. Looking forward to seeing my sister and niece. They'll pick us up at Manassas and take us to my condo. I'd like to have lunch with them. Then we can take my car over to HS and meet with Duff."

"Sounds good," Brad said as he focused on his driving. He glanced at her occasionally to be certain that she was comfortable.

~~~

The first leg of the flight to Vietnam would leave Atlanta at 8:00 p.m. I wanted to get to the airport in time to buy a ticket and interact as needed with airport security. As I drove, I reflected on the events of the last few days, including my meeting with my friend and ophthalmologist, Bill McClendon. I would not be doing the MRI or the appointment with Dr. Dan Gunter. I thought about calling and canceling, but it was low on my priority list. I had bought a prepaid phone that wasn't traceable, but in my paranoia, I had removed the batteries. Same for my personal cell phone. Both phones were in the glove compartment of my truck, and the batteries were in my pocket. I wanted to be as invisible as possible until I got to Vietnam. And getting to Vietnam was all that was on my mind.

I knew that Nguyen Li Minh operated a textile manufacturing business east and north of Saigon. I had purchased a programmable GPS at The GPS Store in Charlotte before leaving for Atlanta and had programmed in the coordinates of my encounter with Minh and his father. But I wasn't certain whether I should go to the jungle location or to Minh's business or home. Safest bet would be to go straight to the jungle. If Jen and the kids weren't there, I could then try to intercept Minh at work or home. Something told me that Minh wasn't a Boy Scout and that he wouldn't be comfortable deep into the jungles of Vietnam, but I wasn't willing to bet the lives of my family on my gut feelings.

As I thought on these matters, my head began to ache. I opened a bottle of Ibuprofen, poured three pills into my palm, and threw them into the back of my throat. I was alternating Ibuprofen with Tylenol to knock down the pain of the headaches. The episodes were unpredictable, from two to twelve hours apart. The throbbing discomfort never really subsided. Anticipating that my vision would soon blur, I looked for a place to pull off the road. I turned onto the first off-ramp I came to and swerved into the parking lot of a convenience store. I stopped abruptly, put the truck in park, and leaned my head back against the headrest with my eyes closed.

"Damn," I said. Desperate and discouraged, I did something I hadn't done in a long time. I prayed. I prayed that my body would not fail me before I got my family back. I smiled to myself as I sat with my eyes closed. My prayers had never been answered. I prayed every day that Claire would get better. She continued to get worse. I prayed that she would live. She had died. I prayed that my children would have good lives. One was widowed in her thirties. The other was stuck with a sense of patriotism that put him in Iraq and Afghanistan for forty-five months in the past eight years. Somewhere along the line, I stopped praying. I stopped attending church services. I stopped thinking about God or salvation or forgiveness or grace or any of the things I had been taught as a child. What good was it?

Life was just a series of fairly unpredictable events. That was the way I saw it. If you wanted to change any of it, you had to take action. Maybe God was out there somewhere. Maybe there was a better place for good people like Claire. Maybe there was a bad place for the asshole who abducted my family. But did any of that really matter in the present?

We live today. That's it. End of story. Do the best you can today. That was my religious philosophy. It was the story of the Good Samaritan. Help the person in the ditch. Give a buck to the dirty, wretched person on the side of the interstate. Maybe he's a con artist. Maybe he really *is* hungry. Who knows? Just hand him a little money, and go on about your business. That was how I had lived my life since Claire died, just doing some good every day if an opportunity arose. I was not so big on faith or hope, but I tried to focus on charity, goodness, and kindness after I got sober. I just lived every day the best I could and didn't think much about what God or a pastor or anybody I knew thought about how I went about my life.

Still, though my track record was abysmal, I prayed that God would let my body carry me to Vietnam to get my family back.

~~~

The engine of the Cessna hummed as Brad and Erin cruised at 8,500 feet, east-northeast, traveling at about 120 knots. Brad was a careful pilot.

He maintained a high level of situational awareness, scanning the sky for other planes nearby.

Erin had engaged her cell phone and had gotten a strong signal. She left her headset on so Brad could hear her conversation with her associate, Sherman Duffy.

"Duff, it's Erin. We're in the air now. Still planning on getting there about three this afternoon." She paused to listen, then said, "No, they didn't want to release me so soon after the surgery. But I didn't give them any choice in the matter. I promised to take it easy at my sister's house for a couple of weeks or more." She laughed at something he said in response. "So what do you have for us?"

Brad saw a small plane about fifteen hundred feet below them. He watched it carefully to ensure that it wasn't moving up and into their flight path.

"Duff, hold on a second," he heard Erin say. "I'm going to put you on speaker so Brad can hear you." She set the phone on speaker and held it to the microphone of her flight headset.

Brad nodded.

"So, here's what we know on our end, Erin and Brad," someone said in a deep voice. "State says that Nguyen Li Minh is a well-known and respected businessman in Saigon. He's also a high-ranking member of the Communist Party. He claims he is the grandson of Ho Chi Minh, but even his closest associates question the veracity of this claim. On the other hand, it wasn't Minh who conducted the mayhem in Virginia and North Carolina. He was participating in a very high-profile meeting of the party in Hanoi when these events occurred."

"But we know that Jen Phillips and her four children were abducted," Erin said, nodding toward Brad, "and, we assume, taken to Vietnam."

"Actually," Duff said, "as far as we can determine, they are *not* in Vietnam. The US Consul in Saigon has made inquiries to the government of Vietnam. He says he's confident that they were not abducted by Nguyen Li Minh."

Erin looked at Brad and was quiet for a few seconds. "So where are they, Duff?"

"We don't know." He paused. "Here's the problem, Erin. This is not a top national security priority. You know the drill. If it's not Islamic Jihadists or weapons of mass destruction about to be unleashed in Kansas or San Francisco, it's not going to get much attention from Homeland Security. Same for the FBI."

Brad shook his head.

"So who's working on it, Duff?" Erin asked.

"Besides you?"

"Yes. Besides me, who's working on it?"

"Me."

Chapter 16

WITH OVER NINETY MILLION PASSENGERS annually, Harts-field International, officially Hartsfield-Jackson Atlanta International, was the busiest airport in the world. Remarkably, it was fairly easy to get around, both outside and inside the mammoth facility. I followed the signs to a long-term parking lot near the international terminal. I backed my truck into a space along a fence, scanned the area for the shuttle bus stop, and dragged my stiff body out of the vehicle. I stretched and suddenly realized that my head wasn't hurting. The absence of pain was a feeling I had nearly forgotten. I liked it.

Anticipating that arriving with no reservations for an international flight, no luggage, and a pocket full of cash would set off alarms with the Transportation Security Administration, I had made a quick shopping trip. I had stopped at a Wal-Mart just outside of Atlanta near the Mall of Georgia, where I purchased a few items of clothing and two pieces of luggage. I would check a midsized bag and carry the smaller one onto the airplane like a normal person.

On the other hand, I didn't consider myself a normal person. Even on long flights across the country, I seldom flew commercial. I owned my own plane and preferred to maintain my own schedule. I didn't like to subject myself to security checks and body searches, which I viewed as completely worthless. The TSA, like most federal and state agencies, is too bureaucratic to be effective and too committed to political correctness to find real threats. They spend too much time ensuring that grandmothers and children aren't carrying weapons and not enough time engaging people who are more likely to kill others and themselves. Occasionally, when they do get it right, they are stopped and locked down by the American Civil Liberties Union or a group of liberal politicians. Ninety percent of the security measures taken at airports could be eliminated with no increase in the risk to flyers. The focus should be on people, motives, and objects—in that order. TSA gets it backwards, but they may have no choice.

I put some personal items and the GPS in the carry-on bag and threw everything else into the midsized suitcase. Slinging the smaller bag's strap over my shoulder like a miniature duffel bag, I pulled the suitcase behind me to the pickup point for the shuttle. I waited patiently for a ride to the terminal. It was about two o'clock, hot as hell, but with more humidity, I assumed. Perspiration ran down my neck and back.

Soon I was sitting on a small shuttle bus with a handful of other passengers. The driver announced that the trip to the airport would take about five minutes and that she would deliver the passengers to the airlines they had requested. The sun was unrelenting as it bore down on the little bus, challenging an inadequate air-conditioning system.

Though uncomfortable in my damp golf shirt and khaki slacks, I sat quietly, avoiding eye contact with my fellow travelers, as though any one of them might challenge my forged passport and driver's license. Glancing around, however, I found that everybody on the bus was engaged with a cell phone or tablet computer. I was thoroughly invisible, and that suited me just fine.

~~~

The long line of customers in front of the American Airlines counter was made less daunting by the efficient air-conditioning system inside the international terminal building. I relaxed, pulled out my documents, and studied them to ensure that I could answer any questions that might be forthcoming.

When an attractive young woman in a red, white, and blue uniform raised her hand, signaling me to advance to her counter, I walked forward confidently, pulling my cheap suitcase along for the ride.

"May I help you, sir?" said a young woman with dark hair and big brown eyes. Her nameplate read *Margaret.* She smiled politely as she waited for me.

"Yes, Margaret," I said. "I want to purchase a ticket, round-trip, of course, to Saigon, Vietnam. I went online and determined that I could fly round-trip from Atlanta to Saigon."

"Just spur of the moment, you've decided to go to Saigon?" she said with a bit of suspicion in her voice.

"Well, yes," I said, preparing to tell my story and thinking that maybe the security system was better than I had judged. "I never thought I would go back, to be honest. I was there during the Vietnam War. One of my buddies, a fellow soldier, called me this morning and said that he's on his way over. He thought about me, then called and asked if I could join him and some other buddies. I'm widowed and retired, and I have a lot of flexibility. So I just got in my truck and drove to Atlanta, and here I am. I got here early enough to work it out, if I can go today. If not, I'll go tomorrow or even the next day."

Her smile broadened. She studied the passport and driver's license that I had placed in front of her. "No reservation, Mr. Evans?" she asked.

"No, ma'am. I looked it up online, but I'm not very good with computers, so I just thought I'd drive down and get an actual person to help me."

She punched in some keys on her computer terminal. "Well, I am an actual person, and, lucky you, there are seats available, quite a few, actually. I suppose it's the recession. Quite expensive, however. Let's see, round-trip, that would be $2,873.42, coach, assuming you are staying more than seven days in Vietnam."

"Oh, yes," I smiled. "I'd like to stay ten days."

"You have just the one small bag?" She seemed suspicious again.

I shrugged. "I prefer to travel light, and I can buy stuff over there if necessary."

"Certainly you can. So shall I book you coach, and do you want to check the one bag?"

"Yes, please. Check this one, and I just have this small carry-on with my camera, a GPS, and some travel guides." I placed a prepaid credit card on the counter. I had purchased $4,000 on an AMEX card during my Wal-Mart stop, so it was perfect.

Margaret ran the card, printed out my boarding pass, a receipt, and a baggage claim ticket.

"It's a pretty long flight," she warned. "Atlanta to Fort Worth to Japan to Saigon. Two hours plus to Fort Worth, then you'll fly all night to Japan, then all day to Vietnam, unless there are delays, which there usually are, unfortunately."

"No problem," I said as I collected the printouts. I thanked her again and headed toward security, hoping it would go smoothly. I would soon be disappointed.

~~~

The line for passenger screening looked like merging fences at a slaughterhouse, nervous cattle bleating and stumbling, sensing their throats were about to be cut. But the livestock here were people, all sizes and shapes, mostly large people, carrying too much weight on their bodies and too many things in their luggage.

I tried to be calm, but calm was not available. I felt like the hapless cattle, certain someone was going to cut my throat as I neared the magnetic imaging equipment that would expose my body parts in stark contrast for some anonymous TSA agent more interested in the end of his shift than the job at hand.

I presented my boarding pass and driver's license to the agent who would direct me to one of eight lines for further scrutiny. Sweat beaded on my forehead and neck. The agent who checked my pass and license was a large Hispanic woman, wearing a tight-fitting uniform and a scowl. She turned slightly and raised her hand.

Two male agents quickly approached, both seriously muscled, one African American and one Caucasian. The gatekeeper handed the driver's license and boarding pass to the Caucasian agent. He looked at me. "You'll have to come with us," he said.

"Is there a problem?" My heart was racing in my chest.

"Just follow us," he said, as though directing a frightened child.

I followed. My gut churned. I felt like I was going to vomit.

Soon we reached a small, glass-enclosed room with a round table and four plastic chairs. One of the men motioned for me to sit down. The two agents sat across from me. The gray plastic chairs were far too small and, perhaps, intentionally uncomfortable.

"Do you have a passport, Mr. Evans?" the Caucasian agent asked. He was bigger than me, maybe six-two, and well over two hundred pounds of hard body, shaped by heavy steel plates and multiple reps. He looked Italian and had a New York or New Jersey accent, probably Jersey, I thought.

"Yes, sir," I said to Jersey.

The African American man was shorter than me, maybe five foot nine or ten, but he had thighs as thick as an NFL running back. He examined the passport that I had laid on the table.

"Do you know why you were pulled out of the line?" Jersey asked.

"Random selection?" I said. I tried to smile, but my lips turned down instead of up.

"Hardly," NFL said. His voice was higher than I would have anticipated. He was from the Deep South, maybe Louisiana.

"Then I have no idea."

"Okay," Jersey said. "You show up with no reservation. You purchase a ticket with a prepaid credit card. You seem nervous." He tried for a look of intimidation. "Doesn't he seem nervous, Ned?" He nodded to his partner.

"He does," Ned said.

I took a deep breath. "Okay. You got me. I am very nervous. Last time I flew was on my way back from Vietnam in 1969. I've lived on a farm in the country for four decades. Never thought I would go back. Got shot up twice over there in '68 and '69." I pulled up my shirt like Lyndon Johnson showing off his gall bladder surgery, and revealed an ugly scar that crossed my chest diagonally. "Eighty-two millimeter mortar round, August '69. I'm nervous as a goat, but my buddies called me this morning and begged me to meet them in Saigon as soon as possible, so I'm on my way if I can get through security."

Jersey smiled. "Ned, let's help this American hero get through this bullshit security. We can run him through the airline queue." Both men stood.

I took that as a signal and stood as well.

"Thank you for your service, Mr. Evans," Ned said in his high Southern drawl. He held out his hand, and I shook it.

"Follow me," Jersey said as he led me toward a fast-check security line.

I breathed a sigh of relief.

Chapter 17

JEN STOOD ON A SHORT porch attached to the guest house where she and the children were imprisoned. She looked down at Minh, made more diminutive by the foot-high porch. He looked up at her as he begged for her cooperation.

"This is not a place for children," he said.

"I will not leave my children under any circumstances," Jen insisted. Her arms were crossed and her back was straight.

"It will be a long drive. The jungle is dark and foreboding." He was getting more emotional with each word. His flat face darkened, and his small, dark eyes stared hard at her. "They will be safe and more comfortable staying here. My wife will care for them."

"No. Under no circumstances will I leave my children." She stood her ground. "You can take me by force, of course, but I will not leave of my own free will. Absolutely not."

She noticed that Minh looked at his driver, who with little effort could have picked her up and thrown her into the waiting Mercedes. He shook his head. "You are a stubborn woman."

"I am a mother," Jen said, her voice rising. "I'm certain that your wife would respond in the same manner, putting your children's safety above all matters."

Minh nodded. "She would." He took a deep breath. "Okay. Put enough clothing together for three nights. The tents and cots are comfortable, but there are no toilet facilities. I will provide spray for the mosquitoes, and we have netting, of course."

"Why?" Jen asked, still not moving.

"Because," he said sarcastically, "the mosquitoes bite."

"No, I mean, why are you taking us out into the jungle?"

"Because that is where I told your father to meet us. I am thinking he is getting close, and that he will be here in a day or two, maybe three. I want to be where I told him to meet us."

"Okay. Give me a little time to get the children ready to go."

"An hour. We leave in an hour," Minh said, trying to reassert his control.

"Fine," Jen said. "An hour."

~~~

Brad glanced at Deputy Director Erin Stephens as they rode the elevator to the fourth floor of a building that housed offices for Homeland Security in Washington, DC. He thought he noticed a hint of makeup on her face. She had been perfectly professional with him, cordial and grateful for his assistance. But on the short ride up the elevator shaft, he observed something different in the way she glanced up at him through her long eye lashes.

A bell rang, and the doors opened to a crowd of men and women in dress clothes. Some held signs welcoming Erin. Everyone smiled and jockeyed for an opportunity to speak with her about the gunfight that had nearly ended her life.

Brad hung back as a tall woman, north of fifty years old, put her arm around Erin's shoulder, careful not to touch her bandages, and gave her a gentle hug.

"Welcome back," the lady said. "You've had us pretty worried about you. Good to see you're healing, but you don't need to get back in the saddle so soon."

"Thank you, Madam Secretary," Erin said. "I'm just here to check on an investigation, and honestly, I agree. I'm not ready to get back in the saddle quite yet. But I'm doing fine, really."

Brad waited as Erin spoke to all her colleagues, one by one, until she came to a tall young man with short blond hair and thick glasses. She pointed toward a conference room and gestured to Brad that he should join them there.

"Brad," she said as he approached, "this is Duff."

The two men shook hands. Duff's hands were thin. His skin was pale.

"What have you got for us, Duff?" she asked as they all sat near the end of an oblong conference table.

"Not much," Duffy said in an amazing baritone voice that sounded like the reincarnation of Bing Crosby.

"What about it not being this Minh character?" Brad asked.

"Well, that's sort of strange. There was a private jet that flew from Saigon to Virginia, Virginia to North Carolina, and North Carolina to Saigon. We can trace those flights. Can't hide from the FAA. But as to Nguyen Li Minh being on those flights or being in the United States during this time, the Vietnamese government flatly denies it. They also deny that any US citizens have been kidnapped and taken to Vietnam against their will."

"But General Bradley and Mia are dead." Erin's blue eyes danced with energy, and her face showed growing anger. "Three of my men were killed near this very building. Two FBI agents were killed in North Carolina. Several men who appeared to be Vietnamese were killed in Virginia and North Carolina. These are facts."

"And Florence Johnson was stabbed in my father's home," said Brad, looking at Erin. "Plus you were shot."

"I know these are facts," Duffy said. "But the State Department has approached the Socialist Republic of Vietnam at the highest levels here and in Saigon, and they deny that a citizen of their country is involved, and absolutely that Nguyen Li Minh is involved."

"Have they questioned Nguyen Li Minh?" Erin said.

"No," Duffy said.

"*No? Are you kidding me?*" Erin's incredulous expression reflected Brad's own frustration. She stood, turning her torso to relieve some tension. "Why not?"

"State says they must follow protocol and allow the authorities of the host country to make inquiries. But they are told that Nguyen Li Minh is a man of high standing and that no one from the government is willing to approach him on these matters."

Brad stood. "This is bullshit. You mean the government of the United States of America is unable to protect women and children from rogue citizens of countries like Vietnam? Are we that impotent?"

He turned toward the door and took two steps before Erin put her hand on his shoulder to stop him.

"Wait, Brad," she said. She turned back to Duffy. "Look, I've got six weeks of medical leave. I may take some vacation in Southeast Asia. What can you give me on this Nguyen Li Minh?"

"Quite a bit," Duffy said. "Quite a bit."

~~~

I settled into a seat in the emergency row on an Airbus A340-600. I had been able to reserve the first aisle seat in the economy section of the plane. Looking around, I saw that there were many vacant seats, so I didn't feel guilty taking a seat that a six-foot-eight-inch power forward might need. Of course, a power forward could probably afford business or first-class seating.

I waited anxiously to see if anyone was assigned to the window seat beside me. It seemed that no one was until the very last minute, just before the door to the plane was closed. An attractive woman, perhaps mid-fifties, wearing a yellow sundress, white sandals, and a few extra pounds, appeared in the doorway. She walked my way and sat down beside me. She wore a yellow straw hat that matched the dress and carried a large yellow purse over her right shoulder. Her natural red hair was cut very short. She turned to me with a big smile. Her big brown eyes appeared friendly beneath large, round glasses. "I'm Martha," she said, holding out her hand.

I took her hand and said, simply, "Travis." I smiled briefly and said nothing more.

Martha stood and placed her purse and hat beneath the seat in front of us, then returned to her seat and engaged the seatbelt.

Within minutes, the plane was taxiing down the tarmac toward the runway and climbing into a clear Georgia sky brightened by stars and a full moon.

I silently hoped that Martha was not a talker. Despite the three pills I had taken just before getting on the plane, I could feel a headache developing. Though we were supposed to take off at eight o'clock in the evening, it was already after nine. I knew that sleep was out of the question. Even in times of less stress and pain, I had never been able to sleep on airplanes. That was a good problem to have when I was the pilot in charge, but it wasn't so good on long international flights. I sat quietly with my hands in my lap, like a bronze statue in a city park.

When the flight leveled off at thirty thousand feet, Martha retrieved her purse and removed a travel guide on Vietnam. "Will this reading lamp bother you?" she asked.

"No, ma'am, not at all," I said quietly.

"I can't sleep on these flights," she said. "There was a time when I used to try, but finally I just decided that it wasn't going to happen, so why fight it?"

"Same here."

"You're not a reader?" She smiled, and two dimples showed on her cheeks. Her teeth were very white and straight. "Most men don't read."

"Well, actually, I do read quite a bit, but my eyes have been bothering me some lately."

"Oh, sorry." She turned to the travel guide and began reading. Ten minutes later she asked, "Are you going to Japan or on to Vietnam?"

"Vietnam."

"First time since you were in the war?"

"Yes. How did you know?"

"I'm a psychologist with the VA, just retired," she said as she closed the book. "You look like a lot of my former patients. I often encouraged them to go back, but few did. My husband died two years ago. I decided to go myself. Why are you going now?"

"Sorry about your husband," I said. "For me, it's complicated."

"It always is. What unit were you with?"

"First Cav, '68–'69."

"Bloodiest years of the war. Most active combat unit. Air mobile got you in front of the bad guys, no matter where they were coming in from."

"True."

"What was your MOS?"

"Eleven bravo, platoon leader."

"CIB. How many purples?" she asked.

"Two."

"What's your story?" she asked, turning toward me and looking me directly in the eyes.

"What do you mean?"

"I'd like to hear your story," she said, her eyes dancing now. "Have you ever told anybody?"

"I don't really have a story. I just went over, did what I had to do, then came home. That's about it."

"Right. And you got a Combat Infantryman's Badge and two Purple Hearts. I'm betting green, bronze, and silver, also. Am I right?"

I nodded slightly.

She nearly chuckled. "Tell me your story, Travis. We've got ten hours minimum flying through the night sky, and we're both insomniacs. You can't read, but you can talk. You can tell me your story. Have you ever told anyone? I bet your wife wanted to come with you, and you said no, right?"

"No. My wife died in 1997."

"Sorry." She paused. "Did you ever talk about Vietnam with her or with your children or friends?"

"No. I came home, put the medals in a drawer, put the uniform in a box in the attic, and tried to forget it all—every bit of it."

"But you have a story, Travis. Tell me."

"I wouldn't know where to start," I said. My head was hurting, but not too bad.

"Start anywhere you like, beginning, end, middle… Just tell me what happened."

I turned slightly toward her. "Okay, I'll tell you something they told me I could never tell anybody, since it was completely off the record, top secret. But they're all dead now, and we lost the damn war anyway, so why not? I'll tell you that story. It was at the end of my tour, the very end."

Chapter 18

MY BEST FRIEND AND PLATOON sergeant, Sergeant First Class Marvin Evans, was killed on LZ Phyllis on May 10, 1969. We were pulling perimeter security for a field artillery battery that was nearly overrun that night. I lost two other men in addition to Pep.

Pep and I were moving around the perimeter that night, looking for any penetration by the enemy. Bullets were flying everywhere. I was running toward an M-60 machine gun position with four belts of ammo draped over my shoulders when I killed a sapper carrying a bag of explosives near a bunker. That's when I realized that Pep was no longer with me. I went back looking for him, but in the confusion of the battle, I never saw him again. The next morning, one of my squad leaders found him in a bunker with an AK round through his throat. It looked like he had gone in to check on a wounded grunt. Both men were dead.

My platoon was in pretty bad shape, so Captain Walter Bradley tried to keep us out of the shit as much as possible. After a couple of weeks, he sent First Sergeant Emerson Trainer to bring me in for a meeting.

"Travis," he said as I stood in front of his HQ bunker, "I've asked battalion to get you out of the field."

"Why is that, sir?" I asked.

"Because you've been out here ten months. That's five months longer than me and seven months longer than any of the other platoon leaders. In fact, I just checked. You've been out here longer than any man currently active in the goddamn company. You're living on borrowed time."

"Like Pep," I said.

"Yeah, like Pep. You and he got here about the same time, right?"

"One day apart."

"Look, pack up your shit. Colonel Drum wants to talk to you."

"Now? The brigade commander?"

"Yes, now. Your replacement is coming in on the chopper that will take you to see the BC."

I took a deep breath. It was the first time in four or five months that I thought I might make it back home. "It's not necessary, sir. You know that."

"I know it, Travis, but it's happening. It's not a suggestion. It's an order. Get your shit, get on that chopper that's coming now, and report to Colonel Drum."

"Yes, sir." I started to walk away.

"Lieutenant Kelly," he said.

I turned back to face him.

He saluted me and held out his right hand. "You're a helluva soldier, and I'm damn proud to have served with you."

We shook hands, and I walked away.

I gathered my poncho and poncho liner, rolled them together and tied them under my rucksack. My new platoon sergeant was a seasoned veteran, second tour in Vietnam. Now in his mid-thirties, he had been a nineteen-year-old grunt in the Korean War. Phil McDermont was his name.

"I've been reassigned, Phil," I told him.

"Sorry to hear that for me and the men, sir, but good for you. You've done your time."

"New LT is on the way. Be gentle with him. Probably just out of OCS like me when I got here."

"Yeah, plus jump and Ranger school and a year with the 82nd. I'd say you were ready when you got here." He smiled as we shook hands.

"Good luck, Phil. Hope to run into you again. Give my air mattress to somebody who needs it. I'm hoping I can sleep on a cot the next couple of months." I left him to say goodbye to some of the other men.

~~~

The brigade sergeant major greeted me as I stepped off the chopper in from the boonies. His name was Mike Nelson. He was from Kansas.

"Lieutenant Kelly," he said, snapping off a salute.

I returned the salute.

He was taller than me, maybe six foot three, and built like an Olympic swimmer, with broad shoulders and a flat stomach. Though he was at least forty-five years old, he could hold his own with any twenty-year-old rifleman. His uniform was clean, his jungle boots were shined, and his hair was cut military short.

I, on the other hand, was skinny and unshaven, with sunken eyes and shaggy hair. My uniform was filthy, and my jungle boots were scraped and battered. I was a little embarrassed, standing in front of him in my condition, but he took all that away with an engaging smile.

"I've been looking forward to meeting you, sir," he said. "Same for Colonel Drum."

"Really?" I said. "I'm surprised he knows my name. Or that you do."

"Hell, everybody at HQ knows your name, and Pep's, too. Damn shame we lost him. I could see him a sergeant major someday."

"Well, you're right about Pep, that's for sure."

"Follow me, sir," he said.

He escorted me into a mobile home that had been buried underground and covered with sandbags. It was air conditioned, powered by generators, and had working bathrooms. The living room and bedrooms had been turned into small offices lined with combat maps. Six or seven officers in clean uniforms stood around a scuffed wooden table, discussing battle plans and reconnaissance. They ignored the sergeant major as he led me to a back room.

Colonel Drum stood from his desk when we entered. He was a full bird, about my height, just over six feet, with short blond hair and a square face.

I walked to his desk, stood at attention, and saluted. "Lieutenant Kelly, reporting, sir."

He returned my salute, then sat back in his chair and said, "Have a seat, Lieutenant."

I sat without speaking as Sergeant Major Nelson left the office and closed the door.

"I've been wanting to meet you, son," the colonel said, his deep blue eyes gazing at me steadily.

I nodded, not sure how to respond.

"You have quite a reputation of accomplishment. Both your company commanders have given you very high marks. You've got a chest full of medals, well deserved, from what I hear, and I'm betting you could have had more had there been somebody to write up everything you did in all the firefights you've been engaged in. I want to personally thank you for the job you've done." He stood and walked around the desk, offering his hand.

I stood and shook hands. "I don't know what to say, sir, but thank you."

"Well, sit down. Let's talk for a few minutes." He leaned on his desk.

I sat again.

"I've got a job for you, a piece of cake for somebody who has been doing what you've been doing. When you leave here, you can go take a shower, get something to eat if you're hungry, and then report back to Major Billings."

"What is it, sir?"

"Reading infrared hits from fixed-wing recon aircraft that fly each night. You'll get reports first thing every morning. You plot the hits on maps and provide the information to our recon specialists. I need somebody who has been in the field to help make sense of it. I think you're the best man for the job. But there is one problem." He pushed a button on his desk and spoke into a speaker. "Sergeant Major," he said.

The door opened, and Sergeant Major Nelson walked in with an arm full of fresh jungle fatigues, new jungle boots, green tee-shirts, and boxer shorts.

"You're going to have to clean up and look more presentable."

I smiled. "Yes, sir." I stood to accept the clothes from the sergeant major.

"Plus, this job calls for a captain. We've taken the liberty of sewing captain's bars on the lapels for you. Congratulations, Captain Kelly."

~~~

The showers were not elaborate by any means. In fact, they were simply large canvas bags that allowed cold water to flow over your body by the force of gravity. But it was the first shower I'd had since R&R, and I stood beneath it a long time. There was actual soap, plus wash cloths and towels. Unbelievable. I scrubbed the jungle grime off my body for nearly an hour. Then I put on the fresh underwear. It was first time I had worn any since my first week in the boonies. I put on the crisp new uniform and boots. I shaved in front of a mirror. That was an experience in humility. The soldier looking back at me was a shadow of the man who had flown to Vietnam ten months earlier. I was just over six feet tall and weighed two hundred pounds when Claire drove me to the airport in North Carolina. My guess was that I had dropped thirty pounds minimum, maybe forty. I looked like shit.

I was directed to a tent where an elderly Vietnamese man was cutting hair. After my haircut, I put a new camouflage cover on my steel pot with black captain bars pinned in the center front, and pulled on my shoulder holster with my forty-five in it. Finally, I reported to Major Billings, who was working in the colonel's headquarters bunker.

Billings was a red-headed man with pale, freckled skin. He was about my size, or the size I was when I'd arrived in Vietnam. He didn't smile, but I liked him immediately.

"You eat, yet?" he asked when I introduced myself.

"No, sir," I said.

"Let's go to the mess tent. We can talk there." He pointed me in the direction of a large tent in the middle of the compound.

Real food, not C-rations or dehydrated meals, was served by enlisted men in a line, as in a cafeteria in the States. It was served on paper plates, but it was real food. Plastic forks, knives, and spoons were provided. Large containers of milk and coffee lined the walls on one side. The large tent could serve two hundred men at one time, but the eating schedule was staggered so that it was never crowded. The midday meal would close down at 1400, which was a half hour away.

Billings and I sat alone at a crudely built side table, much like a large picnic table but not very stable.

"First hot meal in a while?" he asked, almost smiling.

My plate was piled high with virtually everything offered on the service line. "Yes, sir. Now I'm not sure I can eat all this." I took a few bites and drank the milk.

"Give it a while," he said. "Your stomach is probably the size of a walnut. I lost forty pounds on my first tour."

"What did you do?"

"Field artillery forward observer, out humping with an infantry company like the one you just left."

I noticed the field artillery insignia—crossed cannons with a rocket through the middle—on his collar opposite the black oak leaf, indicating both major and lieutenant colonel. I knew he was a major.

I took a few more bites and pushed the plate away as I drank more milk.

"Let me describe your new job," he said.

I nodded, wiping my milk mustache away with the back of my sleeve.

"We fly fixed-wing aircraft all night up and down the Cambodian border. They're equipped with infrared sensors that pick up body heat. The data are transferred to acetate maps that can be overlaid on combat maps in the HQ bunker. You'll have a stack of them every morning by 0600 hours. Your job will be to match the acetate maps with field maps, plot the positions, and try to make some sense out of it. You will be provided coordinates of all friendly positions. You'll need to segregate the bad guys from the good guys, see if any patterns emerge, then provide me with both the raw data and your analysis. You'll work from 0600 to as long as it takes, but generally 1800. Twelve hours of this kind of work is about all your brain and eyes can take. Then you come in the next day and do it all over again." Still he didn't smile. I heard emotion and conviction in his voice, but didn't see it in his broad Irish face.

"When do I start?"

"Oh-six-hundred tomorrow morning," he said as we both stood. "One of my men will get you to your bunk and help you get organized the rest of today. You can sleep, if possible, or generally relax until you go on duty. Lights, or excuses for lights, go on at 0530 in your quarters. There are ten officers in each tent. We'll walk back to HQ, and Specialist Trudinak will take you from there. Got it?"

"Yes, sir." I picked up my full plate of food and empty cup of milk and dropped them in a large steel drum that served as a trash can.

Chapter 19

THE LUSH JUNGLE HOVERED OVER the sedan like a grandmother happy to see her children's children. Unlike the asphalt highways on which they had driven for three hours after leaving Minh's residential compound, this road, though straight and narrow, was built from hard red clay and stone.

Jen sat in the back seat of the Mercedes. She checked LB's blood sugar, found it to be low, and gave him a pack of crackers with a couple slices of cheese.

She smiled to herself as she watched Minh bang on the side of his iPhone, as though it would help obtain a signal in the deep jungle. He said something in Vietnamese. The driver nodded, but, naturally, said nothing.

She glanced back at a midsized truck that followed closely behind. It was driven by the two bodyguards and presumably packed with provisions for their stay in the jungle. It maintained a distance of about two car lengths behind the Mercedes.

Minh turned toward her. "How is your son's health?" he asked.

"He's fine," she said. "But I'm not excited about having him or any of my children go so deep into the jungle."

"Duly noted, and you will recall that I suggested that they stay at my residence."

Jen didn't answer.

The car slowed. The driver nodded to a place where they could pull off the road.

"Yes. This is the place," Minh said. He seemed excited as the car was parked beneath a ring of tall trees.

~~~

The coffee shop was packed. Brad sat with Erin at a small, round table in the corner of the popular establishment.

"So you have no passport?" she asked.

"No. I've been traveling on Uncle Sam for over ten years." Brad sipped his Americano and looked at Erin over the rim of the cup. He noticed her large blue eyes and the fact that she had done something different with her blond hair. "No need for a passport."

"Well, the good news is that I can get you one in less than twenty-four hours, one of the perks of working with Homeland Security. We'll walk down to the passport office from here. Could have one in a few hours, really." She smiled up at him as she cupped her coffee in both hands. "I'm guessing you have a top secret clearance."

"Yes, I do," he said. "So what now?"

"I say get the passport process started for you. Go back to my condo, get on the computer, and book flights and accommodations for a trip to Saigon, or Ho Chi Minh City, as their government prefers to call it." She leaned back and self-consciously touched her hand to the bullet wound above her breast. "We go to the US consulate and then straight to Nguyen Li Minh's home and inquire about your sister and her family. What do you think?"

"I say that sounds like a good plan for me, but I don't want you to get in trouble for helping me." He looked intently into her eyes and felt she was studying him. It was as though they were having a staring contest to see who blinked first.

Erin blinked. "Sorry," she said. "I was thinking about something else. What did you say?"

He smiled, almost chuckling. "I said I don't want you to get in trouble for helping me."

"I'm not worried about that. I'm on leave for at least six weeks. I can go where I want and do pretty much what I want to do."

He glanced down at her white blouse, which was unbuttoned enough so that bandages showed. "Do you think you should be traveling so soon after the surgery?"

She instinctively touched the buttons on her blouse. "I'm fine. I feel better every hour, really. Not going to run a marathon, but I don't see why I can't travel, especially if I have a companion to help me with my luggage."

"No problem," Brad said. "Okay, let's do it."

~~~

A tall steward, handsome in his red, white, and blue uniform, stopped and quietly offered Martha and me drinks. It was after eleven, and most of the passengers were sleeping.

"Water," Martha said.

I nodded. "Same."

After the steward had handed us our cups, Martha said, "Very interesting, but this doesn't sound like top-secret material so far." She smiled, and two dimples punctuated the center of her cheeks.

I noticed the freckles that lightly crossed her nose just below her eyes. "I'm getting there." I took a long drink of the water and a deep breath, then returned to my story.

~~~

I fell into the routine of the job pretty quickly. Brigade headquarters was located on a major, nearly permanent facility at the Biên Hòa Air Base. Planes took off and landed twenty-four seven. One or two enemy rockets whistled in and exploded every night. Still, I had no problem working and sleeping, counting the days until my DEROS, Date Eligible for Return from Overseas, which was 31 August '69. I gained weight.

About the second week in August, I felt great and weighed 185, up ten or fifteen pounds. I was overlaying the infrared hits on my combat maps when I detected a distinct pattern of enemy activity. My small army desk barely held a full array of maps. I stood and moved them around so I could better understand what I was seeing. I pulled out my reports from the prior seven days, then turned and walked to Major Billings' desk.

"Sir," I said. "You need to see this." I walked back to my small corner desk. When I looked up, Major Billings was standing close.

"What is it?" he asked, looking at my maps, his bushy eyebrows raised.

"Look here," I said. I showed him the infrared hits from the prior night. Then I pulled out the report of the night before, and the one before that. "See," I said. "They're massing a large force, very large. It's been coming together over the past week."

"Okay, I see that. But they're well within the borders of Cambodia. Not much we can do about that."

"Yes, but look." I pointed at three friendly positions on the map. "Field artillery units, M101s. This one is five miles from Cambodia."

"Right. We're pretty active in that area," Billings noted.

"We are. But look at our infantry positions. They're all wrong. No help here." I pointed them out on the map. "And look at these enemy hits. And look at where they moved from night before last to last night." My heart was pounding.

"Damn. You're right." He practically ran toward Colonel Drum's office.

The colonel was normally in the field with his fighting units, but he was in his office that morning.

Both men appeared at my desk in seconds. Other officers gathered around.

"Go over that with the colonel, Travis, like you just went over it with me," Billings said between breaths.

I explained it carefully and clearly.

"Holy shit," Colonel Drum said. "They're massing to overrun Charlie Battery."

"Yes, sir," I said. "And they may not wait until nightfall."

The room cleared as though somebody had yelled, "Grenade!"

I could hear helicopter engines cranking up. A lieutenant colonel was on the phone with air support. A major was calling the 2nd Brigade commander. We were the 3rd Brigade. The wheels of combat were swinging into motion. Suddenly I was alone in the trailer, and I had no idea what I was supposed to do. So I just sat there and monitored the radios. It was like listening to Orson Welles's *War of the Worlds*. I was too far away to hear the battles as they began, but I could hear the communications between the Air Force and Army officers as they initiated the process of bringing the full power of the US Armed Forces down on two regiments of North Vietnamese regular army units, nearly two thousand enemy soldiers who were poised to overrun an artillery battery defended by about one hundred fifty American artillery and infantrymen.

~~~

The next day was filled with fist pumping and shouts of bravado. We had won a major victory. I was proud of my role, but I kept my head down and quietly did my job as though nothing had happened.

Mid-morning, however, Major Billings asked me to go with him to the mess tent for a cup of coffee. When we got there, just about everybody in the recon operation was standing around. Sergeant Major Nelson and Colonel Drum walked in. Major Billings escorted me to them. The sergeant major yelled, "Attention!"

To my great surprise, in walked General Creighton Abrams, commander of all American forces in South Vietnam.

"As you were," he commanded, and we all relaxed just a little.

He shook hands with Colonel Drum, who pointed him toward me. Suddenly I was standing in front of a four-star general.

"Captain Kelly," he said, "I want to personally thank you for the work you did, determining with great accuracy what our enemy was planning. You, through your diligence and skill, helped us to orchestrate a major victory against North Vietnamese forces. And, had you not acted decisively and effectively, we could have suffered an embarrassing defeat, and many American soldiers would be wounded and dead today. I have instructed my adjutant to prepare a letter of commendation which I will personally sign and place in your file. You are a credit to the uniform and to the US Army." He offered to shake my hand.

I shook hands, then saluted him as though he had pinned a metal on my chest.

The tent broke out in applause, and I was seriously embarrassed.

~~~

My replacement arrived the next week, and I was asked to provide him with three days OJT. Then I was permitted to start the DEROS process.

Just a few days away from getting on a helicopter that would take me to Tan Son Nhut Air Base and a civilian jet home, I was generally killing time, eating, and sleeping. I had become good friends with the mess sergeant, a fellow North Carolinian named Frank Thompson. We were playing chess in the mess tent at about 1500 hours when a tall lieutenant colonel walked in. We both stood as he walked toward us.

"As you were, men," he said. "I'm looking for Captain Kelly."

"Yes, sir, I'm Captain Kelly," I said.

"May I speak with you for a few minutes?"

"Certainly."

Frank nodded and walked back toward the kitchen.

"I'm from division headquarters, on General Beauchamp's staff," he said. His nametag said *Davis*. "I was sent here to escort you to an important meeting."

"Sir, can I ask what this is about?" I was a little worried. "I DEROS in a couple of days."

"I know. We all know." He looked concerned. "But, no, I am not at liberty to tell you what this is about. General Beauchamp got a call, and he asked me to locate you and escort you to an important meeting. Gather all your gear. You won't be coming back here."

I thought it might have something to do with the battle a couple of weeks ago. Maybe an award of some kind. But it didn't feel that way. It felt like shit.

I nodded to Colonel Davis, and we walked together to get my duffel bag, then out to a chopper that was cranked and ready to go.

I had just written what I hoped would be my last letter to Claire. I told her I would be arriving in Charlotte in four or five days. I was hoping I would beat the letter home. Now I wasn't so sure.

Chapter 20

BRAD SAT ON A SOFA in Erin Stephens's condo in northern Virginia. Though the clock said 8:30, it was still daylight on a hot July night. Soft music played from an iPod plugged into speakers on a bookshelf nearby.

"Would you like to have the wine on the back patio?" Erin asked. "According to their newsletter, the homeowners association sprayed for mosquitoes about a week ago, so it might be somewhat pleasant." She handed him a glass of Shiraz.

"Sure," he said as he stood.

She looked up at him and smiled. "How tall are you?"

"The Army says I'm six feet four inches. My football coach said I was six feet five inches. I'm betting the Army has it right."

"You were at Lenoir-Rhyne University when you joined the Army?" she asked as she led the way to the patio.

"No. I had been out a few years. But I went to LR. It's a small Lutheran school. Expensive, but I got a football scholarship. It's near my home, so my family could come and watch the games. Good school. How about you?"

They sat in two chairs facing the back lawn of the condo complex.

"I went to West Point. My father was in the Army, Vietnam era. He retired with twenty-five years active duty service. I was an Army brat growing up. No boys. He started talking West Point when I started crawling. We're Catholic, but honestly, I couldn't tell you the last time I went to a Mass. It was probably for a funeral."

Brad gazed out over the parched lawn of the housing complex. "My mom was a faithful member of her Lutheran church. I haven't had much opportunity to attend services for the past ten years, but I do confession and communion with the chaplain every time it's offered. When bullets start flying, I don't want to think, 'When was the last time I took communion?'"

She laughed and took a long sip of the wine. "You never married?" She turned to look at him as he answered.

"No. Had a high school sweetheart. But I would not commit while my mom was so sick. When I joined the Army, she never wrote, and six months later, she married a former friend of mine. Took me a while to get over that. Then there really never was much time for relationships. How about you?"

"There was a boy at West Point I thought might have some potential. He was very nice to me, unlike most of the high-testosterone jerks there. I sort of suggested to him one night at a dance that I was interested. He told me that he was gay. It was embarrassing, but sort of funny. We laughed. We're still friends. He's a major now."

"Good for him," Brad said.

"You're okay with gays in the military?"

"I'm okay with people who volunteer and do the job, and as far as I know, everybody who's serving is a volunteer."

"I'm going to cook here since we're leaving so early in the morning. You can sleep in the guest bedroom. Does that sound okay?"

"Sure. Sounds great. Can I help you in the kitchen?"

"No, let me do it. You just relax." She smiled and rose, heading toward the open glass doors leading to the kitchen.

He watched her walk away and thought he might need to reveal the thoughts that were popping into his head at his next confession. He sipped his wine and thought about Jen and the children. The reality of it hit him, and he said, "Damn."

~~~

Colonel Davis told me that we were on our way to MACV headquarters. It stood for Military Assistance Command, Vietnam. He said nothing more as the blades of the Huey chopped through the thick Vietnam air.

We landed at a huge complex on Tan Son Nhut Air Base, where a series of multi-story buildings, heavy on function, light on style, lined the airport like a college quad. Thousands of officers and enlisted men worked in the buildings for the Army, Navy, Marines, and even Coast Guard, plus Air Force, of course.

I followed Davis as he wound through security, showing his ID and escorting me down long hallways. We came to the end of one hallway which terminated at a closed door. Two Marines stood guard, M-16s at the ready. They nodded to him. He knocked once and opened the door, indicating that I should precede him into the room.

A brigadier general, two full-bird colonels, and a four-star general stood around a square table covered with a three-dimensional, raised relief map. The four-star was my new friend, General Creighton Abrams.

"Hey, Travis," he said as though I were his favorite nephew. "Thank you for coming." He offered his hand.

I shook it and smiled, but I was thinking, *Did I have a choice?*

"This is General Gryzbowski, Colonel Fenton, and Colonel Nixon. Gentlemen, this is Captain Kelly." They all nodded, but none offered to shake hands. Their attention returned to the relief map, an elaborate eight-foot-square creation. "Travis, what you're looking at here is a five-square-mile slice of Cambodia, just inside the Parrot's Beak area. I know you've been up and down this border many times on the Vietnam side."

"Yes, sir," I said. I was still completely in the dark.

General Gryzbowski pointed to an area on the map, nodding to the other officers. "Maybe here," he said. It was a meadow probably two or three hundred yards across, oval shaped, with little or no vegetation and flat topography, if you could believe the map.

"I like it," General Abrams said. "Plus, I don't think their attention would be here, but here." He pointed with a long pointer. "Their orientation and complete focus is east, and this is in the westernmost area."

"Steve," he said to Colonel Fenton, "why don't you brief Travis?"

"Sure," Fenton said as he looked at me. "Captain Kelly, I'm sure you're wondering why you're here and what this is all about."

I nodded.

"You remember a couple of weeks ago, the intel you had a big part in led to a major battle along the Cambodian border. We wiped out two regiments of North Vietnamese regulars with virtually no US casualties."

I nodded again.

"We're still bombing that area with any aircraft we can beg, borrow, or steal. Unfortunately, a couple of nights ago, a Marine F-4 was shot down on a bombing run. Both airmen, the pilot and the radar intercept officer, ejected. We know that they survived and were actively engaged in escape and evasion. But we're certain now that they were captured and are being held captive in Cambodia. They will be transported up the Ho Chi Minh Trail to North Vietnam and held as prisoners of war, assuming they survive or aren't simply killed by their captors. We have an asset on the ground inside Cambodia, and he provided these photographs." He showed me two eight-by-ten, black-and-white pictures of men in flight suits in separate bamboo cages. "This is the pilot, Major Ellis," He pointed to one of the men, then to the other. "This is Captain Wendelman."

I nodded again, still not sure how this related to me.

Colonel Nixon took over from there. "We have a Special Forces team ready to go in to try to rescue these flyers before they are transported north. Our asset on the ground, a Vietnamese Chieu Hoi, tells us that the cages are lightly guarded, but the transport date is approaching. The four-man team, like an LRRP team, includes an infantry officer leader, a communications specialist, a medic, and a weapons-specialist-slash-sniper. They're all HALO qualified. So our plan was to drop them, really more a sky dive than HALO, over this area." He pointed to the flat, open area on the map. "They would hook up with the Chieu Hoi, locate and rescue the airmen, then return to this hill." He pointed to a hill marked *Hill 1204*, which indicated just over twelve hundred feet elevation above sea level. "We will extract the team by helicopter from this point."

"We need to go now, as in a few hours," General Gryzbowski said. "But the team leader is in the hospital with malaria."

I was beginning to get the point, and it was like getting punched in the gut.

General Abrams picked up the briefing. "We need a seasoned infantry officer to lead this team. We need someone who has led troops in combat in this very area and knows the nuances of the topography and flora. We need someone who knows how to handle a parachute. Bottom line, Travis, we need you."

"Sir," I said, my pulse racing now, "I'm not Special Forces. I've never led a Long Range Reconnaissance Patrol. I've made only five high altitude, low opening jumps, and that was in the confines of the school at Fort Benning. I was an alternate on the Golden Knights, but that was purely recreational." I didn't mention that my tour was up in a couple of days.

General Abrams put his hand on my shoulder. "Travis, son, we don't have anybody who can do this right now. And we need to do it right now. The weather is perfect. We will drop this team from fifteen thousand feet, so no supplemental oxygen, deploying at two thousand feet. It has to be tonight. We can send the three green berets in without an infantry leader like you, but their chances of success would be significantly diminished. It's a high-risk mission, no doubt. You've done more than your share over here, and your time is up in a couple of days. This is not about what is right or what is wrong. This is about saving two men from possible torture and death at worse, or years of deprivation in a North Vietnamese

POW camp at best. If I had any other option, any other man I could put my hands on who I thought could do this other than you, I would get him. But I don't. It's you or it's nobody."

I swallowed hard and looked back at the map. "Can the Chieu Hoi mark the landing zone with a strobe light? Is he reliable?"

"Yes, he's reliable," said General Gryzbowski. "He'll bury a strobe light, visible only from above."

"What about logistics, extra ammo, water, food, and medical supplies?" I asked.

"They'll be low-altitude dropped here." Colonel Nixon pointed at the map. "Also, here and here. There will be a beacon that your communications man can home in on. Hopefully you're in and out, and you don't need any of these extra supplies."

I walked slowly around the table. "Where do we think the flyers are?"

Colonel Fenton pointed to a trail along the eastern border of the map. "This is the Ho Chi Minh Trail. Our Chieu Hoi says they're about here." He drew a round circle with his finger.

"So, maybe two miles from the drop zone," I said, studying the map carefully. "We'd have to wait until daylight to cover that ground. Couldn't do it at night."

"Right," one of the senior officers said.

"Okay. We land here." I pointed at the map. "We go north into the canopy and set up here for the night. First light, we move east. We identify the target and wait until the following night for extraction. I'd prefer M-14s in this jungle. Can we get flash and sound suppressors?" I said, my mind building a mission checklist. "We can each carry two hundred rounds; heavy, but not too bad."

"Good idea," Colonel Fenton responded. "Yes, we can put flash and sound suppressors on M-14s. You will each have rifles, forty-fives, and survival knives. What else?"

"Jungle hats. Camouflage makeup. Frags and smokes. Strobe lights. Flashlights with red filters. Maps. Compasses. One entrenching tool. Extra dehydrated meals. I bet these men are starving. Two completely full canteens, no sloshing, so we can share with the prisoners. Two extra forty-fives with three clips each so we can arm them." I began to smile. "Okay, I see it now. I want to meet the team. Sounds like the flyers have been in the cages just one day, but it will have been two days by the time we get them out. They may be in pajamas and barefoot. If they're still in their wool flight suits, they will be filthy and hot. I'm sure they have taken their boots. I'd like to take clean jungle fatigues for them, boots, and socks. Can we get their sizes?"

"Absolutely," said General Abrams. "Colonel Fenton will take you from here. He's Special Forces."

Fenton started to lead me out of the room. He turned to General Abrams as we were leaving and said, "Good choice, sir."

Chapter 21

JEN AND HER FOUR CHILDREN were now living in a large tent near the center of a small clearing in the jungle. Three other tents stood nearby. Minh and the big driver had individual tents on either side of Jen's large linen tent. A similar tent had been pitched directly across the fire pit in the center of the campground to house the two bodyguards.

Surprisingly, Minh was the cook. Meals were prepared on an open fire in a large cast-iron pot. The main course was rice, which wasn't good for LB. Side dishes, fish, and vegetables were cooked on small stoves fueled by propane gas.

Jen decided to gather the meals for her family and bring them to the children in their tent. She escorted them to the outdoor toilet facilities. She was especially suspicious of the two bodyguards, small, hard men who said nothing but looked at her in a way that left her with cold chills.

The cots, furnished with blowup air mattresses, were reasonably comfortable. But she slept lightly, like a lioness guarding her cubs. She prayed that her father would come for them, though she was certain this was a setup to ambush and kill him when he fell into the lair.

~~~

Brad carried the luggage, as promised, but there was precious little to carry. Erin walked beside him. She was more than a foot shorter. He liked the fact that she wore comfortable athletic shoes, not fancy high heels. She wasn't a girly girl, but it was impossible to hide her femininity. He liked the confident manner in which she handled herself.

She had their passports, driver's licenses, and boarding passes in hand. He took care of the luggage, a division of labor.

Security at Reagan International was especially tight, with Homeland Security on high alert due to the recent incident involving the assassination of Undersecretary Bradley and the ambush of an HS convoy.

Preferring to fly as a civilian and as far under the radar as possible, Erin told Brad that she preferred not to use her HS status to get through the long lines more quickly. She had discreetly pointed out the cameras to him and had shown him by her own actions how to avoid extra scrutiny as much as possible.

"Just pretend we're a recently married couple on a much-needed vacation," she had said. The way she'd said it made him think she might be making a suggestion. He was not entirely displeased with the thought.

~~~

We wore black flight suits over our jungle fatigues. Our faces were painted black, but we had more camouflage makeup, greens, and dark rust for after we landed. We wore black helmets and goggles. As we sat in the large single-engine plane that cruised toward the Cambodian border, we fidgeted and made repeated checks of our equipment.

I was the only non-Special Forces man on the team. I was also the only officer. The three men, all Green Berets, were seasoned and exceptional. David Robertson was an E-7, sergeant first class, with twelve years of active duty. This was his second tour in Vietnam. He was a communications specialist and carried a compact radio with a ten-mile range. He also had homing devices to find supplies that would be dropped for us in case the mission was extended.

Charles Johnson—we called him CJ—had completed two years of medical school when he ran out of money and enthusiasm. He'd joined the Army and liked it—and he was now a senior medic, also an E-7, sergeant first class, and Green Beret.

Mike Hammer was a weapons specialist, a graduate of the Marines' sniper school, also on his second tour in Vietnam. He was an E-6, staff sergeant.

If you stood the four of us in a line or side-by-side, there would not be a half-inch or ten-pound difference in size. Lay us prone on the floor and draw an outline of our bodies in chalk, and you would never be able to determine which outline belonged to which man. We were all volunteers. We were all Southerners. North Carolina for me, Alabama for CJ, Texas for Dave, and Virginia for Mike Hammer. All four of us had been to the Army's language school in Colorado for immersion in Vietnamese. We were all airborne rangers. Each of us had graduated from the HALO school at Fort Benning. Each of us had made dozens of night jumps like the one that was in front of us.

In the few hours since we had met, we were Travis, CJ, Dave, and Mike. The three men had quickly accepted me as the replacement for their friend and former leader, Lieutenant Pete Peterson.

Everything was black: our faces and hands, our jumpsuits, our helmets, even the wrist bands on our altimeters. It was, technically at least, not a HALO jump. High-altitude, low-opening jumps were usually from twenty thousand feet or more. All of mine had been from thirty thousand feet and pre-dawn, just like this one. This was really just a simple sky dive operation. The fact that we were all HALO school grads, each with dozens of static line and free-fall jumps, was obviously a plus. My sky diving experience was more relevant.

The plane looked like a bush plane, only wider. It was a tail dragger, and its undersurface was painted black. Our parachutes, and even the risers from which they would deploy, were black.

The pilot had met with us on the tarmac at 0300 hours and explained that he would climb to eighteen thousand feet as we flew in the direction of the Cambodian border. A few miles east of the drop zone, he would kill his engine, turning the aircraft into a glider. We had supplemental oxygen, and he said we should breathe the oxygenated air during the flight. He told us we would be at about fifteen thousand feet over the drop zone.

We wore backlit altimeters on our wrists, but we all knew that in free fall, we would be falling about one thousand feet every five seconds, so we would need to deploy our parachutes in about one minute after exiting the aircraft. The ground elevation was around eight hundred feet, so we had to factor that into our calculations.

We each had our equipment strapped tightly to our bodies. Our silenced M-14 rifles were slung over our left shoulders, barrels pointed down. We had access to our .45-caliber pistols if we were engaged by enemy forces before we landed, but a .45 versus an AK-47 would not be much of a fight.

Each of us had extensive experience in steering these relatively high-tech parachutes. We could all find the strobe light and put ourselves close to it. We should be able to see it well from the plane before we jumped.

My heart was thumping as we took off from Tan Son Nhut Air Base. I looked forward to shedding the heavy wool jumpsuit that I wore over my jungle fatigues and equipment. The four of us looked like overstuffed teddy bears, but our arms and legs were perfectly maneuverable for the type of free-fall jump we were going to make.

Noticeably quiet as we approached Cambodia at about eighteen thousand feet, we each took frequent hits of the oxygen so that our minds would be clear. An enlisted man sat in the back with us. His job was to drop the goody packages filled with ammo, water, and other items—supplies I hoped we wouldn't need.

The pilot cut the engine, and the small plane glided in a slightly downward path. I knew enough about flying to know that his main job now was to fly straight and level, avoiding a stall that would send us down in a death spiral. He was an experienced pilot and did his job well.

As the team leader, I would be the first to jump. I saw the strobe light and pointed it out to the others. I prayed a silent prayer that the Chieu Hoi really was on our side, knowing full well that the loyalties of former Viet Cong combatants sometimes swung from one side to the other, depending on who was offering more money, weapons, or food.

We each rose to our knees, our backs to one another, and checked each other's parachute and equipment. "Clear, clear, clear, and clear," we said together as I turned to the open cargo door.

I threw myself out of the plane. The thick jungle night air felt good as I assumed a spread-eagle position with my arms and legs as wide apart as the flight suit and equipment would permit. The moon was as large as a basketball and as bright as a white phosphorous grenade. Stars were the size of tennis balls, bright and flickering in the clear night sky. We had night scopes, but this was prior to night vision goggles. We needed neither, as we could certainly see well enough to maneuver toward the meadow that was coming up at us at about over one hundred miles per hour.

One minute after exiting the aircraft, I squinted at my illuminated altimeter, took a deep breath that lasted a couple of seconds, and deployed my parachute. The dark ground stopped charging toward me, and I began to make out the outline of tall trees and hills on the horizon. A minute later, I could see the flora and the target strobe light. There was no wind at all, so it was easy to maneuver the parachute toward the landing zone. I hit the ground, stumbled slightly over some low-growing shrubs, recovered, and collapsed my parachute, folding it in my arms in a figure-eight motion.

Dave, CJ, and Mike landed, in that order, just seconds later. We stripped off our flight suits and carried our gear toward the trees north of the drop zone. As we squatted together, we heard two clicks from a handheld cricket, the signal that our Chieu Hoi was nearby. Then we saw a small shadow run toward the buried strobe light, retrieve it, and come toward us. I pulled my .45 and cranked a round into the firing chamber, released the safety, and held it by my side, pointed toward the ground.

The Chieu Hoi smiled, his big teeth shining in the clear night. An M-16 hung across his right shoulder. He said simply, "Li," meaning his name was Li, pronounced Lee, and motioned that we should follow. He pointed toward a hole that he had dug to bury the equipment we would no longer need, including our parachutes. We threw everything in, and Li began covering it with a small shovel, pushing dirt into the hole from a dark mound.

As he worked, I pointed each man to a defensive position, creating a small triangle with me in the middle. We would wait until daylight to make our way toward the American prisoners, presumably just two or three miles east. I kept my eyes on Li while the rest of the team watched for any movement outside the small perimeter. I released the hammer on my forty-five and put it back in my holster, then pulled my M-14 off my shoulder and made certain that it was locked and loaded with heavy .30-caliber rounds. Instinctively, I played with the muzzle flash and sound suppressor, ensuring that it was screwed on tightly. The silencer would be effective with low-volume fire, but if we got into a real firefight, the clunky metal tube would be more nuisance than benefit.

I pulled the jungle hat out of my back pocket and put it on, then retrieved the can of paint and added greens and rust to my black face. I saw that the others were doing the same.

I thought about Claire and the last letter I had written. I figured I had about a twenty-five percent chance of making it through this mission alive. My worst fear was to end up a POW in a North Vietnamese prison camp in Hanoi. I realized that the seventy-five percent chance that a bullet would take care of that alternative was more likely. Also more preferable. *Damn*, I thought, *I almost made it.*

Chapter 22

JEN SLEPT JUST INSIDE THE tent's opening, so nobody could enter without disturbing her. Each child had a cot, cover, and mosquito netting, just like she had.

Though it was nearly midnight, the air inside the tent was uncomfortably hot. She could reduce the heat by opening the flap, but she chose to keep the children and herself out of sight as much as possible.

She prayed for her father, that he would come for them, but also that he would not be hurt or killed. She knew that she and the children were simply bait, like the cheese in a mousetrap, to draw her father in for the kill. But she also knew that her father was a formidable man, and he would rescue them if and when he could. She lay on her side, watching the children sleep in the ambient light and hoping this ordeal would soon end.

~~~

The flight from Reagan International to New York's JFK had been easy and relatively short. Now it was time for the long leg from New York to Japan.

Brad's six feet four inches and military bearing had gotten them assigned to an emergency aisle with just two seats. Erin took the window. Brad took the aisle.

He looked across Erin and out of the small airplane window at the orange and pink hues of the setting sun and early evening. A reasonably good meal featuring pasta, shrimp, and broccoli had been served, and the dishes had been cleared away. Erin lay her head back on her seat and closed her eyes.

"Tired?" he asked as he studied her profile in the dimming light.

"A little."

"Can you sleep?"

"Yes, no problem," she said through closed eyes.

"Me, too." He closed his eyes and soon relaxed. He was almost asleep when he felt her head settling on his shoulder. He leaned just slightly toward her, and sleep soon overtook him.

~~~

As the night grew longer, I drank black coffee. Martha drank hot tea. She cupped both hands around her cup and held it to her mouth. "You never told anyone this story?" she said, looking at me over the cup, her lightly freckled forehead slightly wrinkled.

"No. It was top secret at the time. I never really talked about anything I did over there, especially this." I put the coffee down. "I need to use the bathroom."

"Me, too," she said.

"Okay." I smiled. "You go first."

"Thank you. And when you get back, I want the rest of the story. I figure we'll be in Japan in about five hours."

I nodded.

~~~

After Li buried our discarded equipment and parachutes, I asked him to stick close by me. He nodded that he understood, though I wasn't sure how much English he spoke or comprehended.

At 0600 I told him that I wanted to go east toward the prisoners' cages, but when we got close, I wanted to wait until dark to try to extract them.

Again, he simply nodded, but said nothing. He did, however, lead the way through the thick jungle.

I put Mike directly behind Li, then Dave, then me. CJ was rear guard. If we were ambushed, I would need CJ to attend to the wounded. I knew that the order of importance was medic, leader, communications, and weapons. These men knew it, too, and needed no explanation. My first company commander in Vietnam was Captain Barry McCaffrey. Barry's first rule for platoon leaders was not to get killed in the first ten minutes of a firefight. Once the platoon leader and platoon sergeant were killed, the platoon was in seriously deep shit. I put myself third so I had a greater chance of surviving an ambush and could therefore stay alive and on mission. Only reason. End of story.

Fortunately, we were not ambushed, and I was beginning to trust Li just a little. He led us to a ridge that overlooked the Ho Chi Minh Trail. I had heard about it, but it had always been just out of sight, generally to the west of our unit. It wound hundreds of miles south from North Vietnam, just inside Laos and Cambodia.

I was surprised by its crude construction. It was merely a simple beaten path surrounded by bamboo and jungle. It was certainly wide enough for the occasional tank or truck, but in reality, it was merely a way to walk through jungle quickly and easily without chopping your way with a machete one step at a time.

"The prisoners are down there, half mile south," Li said. It was the first time I had heard his high, soft voice.

We were now spread over a thirty-meter area, each man lying on his belly, M-14s ready to fire.

"When did you see them last?" I asked Li.

"Last night. Maybe ten hours ago," he said. His English was very good, which surprised me.

"Can you take me close enough to see them now?"

"Just you?"

"Yes. The others will wait here."

"Okay, we need to go this way." He started walking.

I pulled the team together and told them that I was going to confirm the targets and they should stay spread out and quiet. But they already knew this, and I was a little embarrassed to have said it.

I caught up with Li, who was climbing over, under, and through the tangled limbs, vines, and flora that comprised the floor of the triple-canopy jungle. This was easier for a small man like him than for me. My face and hands were lacerated by sharp limbs and elephant grass. Though uncomfortable and frustrated, I pushed on.

Thirty minutes into the march, Li raised his hand and closed his fist.

I knelt with my M-14 held to my shoulder.

He turned and indicated that I should come slowly and quietly toward him, which I did. He pointed ahead, along what looked like an animal trail.

I pulled out my binoculars and scanned the area in the direction he pointed. I saw him immediately—a barefoot Marine airman, still in his green wool flight suit. His head was bowed. He looked under-standably discouraged in a cage that was probably four feet square. He could not stand or even sit comfortably. He could only squat. His legs were probably cramped. With the benefit of the strong lenses of my binoculars, I could see flies and other bugs buzzing around his head. His eyes were closed as though he were praying. Perhaps he was, I thought.

I nodded to Li and indicated that we should return to our team.

He shook his head no and pointed in another direction. He began walking, and I followed. Soon he stopped and pointed.

I raised my binoculars and saw another cage, but I saw no one in it. I stood slowly and raised myself up as high as possible. Then I saw him—

another Marine airman, lying in the cage in a fetal position. I could see blood on his face. Flies and gnats swarmed all around him, but I never saw him move. Maybe he was sleeping. Or dead.

I nodded toward Li. "Let's go," I whispered. "We'll come back tonight."

Li said, "Affirmative," and turned back toward our team.

~~~

"Okay," I said to the men when we returned. "Targets confirmed. We go at twenty-two hundred hours. They're in four-by-four cages. Can't judge their condition or their ability to help themselves. It's only been a day plus a few hours, so they should still be okay. Of course, they were doing E and E before they were captured. Escape and evasion isn't much better than being captive. We may have to carry them. If so, we'll take turns, hundred-yard pulls and swap. CJ and I will low-crawl to separate cages at the same time, cut them loose, see if they can help themselves, and get them the hell out of there. Mike and Dave will cover us. We saw no guards, but there have to be some. Best case, one or two. More likely, three or four. If we're undetected, we shoot nobody. Otherwise, try to kill them before they get any shots off. There are probably a thousand NVA within two miles of the cages. We meet back here with the prisoners. Change their clothes. Give them boots and weapons. Hopefully they can walk and fight. Got it?"

Each man nodded. Li smiled, his big teeth sparkling.

I patted him on the shoulder and said, "Good job, Li."

The other men congratulated him, as well. His smile broadened.

I took a deep breath and thought about those thousand NVA soldiers.

~~~

We waited quietly, ever vigilant for any movement in any direction. The time passed slowly, but finally darkness invaded the jungle like a primeval demon. There is no darkness darker than night in triple-canopy jungle. But the five of us had experienced it many times, and we knew that our eyes would adjust. Soon we would be able to see well enough to move along familiar terrain. And that's what we did.

What had taken twenty minutes to walk in daylight took two hours in the darkness. We used our flashlights with red lenses sparingly and only on an as-needed basis. We were quiet, careful, and determined as we made our way toward the two cages.

Sometime after midnight, CJ and I separated. He and Li went toward one cage while I began crawling the last fifty yards toward the other. Mike and Dave circled what we assumed was an encampment. They put themselves in a position where they could kill the guards, regardless of how many. We hoped we could get the prisoners out without firing a single shot.

It took me a good thirty minutes to crawl fifty yards to the back of the cage.

From my position, I could clearly see a small encampment with three guards, all sleeping peacefully beside a dying fire.

The prisoner was slumped in his cage. Gnats and flies had been replaced by mosquitoes. I noticed that he occasionally swatted one on his neck or face. His eyes were closed. From my location, I could not tell if he was the pilot or the RIO.

I crawled to the edge of the cage, reached through with the butt of my survival knife, and touched him on the heel of his bare foot.

He didn't notice at first. I did it again. He put his hand on his foot and I touched the knife to his fingers. He opened his eyes and turned to look at the knife. Then he understood what was happening and slowly looked at me.

I put my hand to my mouth, indicating quiet. He nodded. I began cutting the ropes that tied the bamboo stakes together. I moved the knife back and forth like a saw blade as I cut through the hemp fibers very slowly. It took a long time, but I finally could remove one piece of bamboo in the back of the cage and then another until I had made an opening large enough for him to slide through.

He slid between the stakes and moved to speak, but I pressed my hand over his mouth.

"Can you crawl?" I whispered.

He tried to crawl on his knees like a baby. At first, he was wobbly, but soon he was able to move at a reasonable pace.

I pointed him in the direction from which I had come. He crawled a few feet while I sat watching for any response from the guards. We repeated this process again. When I thought we were far enough from the encampment, I whispered, "Can you walk?"

He tried to stand, but his legs wouldn't straighten completely.

I pulled his right arm over my shoulder and helped him with his mobility. The more steps we took, the stronger he seemed to get. Soon he was hobbling on his own, his bare feet taking the punishment of the jungle floor.

After a while, I stopped him and told him to lie down and wait.

"Are you Ellis or Wendelman?" I asked.

"Wendelman," he said. "Thank you for coming for us."

I nodded.

That's when I heard the first shots.

Damn.

Chapter 23

JEN LET THE CHILDREN SIT with her by the fire as Minh prepared breakfast. She moved from one child to the other, gently applying mosquito repellent. All four children had become quiet, almost catatonic. She could feel the tension in their small bodies as she touched them. LB's blood sugar readings were erratic.

The big driver stood opposite her family, assisting Minh with the cooking. The bodyguards walked the perimeter with rifles slung over their shoulders. Apparently, they had already eaten.

"I have to drive back into town this morning, to my business," Minh said.

"Okay. I'll get the children ready to go," Jen said.

"No. Sorry. You will be staying here. I will be returning tomorrow."

Jen looked at the guards. "No. That's not acceptable. I do not trust those men." She nodded toward the guards.

Minh stopped cooking and put his hands on his narrow hips. "Jen, let me explain something to you very clearly."

Jen raised her hand and pointed to an area away from the children. "Can we talk over there?"

Minh looked at the four children. He gave each of them a glass of apple juice and a piece of baked bread, and then handed Megan a small plastic knife and a jar of preserves. She began spreading it on each child's bread.

"Yes, okay," he said to Jen, and started walking toward one of the tents.

When Jen felt that they were far enough away from the children, she confronted him. "You can't possibly think about leaving my children and me with your bodyguards."

"They are not bodyguards," he said sharply. "They work for my company."

"And carry guns?"

"We are awaiting a visit from your father, and we know what he is capable of doing, don't we?" He crossed his arms. "You will stay here. I will return tomorrow as early as possible."

Jen stared at him. "Take us back to your residence."

"No."

"What about your driver?"

"What about him?"

"Can he stay with us? Let one of the others drive you?"

"Chinh. His name is Chinh."

"Can Chinh stay with us? I trust him more than the bodyguards, and they seem a little fearful of him."

"The bodyguards, as you call them, will not harm you. They work for me. They follow orders. Chinh and I will leave in an hour."

Cold chills ran up and down Jen's spine. She didn't want to be left alone with the bodyguards. They were hard men with cold eyes.

"We'll run away, into the jungle," she said.

Minh waved a hand dismissively. "Then you will not survive. A woman and four children cannot survive in this type of jungle."

"We're not going to survive either way." Tears filled her eyes, though she tried with all of her will not to show fear. "I'll take my chances with the jungle, rather than stay with these men. I saw them kill the FBI agents. I know what they're capable of doing."

"They didn't kill the agents, but that doesn't matter." He said nothing for a minute. He looked away toward the foreboding jungle, then back at

Jen. "Okay, Chinh can stay with you. I will give clear instructions to my men not to bother you or your children. They will follow my orders. I will drive myself back to the plant and come back tomorrow." He walked away without further comment.

~~~

I gave Wendelman the jungle fatigues, socks, and boots, then pushed a magazine into the butt of a .45-caliber pistol and cranked a round into the firing chamber. I handed him the weapon and two additional clips of ammunition.

"Stay here," I instructed. "If CJ and Ellis get to this point, his clothes and weapon are here." I pointed to the place where we had left them. "There are dehydrated meals and a canteen of water there." Again, I pointed. "I'm going to help my guys." Leaving Wendelman sitting there with the clothes and gun in hand, I moved as quickly as I could toward the gunfire.

I heard the low thump of the silenced M-14s, probably from Mike Hammer. No problem there. But the volume of AK-47 fire worried me. More than three guards for sure, plus a host of others nearby and probably on the way.

Fortunately, it was dark, and moving through the jungle at night was extremely difficult. Reinforcements would take time.

I found a vantage point where I could see the flash of the weapons and could try to determine what was going on. Mike and Dave seemed to hold strategic advantage. They had killed the three guards by the fire; I could see their bodies. But two other NVA were still fighting and had good positions. They were firing from the east, which would have been toward the Ho Chi Minh Trail from the campsite. Any movement by Mike or Dave brought heavy fire. They were pinned down and reluctant to use grenades.

I heard movement to my left and turned quickly. It was Li. I almost shot him.

He gave me a big smile. "This way," he said.

I followed him, still careful and alert. He led me in a flanking movement around the two NVA soldiers. Soon we were near them and had the benefit of a break in the jungle canopy and some ambient light from the moon and stars. We had clear shots.

He raised his M-16, but I stopped him and pointed to the silencer on my M-14. He nodded.

I stood very slowly and deliberately and braced myself against the trunk of a large tree. I waited until one of the NVA soldiers fired in the direction of Mike or Dave's position. I fired three quick rounds four feet behind the muzzle flash and knew immediately that I had taken out one of them.

Then AK rounds started cracking everything around me. The other soldier had heard my shots and had me zeroed in pretty well. A burst of thumps from Mike and Dave put him down.

The two Green Berets quickly made their way to us.

Li led us back to our rendezvous point on a much better path than I had used.

CJ was on his knees, attending to Major Ellis, who lay on his back unmoving.

"How is he?" I whispered to CJ.

He shook his head side-to-side. "Not good."

I walked over to Wendelman, who seemed alert in his new clothes and boots. "How are you?" I asked.

"I'm fine. They pulled him out of his cage yesterday and beat him with bamboo stakes and their rifle butts. I guess they knew he was the pilot. Not sure why, but they left me alone in my cage while they beat the shit out of him. I thought he was dead."

"Was it the guards?" I asked.

He nodded. "Yes."

"Well, they won't be beating any more prisoners. We've got to move," I told the group.

"He can't walk," CJ said. "We'll have to carry him. Both legs are broken. He has a concussion. Could have some internal bleeding, but nothing we can do about that. He's alive, and we can do our best."

"Okay. Let's make a stretcher," I said.

The Special Forces men did this in minutes, stretching fabric from the discarded flight suits and securing it around bamboo stakes. We laid Ellis on it and started carrying him gingerly through the dark jungle.

Li led the way toward Hill 1204.

I took up a rear guard position, stopping often and listening for anyone who might be following. Our progress could be measured in meters per hour. It was exceedingly slow. But we plugged ahead by simply putting one foot in front of another. We used our compasses and flashlights with red filters and the familiarity of the terrain that Li provided.

It was about 0500 hours when I realized that we were climbing the hill. Each step was now a little higher than the last. If our maps and compasses were right, we were at the base of Hill 1204. If we could make it to the top and Dave's communications equipment worked, we could get a signal out to the rescue team. I was beginning to feel more and more confident with each passing minute.

I moved quickly up the line to check on Ellis. He was moving around, which looked promising. CJ and Mike had been carrying him, CJ refusing to take a break. I pointed Mike back to the rear guard position and took a turn carrying the airman. Within two minutes, my body was drenched in sweat. An hour later, my arms and legs were trembling. I thought CJ must be exhausted. I stopped the patrol and told everybody to take a break.

Li came back and squatted down beside me in the familiar way that Vietnamese soldiers rested, their butts on their heels, their knees fully bent, their arms resting over their legs. "It is only a hundred meters to the top from here," he said in remarkably good English.

"Your English is good," I said to him.

"I was a teacher before the war. I taught languages, including English." He smiled. "I graduated from Ohio University in Athens, Ohio. My parents and sister live in the States now, in Cleveland."

"But you joined the Viet Cong?" I said.

"Yes. I was young. As George Bernard Shaw said, 'Youth is wasted on the young.' I had witnessed the corruption of colonialism and capitalism, and I was idealistic. But the greed of the French and the corruption of the capitalists paled in comparison to the cruelty of the communists. I joined the American forces two years ago and have been working the Ho Chi Minh Trail since then." He smiled.

"Thank you," I said.

That's when I heard the thump of an 82-mm mortar tube, close—very close.

We all lunged for the ground. A heavy, high-explosive round hit several hundred meters away. They were firing in the wrong direction. The mortar crew was closer to us than the targets at which they were firing. In fact, they were firing directly away from us, one hundred and eighty degrees off and a mile or more away. We could have thrown grenades at the mortar crew, but that would have been foolish.

I stood and walked to each person and told them that we had to be as quiet as possible as we made it up the last one hundred meters of the hill. The enemy didn't know where we were, but they knew we were out here somewhere. The men all nodded.

CJ and I picked up Ellis's stretcher and started carrying him through the tangled jungle and up the hill.

I heard the thump of the mortar tube again and again, but the rounds were exploding far away. *Maybe we'll make it*, I thought. I was gaining confidence with each labored step when Li stopped Dave, our point man. We all came to a stop like a line of cars approaching an accident on the interstate.

Dave and Li walked back to me. Dave gave me the bad news.

"The hill is occupied," he said.

"Really?" I said. "Looks like we would have known that?"

"First night they are there," Li said, breathing hard from hustling up and down the hill. "They were not there last night, for sure."

"How many?" I asked.

"It's an open area, maybe forty yards across," Li said, still a little winded. "Good landing area for a helicopter. Could be a small squad just camping out for the night. Maybe ten or twelve men."

"Maybe we could hide out and wait for them to leave in the morning," I suggested.

"This way," Li said. He started leading us away from the direction of the summit and to the west of Hill 1204.

Chapter 24

BRAD FELT ERIN MOVE AND opened his eyes. She had been sleeping with her head resting on his shoulder. He pretended that he was sleeping as she stood quietly, gathered her carry-on bag, and tiptoed to the bathroom. A few minutes later, she returned to her seat.

Brad moved as though just waking and opened his eyes. "Good morning. What time is it?" He stretched his arms in front of his body.

"Hard to say what time it is where we are," Erin replied. "Somewhere over Alaska, I think. It's eight hours later than when we left New Jersey."

Brad retrieved his shaving kit from his carry-on bag and went to the bathroom. Inside, he used the facility, washed his hands and face, and brushed his teeth. When he returned to his seat, he asked Erin, "So, do you have a plan of action once we get to Saigon?"

"Yes . . . well, sort of. I say we go first to the United States consul general's office. It's in the old consulate building, the one made famous in the newsreels of the fall of Saigon in 1975."

Brad nodded.

"The consul general is Tran Le, a US citizen of Vietnamese descent. Duff is supposed to be getting information to his office. Hopefully they will help, and we can get to Minh through them. I think that's the best starting point."

"That sounds like a good plan. But I'm disappointed that we're not getting more help from Homeland Security and the FBI," Brad said. He thought about his last conversation with his father. "I'm beginning to understand my father's attitude toward the government."

"I know. We haven't had a lot of support. But we should still try to use all of the resources available to us. Agreed?"

He smiled at her. "Agreed."

~~~

Jen kept the children in their tent as much as possible with the flaps open and the mosquito netting in place. The hot, humid air left them constantly damp with perspiration. They played games to pass the time. Jen made up games about animals, and the girls played imaginary card games with their young twin brothers. Jen was proud of her children.

She gazed across the campsite. Chinh sat in the shade near their tent, putting himself between them and the guards, intentionally or not. He leaned against a large tree, occasionally dozing lightly, but generally passing the time simply staring off into the dark jungle.

Jen could see one of the guards walking the perimeter. The other lay in their tent in the shade. The guard on duty occasionally glanced in her direction but seemed more focused on keeping watch for intruders, as instructed by Minh.

Jen was wary of the guards and glad that Chinh's big body was between her family and them. She didn't know why she trusted him, but she did.

~~~

Minh drove his expensive sedan toward Saigon. "That damn woman," he muttered to himself. He did not like driving himself. It diminished his stature. After all, he was the most successful businessman in all of Ho Chi Minh City. It was nearly two o'clock in the afternoon when he pulled into the parking lot of his textile plant, located about sixteen miles northeast of Saigon.

He smiled to himself as he parked the vehicle. No one was around to notice that he had no driver. Everyone was working. He liked that best.

His suitcase was in the trunk. He had packed for this eventuality, though he had hoped it would not occur. He used the private entrance to his executive suite, which included a small bedroom, a full bath, his office, and that of his secretary.

He took a hot shower and changed into a freshly cleaned business suit, including a handsomely starched white shirt and appropriate tie. His shoes were shined to a high gloss.

His visitor would be arriving in one hour.

When he was settled behind his desk, he pushed a button and requested a hot cup of tea. A moment later, his secretary brought the tray to him. He informed her than Nguyen Van Dang would be arriving very shortly. She should bring him into the office immediately and offer him a cup of hot tea.

Dang was the head of the Communist Party's Committee on Commerce. He was essentially Minh's boss. Unlike Minh, Dang was a big man. He was not as big as Chinh, but certainly large enough to intimidate someone as small as Minh. He did not feel comfortable in Dang's presence, but he knew how to handle him.

Within forty-five minutes, Dang arrived. "Good afternoon, Minh," he said in English as he entered the office. Both men had been educated in England.

Minh walked around his desk and shook hands with the party boss. "Good afternoon. Would you care for a cup of tea?"

"No, thank you. Your secretary offered."

"I am sorry for the delay," Minh said as the two men settled into facing chairs. "I was in the country, and my cell service was erratic. Your message just arrived on my phone this morning."

"I understand," Dang said. "However, our agreement is that you will maintain full and constant contact with our office."

"I am sorry. Please tell me what it is that you need, and I will do all within my power to accommodate you and the party."

"I saw your brother recently," Dang said.

"My brother?"

"Yes, at a conference in Hanoi. I waved to him. He did not seem to recognize me as he hurried into a seminar."

"I see," Minh said.

"Is there something you need to tell me?"

"No."

"There have been inquiries from America about a family that was abducted."

"I see," Minh said.

They were both quiet for a minute or more.

Dang broke the silence. "I suppose you have something for me."

Minh pulled an envelope from inside his coat pocket. "Yes, I have a contribution to the party. It is made payable to you. I know that you will ensure that it is properly noted." He handed the envelope to Dang.

Dang glanced at the check inside the envelope and noted the amount. He nodded and said, "Yes, it is properly noted." He stood. "We assume that we will not suffer any embarrassment."

"None," Minh said. He stood and bowed slightly. "I assure you."

The party boss put the envelope in an inside pocket of his suit jacket, then turned and walked out with no further comment.

~~~

Martha sat with her hands folded in her lap, absorbing what I had told her so far. My first impression of her had been that she was a little overweight, but now that I'd studied her more, I had changed that opinion. She had a sort of old-fashioned, voluptuous figure, like a Marilyn Monroe or a Jane Russell. But she looked like neither one with her bright brown eyes and round face. Her short haircut suited her just fine. The light sundress allowed a flattering view of her freckled shoulders and the rise of her round breasts. She wasn't a swimsuit model, but I liked the way she looked.

"Do you have children, Martha?" I said as I took a bite of an apple.

"I do," she said, nibbling on an orange slice. "Three girls, ages twenty-six, twenty-three, and twenty."

"Are they all going to be psychologists like you?"

"Heavens, no." She laughed. "Elaine, the oldest, married a bachelor fifteen years older, a banker. They have two boys. She has her hands full. They're actually in Charlotte. I go there often, as you can imagine. Elizabeth is a teacher, not married, but engaged. Emily is a junior at the University of Cincinnati, studying geology, of all things. She loves rocks and dogs. Lives with me. Good company. What about your children?"

"Two. Jen lives nearby. She has four children. Brad is a career military man. He's single."

"Are you going to finish your story, or do I have to beg?"

"I'll finish it," I said. I closed my eyes and returned to my story as though dictating notes to a typist.

~~~

Li led us away from Hill 1204. We found a small area that we could defend and deployed in a thirty-meter perimeter. CJ stayed in the center of the circle with Major Ellis. Wendelman took a position like the rest of us. CJ had given him his M-14 and web gear, which carried full magazines of ammunition and grenades.

I had time to decide what to do if the patrol didn't vacate the hill the following morning. There were too many enemy soldiers to engage, and a firefight would attract other forces. The mortar fire told me that the NVA knew we were out here, but didn't know where. My hope was that the patrol would move on, and we could take their place. Otherwise, we would have to find another evacuation point. Nothing to do now but wait.

After a sleepless night, daylight finally began filtering through the high trees in the jungle. I found Li in the green jungle haze.

"Let's you and me go see what that patrol is up to," I said.

"Good idea," he said.

I told the others what we were going to do, but didn't tell them how to do their jobs while I was away. I knew now that these were professional soldiers, not nineteen-year-old kids like I had once been managing.

Li pointed the way through the brush. We slowed as we neared the clearing at the top of Hill 1204 and made ourselves human chameleons, waiting and watching.

At about 0700 hours, I heard the NVA breaking up their camp. They were talking loudly with no field discipline. After all, they were five miles inside of Cambodia, so there should have been no enemy soldiers nearby.

Li and I waited silently and patiently for them to move away from the crest of the hill, and they did. By 0800, the hill was unoccupied and available to us for evacuation.

We made our way back to our unit and organized them in a line to move up Hill 1204 once again. Within an hour, we were within a hundred meters of the crest of the hill. Thoroughly exhausted, we plowed forward. Dave and CJ carried a still-lethargic Major Ellis. The rest of us dragged one foot in front of the other and plodded up the hill.

In the open area at the top, Dave pulled out and assembled his communications equipment. He called in our coordinates to the Marine Chinook, a CH-46 helicopter with two .50 caliber machine guns and six Marines in full battle gear. The chopper and crew had been on call since our mission began.

I now felt very confident we would make it, but my confidence eroded rapidly when I heard the thump-thump-thump of an 82-millimeter mortar. Unlike the day before, this time we heard the distinct whir of the fins of mortar rounds as they left their highest arc and sped toward the ground. The first round hit about fifty meters outside our perimeter, the second closer, and the third close enough to send hot shards of shrapnel whizzing over our now-prone bodies.

We made ourselves as flat as possible in the thick elephant grass.

Another round hit close, near the crest of the hill, not a lucky shot.

This told me that there was a spotter, so I sprang to my feet and ran into the tree line, pulled out my binoculars, and started surveying the area. I found him in seconds on the opposite side of the clearing. He had a 1950s-era field radio and small binoculars like those you might see at an opera house. I raised my M-14, sighted carefully, and shot him in the chest. He went down like a silhouetted target on a firing range.

Random mortar rounds from the mortar followed, but with no spotter, they were ineffective.

Dave was in contact with the rescue team. We soon heard the big double-bladed helicopter in the distance.

I got on the horn with the pilot and gave him an azimuth and distance from the crest of the hill to where I thought the mortar crew was set up.

I ran to the center of the landing zone and popped a green smoke grenade and laid it in the tall grass. Then I got everybody back into the tree line.

Before the chopper was visible, I heard the rattle of their .50-caliber machine guns. They were taking out the mortars. It was quick.

The Chinook came in low over the tall jungle trees. It circled and suddenly turned. I could see the door gunners at the front of the aircraft. They directed their big .50-caliber machineguns toward the lower elevations of Hill 1204 and opened up, full force. The sound was deafening.

The Chinook pilots took the aircraft up another two hundred feet, and the gunners laid down a steady barrage of deadly fire.

The pilot told Dave there was a large force of NVA at the base of the hill. He couldn't tell how many were already closing on our position. He told Dave to prepare for an attack.

I called my team to me and deployed each of the three men, plus Li and airman Wendelman. We had to defend the hill.

Suddenly, AK-47 fire filled the area, and the Chinook rose even higher, the twin .50-calibers screaming.

I walked into the opening and unscrewed the sound and flash suppressor from my M-14 and made a show of discarding it in view of my team, indicating to them that they should do the same. It was probably unnecessary, but it made me feel better.

I set myself up behind the trunk of a fallen tree and waited for the advancing enemy.

The first three NVA came running directly at me, and I cut them down easily, one shot each, *bam, bam, bam!* AK rounds whizzed through the air, cracking over my head and cutting the trees and brush beside me. We had the high ground, however, which meant they were firing uphill and we were firing down. Better for us.

The Chinook was raining .50-caliber rounds on enemy soldiers we couldn't see.

To my left, in my peripheral vision, I saw two NVA running toward the clearing. Li stood and shot them expertly with his M-16.

I pulled all the fragmentation grenades I had attached to my web gear—four, I think—and pulled the pins and started hurling them down the hill. As they began to explode, I heard similar explosions all around the hill as Dave, CJ, and Mike did the same.

I followed the grenades by advancing down the hill, firing my M-14 at any movement I saw.

The AK fire subsided.

I saw Dave call into his radio, communicating with the Chinook.

The Marine helicopter landed in the middle of the clearing at the top of the hill. Six Marines ran out of the back of the chopper and set up defensive positions.

CJ and Dave carried Major Ellis toward the open rear door of the CH-46.

Mike and Wendelman ran toward the opening and scampered into the helicopter.

I gave a hand signal to Li, directing him to board the helicopter. He started running toward the aircraft, but was hit in the back by small-arms fire. He spun around and slammed into the thick elephant grass.

"Damn," I said. I looked back toward the tree line and saw four or five enemy soldiers with AK-47s at their shoulders.

I sprang to my feet and ran directly at them, firing my M-14 from the hip. Out of nowhere, a mortar round exploded not too far from me and a piece of shrapnel sailed like a Frisbee across my body, slicing me like a piece of fish. Blood shot from my chest and soaked my jungle fatigues. I was so pumped with adrenaline that I completely ignored it and kept firing.

The Marines saw the NVA I was charging and opened up on them. They fell like bowling pins.

I ran to Li, picked him up like a rag doll, slung him over my shoulder, and carried him toward and into the back of the chopper.

The six Marines laid down a withering barrage of fire and returned to the Chinook, circling it and continuing to fire into the tree line. Then they scrambled onboard.

As the helicopter rose into the thick air, the door gunners blasted the area with their .50-caliber machineguns. The Chinook shuddered. The sound was off the charts.

Within minutes, we were at a high altitude and heading east toward a friendly air base inside South Vietnam.

CJ applied a field bandage to Li's right shoulder, badly damaged by an AK round, but probably not a mortal wound. He laid him on his stomach and applied pressure, looked at me and nodded affirmatively, indicating that he might make it.

Mike and Dave applied a field bandage to my chest wound. The bleeding had slowed, but the pain had increased exponentially.

I laid my head back against the skin of the chopper, closed my eyes, and gritted my teeth.

Dave took CJ's place with Li so he could look at my wound. He took out a vial of morphine and punched it into my thigh before I could stop him.

A few seconds later, the pain subsided. Soon I felt nothing but a round of nausea, and I vomited on the floor of the Chinook.

Major Ellis opened his eyes and seemed to comprehend what was happening.

Remarkably, we had made it. CJ, Dave, Mike, and I, plus the two airmen, had gotten out. Li was wounded pretty badly, but he would probably live. I had a superficial chest wound, that's all. But my head was spinning and my stomach was churning. I was allergic to morphine.

Through the haze of the drug, the steady chop of the helicopter's blades, and the sound of my heart beating, I counted the days since Colonel Davis had picked me up. I figured it was now 31 August '69, the date of my DEROS.

Time to go home.

Chapter 25

"HAVE WE BEEN SLEEPING TOGETHER?" Brad asked with a smile as he felt Erin sit up straight, taking her head off his shoulder.

"Sort of," Erin said.

He straightened and smiled at her. She seemed a bit embarrassed.

"No cigarette?" Brad said.

She gave him a lopsided grin. "Non-smoking flight. Thankfully."

"Yes. I hate cigarettes," Brad replied. "No one in our family smokes. I never have. My coaches wouldn't permit it, but it really had no appeal to me."

"Neither have I. There were a few cadets who smoked on the sly while we were at West Point, but I never participated. I was a good soldier."

"A lot of my men smoked in Iraq and Afghanistan. My mother said my father smoked some in Vietnam, but never before or after." He reached across her and opened the window shade. The sky was getting a little brighter.

"Speaking of your father, how did he get his DSC?"

"DSC?" Brad said.

"Yes. He got a Distinguished Service Cross, a Silver Star, Bronze Star with V, Air Medal with V, two Purple Hearts, and on and on. He never told you about his tour in 'Nam?"

"Are you sure? A DSC?" Brad said. His blood pressure was rising. "I can't believe that. I knew he was a platoon leader in Vietnam and got out a captain. He never said anything to me about the war. I got all my information on his military service from Mom before she died. And she said very little."

"Well, I saw his military record. He definitely got a DSC and served with great distinction. Didn't you see the scars on his right knee and chest?"

"Sure," Brad said. "Seems like, especially after I joined and stayed in the Army, he would have maybe mentioned that he had a DSC and two Purple Hearts. He said the scars were from an auto accident. Don't you think you would tell your only son about your military service when he decided to join the Army?"

"Or my only daughter, when she leaves for West Point." She smiled up at him.

~~~

Jen stood outside of the family tent as the sun faded behind the tall, twisted trees in the jungle. Minh had not returned. Chinh and one of the guards were in their respective tents. The other guard walked the perimeter. Jen didn't like the situation and dreaded the night ahead.

As she was about to go inside her tent, she had a thought. She looked at the dying fire and walked toward it. A small paring knife was among the cooking instruments. She glanced at the guard, saw that he wasn't watching, picked up the knife, and slipped it in her pocket. Then she returned to the tent and her children.

~~~

"Travis, please tell me that's not the end of the story." Martha smiled and put her hand on mine. "What happened to the men? Where did you go? What about Ellis and Li? Did they survive? You can't stop telling a story before it ends."

I returned her smile. Her hand was cool, reminding me of Claire. I had loved the cool touch of her hands. I would wrap my hands around hers to warm them.

"Okay," I said, "but after this last part, let's talk about something else. I want to hear *your* story."

~~~

The Chinook carried us to an LZ just inside South Vietnam. I think it was Cindy. I was in a morphine haze and violently sick from an allergic reaction to the drug.

Medevac picked us up at the landing zone in two Hueys. They put Li and Ellis in one helicopter and me in another since my injury was less serious, other than the allergic reaction to the morphine. They took us to a hospital near Saigon.

CJ, Dave, Mike, and Wendelman stood around me as they carried me to the Huey. I could have walked, but the medics required me to lie on the stretcher. It was all a little hazy. None of us had slept in at least three days, and we had been humping through thick jungle and getting shot at. We were completely spent. Still, we shook hands and thanked each other for doing the best we could. Wendelman cried like a small child as he thanked us for coming after him. I do remember that.

Then it all faded away as I lay on the stretcher and the Huey beat its way toward Saigon. I don't remember getting carried into the hospital or any of that. Sometime later, I woke up in a ward with seven other patients. I was wearing a peek-a-boo gown and had a serious bandage around my chest. My bodily functions were working, however, and that's what brought me to my feet. I had to go to the bathroom badly.

A big male African American corpsman with a round face, a mini Afro haircut, and a perpetual smile came running toward me as I swung my feet toward the floor.

"Hold on there, Captain," he said. "You might be a little wobbly."

His nametag said *Johnson*. I immediately thought of my childhood friends, Florence and James Johnson. "Bathroom," I said.

"No problem. But you've got an IV in your arm." He smiled, and his white teeth lit up the room. He carried a stand from which the IV bag hung as I started walking. "Just let me walk with you."

I urinated for a long time. I was aware that the gown had no back and concerned for his view, but I was in bad shape.

"That's good, sir," he said. "We were about to catheterize you."

I turned around, pulling the gown around me somewhat. "Glad I made it without the catheter."

"How do you feel?" he asked as we walked back to my bunk.

"Hungry. Warm. I could smoke a cigarette, I think."

"You're running a low-grade fever. The wound may be a little infected." He stood by the bunk after getting the IV stand in place. "They've got you on an antibiotic. I'll get you something to eat, and then you can have that cigarette."

"Thanks, Specialist Johnson," I said as he walked away.

My life in the ward was pretty boring. The other seven men were badly hurt and were understandably not up for conversation. Specialist Johnson brought me some books from the hospital library. I was starting *Darker than Amber* by John D. MacDonald. Travis McGee had just rescued the beautiful ex-prostitute, Vangie, from the water, when I heard sounds outside the ward that reminded me of a hen house at dawn, something about which I was informed by personal experience. There were many voices, high and low, loud and soft. A female nurse scampered into the ward and started pulling covers neatly around the patients and picking up litter.

A group of men burst through the door farthest from my bunk. Among them were a general, three colonels, a captain, and a sergeant major. The general went from bunk to bunk, speaking with the troopers. The sergeant major handed him Purple Heart medals to pin on the men. He pinned the medal on the pillow of a very badly wounded soldier whose head and upper torso were completely wrapped in bandages. The general put his big hand on the poor grunt's arm, bowed his head, and appeared to pray a quiet prayer. That's when I recognized him.

When they stopped at my bed, I stood in my pajamas and smiled.

"Travis," General Creighton Abrams said. "I can't tell you how good it is to see you." He shook hands with me. "Sit down, son. Let's visit for a while."

I sat on the side of my bunk. A chair appeared almost immediately, and he sat down facing me. The other officers and the sergeant major stood in a small circle around the bed.

"I would have been to visit you sooner, but I've been in Washington talking to politicians and to the chairman of the Joint Chiefs of Staff." He put his hand on my shoulder. "You did it, son. By god, you did it."

I started to say something, but got choked up. Tears began filling my eyes and rolling down my cheeks. I couldn't say a word. I just nodded.

"Damn, Travis." He started crying, too. "You did it. I am so proud of you." He turned to the group of officers and the sergeant major. "Gentlemen, this is a real soldier here." Tears poured from his eyes, and from mine. "A real soldier. Generals aren't supposed to cry, Travis. Damn."

When I regained my composure, I said, "Thank you, sir. You know that Ellis didn't make it?"

"Yes." He wiped his eyes with a handkerchief that the sergeant major provided. "But he wouldn't have made it either way. And you got him back, gave him a chance. Wendelman will be fine. He'll go home to his family because of you."

"And the others, CJ, Dave, Mike, and the Chiêu Hồi, Li. He got the worst of it," I said, my emotions now under control. "They all did a remarkable job. Unbelievable, really."

"Yes, they did. And you did. I'm making arrangements for Li to get the best treatment possible and, hopefully, to stay in the States and become a citizen. His parents live in Ohio."

"I know. What about some recognition for the three Green Berets?" I asked. "I can write up what they did. It was incredible. All of them, really. I have never seen such professional soldiers—well, other than Captain McCaffrey and First Sergeant Trainer." I looked across the sick bay, remembering two of the bravest and best men I had ever known. "I would put these three in the same class with McCaffrey and Trainer, and that's a pretty high class."

"My adjutant, Captain Henry"—Abrams pointed to the captain at the end of my bed—"has interviewed the three Green Berets, plus the pilots and gunners on the Chinook, plus the six Marines. I have personally nominated all three men for the Distinguished Service Cross. I'm confident they'll receive it."

"They deserve it," I said.

"Travis, will you stand for a minute?" He nodded to the sergeant major and stood. The chair disappeared.

I stood facing him.

He held out his hand, and the sergeant major handed him a Purple Heart.

"I know this is your second Purple Heart, so we have affixed the oak leaf cluster to this one and the ribbon for your uniform, also." He pinned it on my pajamas. "Travis, I want you to know that I have nominated you for the MOH."

I nodded, then thought, *MOH? Medal of Honor?* "Sir, I don't think I deserve an MOH."

Abrams turned to Captain Henry, and the captain handed him what looked like a hundred pages of unlined typing paper. I could see handwritten sentences on the pages.

General Abrams held the stack of pages in both hands and showed it to me. "Do you know what this is?"

"No, sir."

"These are handwritten statements by each of the three Green Berets, plus the Marine rescue team, pilots, and door gunners. Based on what is written on these pages, if anybody ever deserved the Medal of Honor, it's you. I took these statements to Washington with me and personally placed your name in nomination for the MOH."

"I don't think I deserve an MOH or any medal, sir. I was just doing my job."

"And why did you do it?" he asked.

"Because you asked me to, sir. From what I know about you, as a soldier under your command, I would do anything you ask me to do. End of story."

"Thank you, Travis. I wish I had an army of men like you." He put his hand lightly on my shoulder. "I have to tell you that you may not get the MOH, even though I know you deserve it. The politicians in Washington, including some of the top-ranking military men, don't want to authorize an MOH for action inside Cambodia. I told them exactly what you did, but they were more concerned about where you did it. So"—he turned back to the sergeant major—"I have been authorized to give you a Distinguished Service Cross, which may be upgraded to a Medal of Honor." He pinned the DSC on my pajamas beside the Purple Heart with oak leaf cluster. "Captain Henry will type up the citation based on these firsthand reports." He held up the stack of typing paper.

"I don't know what to say, sir," I said. "I really don't. Thank you."

We shook hands.

"Well, there is one more thing," he said. "I brought a surprise back from the States."

The men parted, and standing behind them in a yellow suit with a straight skirt that stopped just above her knees, a pillbox hat, a corsage on her jacket, white gloves, a broad smile, and tears in her eyes was the most beautiful woman in the world, my twenty-one-year-old wife, Claire.

She stepped toward me as General Abrams moved aside. We embraced, and both of us began to cry. We held onto each other as though we were afraid we would be torn apart at any second.

I separated from her long enough to look into her wet blue eyes and wipe tears from her cheeks. We kissed each other on the lips for the first time since our R&R in Hawaii, more than eight months ago.

"I love you," Claire said. "I am so proud of you."

"I love you, too, honey." I looked at General Abrams and said, "This is a lot better than an MOH."

He smiled. "The doctor says you can go home today, and we have arranged a private jet to fly you and Claire back to Charlotte, North Carolina. Captain Henry has put together a khaki dress uniform for you with all your medals and citations, including your DSC."

I didn't care about any of that. I was holding onto Claire for dear life, and she was holding onto me. A couple of hours later, we were on a plane back to the States. All I had with me was the uniform on my back, a pith helmet I had taken off a dead NVA officer, a shaving kit, and a small box of medals in which Captain Henry had put the stack of pages testifying to the events of that last mission.

Twenty-four hours later, I had packed my uniform in a box with the medals and the statements and put it all in the attic of the small house in North Carolina that Claire had bought with a VA loan. I kept the pith helmet with the red star on a shelf as the only evidence of my tour of Vietnam. I sat in a swing on the front porch, holding Jen, my fourteen-month-old daughter, on my lap and sipped a cup of real coffee. Claire sat beside me, her left arm around my shoulder and her soft body pressed against me. We were barefoot, in shorts and tee-shirts, all three of us. We watched the summer sun as it dipped below the longleaf pines that lined a field in the distance. Crickets chirped as children road their bikes up and down the sidewalk in front of our house. I kissed Jen on the top of her head, and she giggled. Claire cried happy tears, and I tried to forget everything I had done for the past twelve months.

Chapter 26

NARITA INTERNATIONAL AIRPORT IN TOKYO had a modern terminal, mostly for international flights. Our flight to Vietnam was scheduled for a two-hour layover. During this time, the plane would be cleaned, fueled, and serviced. The flight was seriously behind schedule. We would arrive in Vietnam nearly eight hours later than expected. I was anxious to get there as soon as possible, but I could do nothing about the schedule. We were required to disembark for the layover and take all of our possessions with us.

Martha and I walked down the concourse. We looked more like pack animals than tourists. We detoured into bathrooms to use the facilities and freshen up.

I was waiting when she walked out. Our eyes met and I smiled.

"I haven't had a man waiting for me in a long time."

"Nor have I been waiting for anyone."

We turned and walked toward a restaurant where we planned to eat and relax.

Martha touched her forehead and said, "I feel like I'm still moving."

"Yeah, that's a sensation that goes with long flights like this one. I have a small plane. Sometimes I just take off across the country and fly for hours at a time. When I get off after about three hours, I can't stop the sensation of moving."

"It just feels good to get off the plane," she said.

I nodded as we walked toward an upscale restaurant.

A cute Japanese hostess wearing a long dress that was slit up both sides to mid-thigh escorted us to a seat at a table for four. This provided enough room to place our carry-on luggage in vacant seats. We settled in and ordered a glass of wine.

"I've told you my story, Martha. What's yours?"

"Not as exciting as yours, that's for sure. I married Bill when we were both in graduate school at Ohio State. He became a psychologist and established a private practice. Unfortunately, he was manic depressive. We lived as normally as possible for twenty-five years, had three beautiful daughters, and were, to those looking in from the outside, a typical American family. Inside our house, however, it was anything but normal. Bill would go off his medications and fall into deep states of depression. He would sleep and stay in the house for weeks, never coming out of his room. I would move in with one of the girls. Then he would recover, get back on his meds, and be perfectly normal—a good dad and husband. A little over two years ago, he became profoundly depressed. While my youngest daughter and I were away from home one day, he drove himself out into the country, pulled his car into a grove of trees, and killed himself with a pistol he had purchased a few weeks prior. A man who trains hunting dogs found him that very day. Otherwise, he could have been in that field for weeks or longer." She removed a tissue from her purse and wiped her eyes.

I put my hand on hers on the table. I noticed how coarse my hand appeared on top of hers. The man looking back at me from the mirror in the bathroom was tired, old, and in need of a shave. I had washed my hands and face and brushed my teeth, but had not taken time to shave.

I smiled at Martha. "I understand a little of what you've experienced. Claire was sick a long time… ten years. But it was cancer, and we fought it together, virtually every day from the time she was forty to just after her fiftieth birthday, when she died."

The waitress stopped at our table again and asked if we were ready to order.

I looked at Martha. She was fishing her reading glasses from a large purse. "Give us a little more time," I said.

She nodded politely and walked away.

We looked at the menu and made our decisions. The waitress reappeared and took our orders, soon to return with two glasses of chardonnay.

Martha took a sip of wine. "Did you ever have any contact with the men on that last mission? Do you know what happened to them?"

"A couple years later I got a letter, addressed 'general delivery' to Darden and forwarded to me at college. It was from Mike Hammer, who was then at Fort Bragg, North Carolina. He said that CJ had gotten out of the Army and was a physician's assistant in Mobile, Alabama. He and Dave had re-upped and were going for thirty. Li had survived and was teaching at a small college in Ohio. He didn't know what had happened to Wendelman."

I drank my wine and looked toward the concourse, then back at Martha. "Claire, Jen, and I had moved to Chapel Hill, where I had enrolled at the University of North Carolina. I earned a degree in economics and got a master's degree. We had another child, Brad. I named him after my second company commander in Vietnam, Walt Bradley.

"A year or so after I graduated, I returned to the campus to attend a seminar. As I was walking across the quad, I saw somebody who looked vaguely familiar. I walked over to him and stood directly in his path. He was carrying an armful of books and looking down at the sidewalk. As he got close to me, I said, 'Captain Wendelman?' He looked up and dropped his books, saying, 'Damn! Never thought I'd see you again.' Turns out he was a law student there.

"We went to Y Court and had a cup of coffee. He was in his third year of law school and had accepted a job in Huntersville, a small firm, he said. I told him that we lived nearby, just west of Charlotte. I was working in a small business and had returned to campus to attend a seminar on the economy and also to return some books. We talked a long time, but it was the last time I saw him. I never drove to Huntersville. He never came to Darden."

"So that was it?" Martha said.

I stared beyond her, toward the concourse, now lost in my own thoughts, talking to myself as much as to her. "One morning three years ago, I read in the local newspaper that an attorney in Huntersville was killed in a car crash. His name was Wendelman. I went to the funeral, slipped into the back of a large Methodist church, and sat at the end of the last pew. I cried softly as the pastor prayed over the coffin at the end of the service." I stopped speaking and wiped my eyes with the back of my hands. "I think it was like that for a lot of us. We were thoroughly connected to one another, but we couldn't take the pain of being together. It reminded us too much about what we had done, what we had to do. I couldn't spend any time with Wendelman without walking through the jungle in Cambodia at night, without killing people and almost getting killed. I think we all had to think about it in the abstract just to live with it. When some young man in my shop would ask me how many people I killed over there, I would just walk away without answering. But, yes, I killed people. People who were trying to kill me and my men. I've—" I started to say that I had killed men recently in self-defense, but I swallowed the words. "We all lost so much over there. For me, and probably for a lot of men who were in actual combat, maybe one out of ten who were in Vietnam, it was just better to forget about it. Leave it in the past. Just go forward. That's what I did. I moved on."

Our food arrived. We ate quietly. I assumed that Martha, like me, was thinking about painful memories perhaps better left in the past.

~~~

Jen slept very little the first night that Minh was away. She held the small paring knife in her right hand, occasionally coming fully awake when it slipped from her grip. She watched over her children like a hen caring for her brood of chicks. She took comfort, but only a little, in knowing that Chinh was in the tent beside her. She didn't know if she could trust him any more than the guards, but his body language was less threatening. In fact, she perceived that he was protective of her and her children. She liked to hold on to that thought, at least.

Late in the afternoon of the second day after he left, it appeared once again that Minh would not return. She would have to get through another night in a dark and strange place, alone with her four children and three men she didn't know. She had fed the children and had eaten a few bites of food when one of the guards wandered over. He said something in Vietnamese to the other guard and laughed. She didn't understand what he'd said, but he looked at her and nodded at Megan. Chinh must have heard it. He immediately emerged from his tent and went straight to the guard. He stood within a foot of him, saying nothing, of course, but he looked down on the small man like a boxing champ measuring the challenger before a title bout. The small bodyguard just smiled, tightened his grip on the strap of his AK-47, and stepped around Chinh. Chinh watched him until he was on the other side of the campsite.

Jen moved the children back into their tent. She later peeked outside and saw Chinh sitting near the fire, placing himself between the guards and her family's tent.

~~~

Brad stretched his arms in front of himself, bending his wrists backward and releasing some stress. The plane was parked on the tarmac in Anchorage, Alaska, while it was refueled and serviced. Passengers were not allowed to disembark, so he did his best to get blood flowing to stiff muscles.

Beside him, Erin stood and stretched her arms over her head, causing her blouse to rise and exposing her midriff. Brad noticed and felt a little embarrassed. As she held the pose, he averted his gaze and decided to take a walk to the front of the plane.

When he returned to his seat, Erin was still stretching, but showing less skin.

"How much longer to Tan Son Nhat?" he asked.

"Twelve hours from here, with good wind and, fortunately, the new treaty with China." Erin sat back down and turned toward him. "You've told me a little about your father. What about your mother?"

"She was a great person. Perfectly disciplined. Drove my sister crazy. 'Do you really need that cookie?' was her constant mantra to Jen. But we both loved her dearly. Dad worked long hours, buying and running his business. He was very successful and around as much as you might expect. But Mom was there for us always, every day, twenty-four hours, seven days per week. They were an old-fashioned couple. He worked and made the money, and she took care of the house and kids. He loved us, no doubt, but he was completely devoted to her. He used to say that the greatest gift a father can give to his children is to love their mother." Brad stared down the aisle, not looking at Erin.

"That is so sweet and so true. My father was career military. My mom always had a job. They sort of lived separate lives, and their marriage eventually ended. They seem to love each other still, but both have moved on. My sister and I were in our late teens when they split. We loved them both and divided our time between them as much as possible, given my father's deployments. I had already decided to go to West Point, and both of my parents were proud of me. My sister and I are still close, but my career keeps me separated from my parents, except on special occasions. I love them, and they love me. But we each have busy lives, and it's difficult to maintain close family relationships. Sounds like it's not a lot different with you. You're close with your sister and her children, but not your father."

Neither spoke for a few minutes.

"My sister and her children are the anchor in my life," Brad said. "That's true. I've got to get them back, safe and unharmed. I just pray they're okay."

"Minh is clearly a man with significant financial means. I don't think he would harm your sister or her children. He seems obsessed with your father."

"My best friend from high school is the general manager of the Majestic Hotel in Saigon. His name is Van Trang Phai, but we called him Tommy. He was valedictorian of my high school class. Tommy appears to have some political contacts there. Maybe he could help." He thought about his friend. "But, back to what you were saying, I would say Minh is about to get something he didn't bargain for. When my father sets his mind on doing something, nothing short of an earthquake, a big one, and a tsunami are going to stop him."

"I think you're right. I just hope whatever Travis does won't jeopardize Jen and the children."

~~~

On my only other trip to Vietnam, I had flown into Cam Ranh Bay from Seattle via Hawaii and Guam. That was August 1968. Four young Braniff Airlines stewardesses in pillbox hats and miniskirts did their best to keep the atmosphere as light as possible. I remember walking down the steps onto the tarmac and watching the perspiration rise on the sergeant in front of me. By the time we reached the terminal, his khaki shirt was drenched in sweat. So was mine. And this was about 9:00 p.m.

When I arrived at base camp at Camp Evans, north of Huế, the captain who was responsible for my orientation told me that more men died in their first thirty days in the country of heat exhaustion than from enemy bullets. I was told to drink plenty of water and take salt tablets.

I thought about the heat as we landed at Tan Son Nhat International Airport in Ho Chi Minh City, better known as Saigon. Martha and I had been relatively quiet during the last leg of the flight. We had even slept lightly from time to time. The painful emotions we had shared on much of the trip—the shared losses, tender memories, and the trauma that had buffeted our lives—had driven us back into ourselves.

Martha understood the pain, both personally and professionally. She didn't pry deeper into my past, but chose small talk and simple quiet to balance her feelings and mine.

A headache hit me an hour after taking off from Japan. The pain was like a baseball bat to the front of my forehead. I called for a bottle of water and took a handful of Tylenol.

"Are you okay, Travis?" Martha asked.

"Headache," I said with my head pressed on the headrest.

"How often do you have these headaches?"

"Varies," I said softly, as though speaking louder would worsen the pain. "For a while, every day, once a day. Now, somewhat more often. I've been to the doctor. Tests are scheduled." Of course, this wasn't the whole truth.

"This sounds serious." She looked at me intently. "You should really check it out thoroughly."

"I know."

After landing, I gathered my carry-on items and let Martha out in front of me. She was connecting with a tour group and staying at the Renaissance Hotel. She quickly found the tour guide, who was holding a big sign and a red umbrella, prepared to lead his customers through baggage claim. I waited for my luggage and helped Martha retrieve hers from the revolving belt. We waved goodbye, and I walked through a covered concourse that was pleasantly air-conditioned.

Passengers who were not with tour groups were herded through customs, where bags were searched. I draped the rain jacket I had filled with cash over my arm. Almost four thousand dollars was stuffed in the pockets, a large sum, considering that the per capita income in Vietnam is just over thirteen hundred dollars per year. I had declared the money on a form provided prior to landing, but needed to protect it since I could not use credit cards. On the other hand, I had kept my real driver's license for emergencies so I could be Travis Kelly, instead of Marvin Evans, if and when necessary.

A young customs agent greeted me with a smile as I presented my forged passport for inspection.

"Welcome to Vietnam, Mr. Evans." He stamped the passport. "Will you step over here to speak with these agents?" He pointed toward two men in military uniforms.

"Is there a problem?" I asked.

"No problem, sir, just step this way," said one of the soldiers.

My heart raced as I walked away, wedged between the two soldiers, one on my left and the other on my right.

Chapter 27

THE SOLDIERS WERE NON-COMMISSIONED OFFICERS, perhaps staff sergeant level in the US Army. This was somewhat reassuring to me. Had they been officers, I would have been more apprehensive.

They led me to a small room, not unlike the room in which I had been interviewed in Charlotte. A large map of Vietnam hung on one wall.

"Please sit, Mr. Evans," one of the men said.

I placed my luggage behind me and sat in a small wooden chair. I crossed my hands in front of me on the cool surface of the table.

"Have you been to Vietnam before now?" one of the soldiers asked in fairly good English.

"Yes. In 1968," I said.

"You were in the war?" the other soldier asked.

"Yes." I knew enough about interrogations to know that the less said, the better. I waited.

They were equally patient. They studied my face carefully. Then one of them pulled out what appeared to be a picture printed on a letter-sized piece of paper. Both soldiers studied the paper without allowing me to see it.

"What is your height, Mr. Evans?"

"Five feet eleven inches," I said, shortening myself an inch or so.

"And your weight?"

"One hundred and eighty-five pounds," I said, hoping they wouldn't measure or weigh me.

"Your eye color?"

Couldn't lie on that count. "Green."

They nodded. Both looked at the photograph.

"Okay," one soldier said. "You are free to go. Sorry for inconvenience."

I stood without saying anything. As I gathered my bags, I sneaked a peek at the photo. It was a forty-year-old picture of me in my dress military uniform, probably from the file that Minh's people had taken in Virginia. I thought that I once was a fairly handsome man, but now, forty years later, with a three-day beard, rumpled clothes, and the strain of my recent struggles, I barely resembled the young soldier in the photograph.

I gathered my luggage, walked out of the office, and then outside through an automated glass door. The black rubber soles of my shoes burned as I stepped onto the concrete sidewalk where taxis were waiting. A middle-aged man in a white linen uniform and a white pith helmet, very similar to the one that Minh had taken from my closet, blew a whistle and motioned for a taxi to move up for me.

I handed him two dollars and got into the open door of the cab.

"Where go?" the driver asked.

"Majestic Hotel in city center," I said, looking at his reflection in the rearview mirror of the cab.

"Okey dokey," the driver said with a big, nearly toothless smile. "Very nice."

As we headed toward the heart of Saigon, the driver started talking. "Your first time in Vietnam?"

"*Số này của tôi là lần thứ hai tại Việt Nam,*" I said, telling him that this was my second time in Vietnam.

"*Bạn nói tiếng Việt rất tốt,*" he said, complementing me on my Vietnamese. Then, in English, he said, "You here for war?"

"Yes. A long time ago. I took the Vietnamese language course in the Army."

"No war now," he smiled. "Just business. My name Le Loi. I learn English in night school."

"*Xin chào, Lợi*," I said in the tonal sounds for *Hello, Loi.* "Your English is very good."

"Thank you, sir. What your name?"

"Travis," I said, then I hesitated. "Marvin."

"Travis Marvin. Famous actor?"

"No. Just Marvin," I said, stammering a bit.

"Okey dokey. Hello, Marvin." He smiled broadly.

We drove a few minutes in the chaotic city traffic.

"We almost at Majestic," he said.

He pulled the taxi to the front of a beautiful six-story building that sat on the Saigon River. I thought, based on my rumpled clothes and grungy looks, I might not be permitted on the premises of the very expensive, five-star hotel.

The hotel doorman opened the cab door. Before he could say anything, Loi said something in Vietnamese that I couldn't understand. I thought maybe he said I was a famous actor, in spite of my personal appearance. The meter indicated that the fair was about 68,000 dong, which was less than four US dollars. I handed Loi a five-dollar bill.

"Can you wait for me, Loi? I have someplace else to go."

He took the money and nodded, smiling. "Okey dokey. You tip doorman and tell him you want me stay."

"Welcome to the Majestic," the doorman said as I got out of the taxi. "Are you checking in?"

"No, I have a very brief meeting here." I handed him a five-dollar bill. "I need my taxi to wait for me. Is that okay?"

He took the money and smiled. "I tell him to wait here." He pointed to a painted parking space at the curb.

I nodded and walked into the hotel.

In 1981, the church that Claire and I attended had sponsored a Vietnamese refugee family. I was among those who met them at the airport in Charlotte. It was my first up-close and personal contact with a Vietnamese family since the war. At first I stood in the back of the small entourage that waited for the refugees, but when I saw the young father and wife, plus four children, struggle to communicate with the pastor and others in the congregation, I stepped forward and became an interpreter. Van Loc Tran and his family were thrilled to meet an American who spoke Vietnamese, and it made me feel good to help. Tran and I became good friends over the years. He was an expert machinist, and I hired him to work in my small business. Eventually, he became a shift leader, and later, a supervisor. Over time, I arranged for him to have a small percentage of ownership in the company, as I did for all my long-term employees. When I sold the business to my brother and a private equity firm, thirteen people, including Tran, became millionaires. Unlike many in that group, Tran kept working and was now general manager of Kelly Industries.

Tran's oldest son was Brad's age. He was a top student at the local high school and attended Davidson College undergraduate and Harvard Business School, both on full academic scholarships. For the past five years, he had been a senior manager of the Majestic Hotel in Ho Chi Minh City. His name was Van Trang Phai, but to his American friends, he was Tommy.

I walked to the registration desk inside the luxurious lobby of the Majestic. A pretty young woman in a white blouse and black skirt stood patiently behind a high counter as I approached.

"Welcome, sir. Are you checking in?"

"*Tôi đang tìm kiếm cho Văn Trang Phái.*"

"*B ạn có biết ông Văn.*" She smiled. "I will tell him you are here. What is your name, sir?" she asked in perfect English.

"My name is Travis Kelly."

She walked into an open door behind the counter. She was beaming when she returned a few minutes later. "He is so excited that you are here. He says please sit in the lobby, and he will greet you immediately."

"*Cảm ơn bạn, bỏ lỡ.*" I thanked her and asked if she could exchange ten US dollars for Vietnamese currency, then took a seat facing the counter.

Tommy practically ran out of an office behind the registration desk toward me. "Mr. Kelly? It *is* you. I thought somebody was playing a practical joke on me."

I stood, and we hugged one another like son and father.

"Tommy, wow, you look great! I haven't seen you since you left for Harvard. That was twelve years ago, just after—" My voice broke off.

"Just after Mrs. Kelly died," he finished my sentence. "My mom sends me a daily text message with news from home. Plus, you may know, they visited this past winter. You know that you will always be my father's hero. He credits you with everything he has accomplished in the past thirty years. Please sit. You look tired."

We sat on a blue leather sofa, still smiling at one another.

"Your father needs to credit nobody and nothing but his hard work and ability," I said. "He deserves everything he has accomplished and accumulated. My brother would be lost without him at Kelly Industries, and that's a fact."

"I wish I had known you were coming. I could have arranged some time off, but we're shorthanded and I'm slammed."

"It's okay, Tommy. I am here on a serious matter that I am not at liberty to discuss. I need a big favor."

His brow creased. "Serious matter?"

"Yes. I think Brad will be coming over in a day or so. He's probably right behind me. It's about Jen and her family. That's all I can say, but I want you to deliver a message to Brad if he looks you up, and I bet he will." I handed him a sheet of paper with some numbers written on it and a message: *Go to consulate first.*

He looked at the message and read the numbers. "What does it mean?"

"Brad will know what it means. Just give it to him and tell him when you saw me, the exact time and day. Will you do that?" I pressed the paper into his palm. "Tell him if I'm successful, I will meet him at the US consulate."

"Are Jen and her children okay?" he asked. "Perhaps I could help."

"I don't think so. I'm on my way to meet with them. They're here in Vietnam. I wish I could tell you more, Tommy, but it's better to say no more about it." I was firm. "I have to go now," I said as I stood. "But if you see Brad, please deliver this information and tell him to meet me at the consulate. Okay?"

"Sure, Mr. Kelly. You know I will."

We shook hands.

I walked toward the exit as Tommy returned to his office. When I reached the revolving front door, I hesitated and turned to see if he was still watching me. I saw that he had disappeared behind the registration counter.

I turned and walked toward a large restaurant on the first floor of the hotel. It was between meals. No patrons sat at the dining tables. I found my way into the kitchen, which was also deserted. There I found a large butcher knife. I slipped it from a stainless steel table and hid it beneath my shirt before hurrying out of the hotel.

Chapter 28

JEN WORRIED THAT MINH WOULD not return. Chinh, though initially alert and concerned about the guards' behavior, now seemed distracted and bored. The children were tired and frustrated. As usual, it was unbearably hot. She tried to keep the children in the shade and applied mosquito repellent frequently.

Without the benefit of Minh's cooking skills, Jen could only offer bland food. She knew that her fears would worsen as the light of day faded into early evening. The guards continued talking and looking in her direction. When they saw her looking at them, they laughed and spoke loudly to one another in Vietnamese. She didn't like the way they looked at her or her oldest daughter, Megan. She put her hand in the right front pocket of her jeans and gripped the handle of the small paring knife. It gave her little comfort.

~~~

The visit from Nguyen Van Dang had upset Minh. He had checked the scheduled flights from America to Vietnam. It seemed clear to him that Kelly was delayed. Would he come at all? Minh was no longer certain.

He decided to spend at least one more night at his plant, perhaps more. He had plenty of work to do to keep his enterprise humming. There were comforts nearby in Ho Chi Minh City that he could call upon after the workday. A very young and attractive woman who liked his money was a quick telephone call away. Perhaps he would return to the jungle in a few days.

~~~

Loi was waiting in his cab with the engine and air conditioning running. I slipped into the back seat.

"Where to now, Marvin?"

"I need to go to a store for some supplies."

"What kind of store? What you need?"

"I need tape, a flashlight, and bottled water." I looked at Loi to see if he was getting what I was saying. I tried to remember the Vietnamese words.

He smiled. "Okey dokey, I know good place."

I wasn't sure if he did, but I sat back and took in the city as the cab moved from the curb. I had been in Saigon only once, and that was en route from the hospital to a jet waiting to take Claire and me home. That was September 1969.

The Saigon I vaguely remembered, and which had been described to me by fellow soldiers, consisted of neon signs, bicycles, strip bars, and prostitutes. Saigon was now a modern city with nice shops and small cars jockeying for position on broad streets packed with motorbikes. The cacophony of sounds was more diverse than those in the heart of New York City. Whistles, horns, shouts, clanging noises, skidding, crying, laughter, and other babel competed for attention. Motorized scooters often carried three or four riders. Some carried dead chickens. I even saw one with a live pig. At one intersection, there were as many as four motorbikes on either side of the taxi. That the scooters and cars moved through the streets without colliding with one another was amazing.

Loi stopped his taxi in front of a large store on a main street in the city center.

"You go here," he said. "I wait."

I got out of the taxi. I was careful to avoid the rush of motorbikes as I struggled through a horde of street vendors and beggars. I dropped a few coins into the outstretched hands of several beggars as I parted the mass of people to get into the store.

Once inside, I found a general store, much like a Wal-Mart, but somewhat smaller and much more personal. I approached a clerk in a light blue blouse with her Vietnamese name over her pocket. When I spoke English, she raised her hand and said, "*Tôi không nói được tiếng Anh.*" I was pretty certain she was saying that she didn't speak English. She pointed to another clerk. Before I could tell her that I spoke some Vietnamese, the other clerk was in front of me.

"May I help you?" the new clerk said in a British accent. Her nametag read *Rebecca*.

"Yes, thank you. I need some supplies for a trip into the country-side."

"We have just about anything you might need."

"I can see that. This is a nice store, and your English is very good. I speak a little Vietnamese, but it's been a while since I've used it."

Rebecca nodded. "I was raised in England and moved back here to learn more about my parents' family. What do you need?"

"A machete, flashlight, batteries, tape, mosquito repellent, and bottled water."

"We have all of that. Follow me."

I followed her through the various aisles in the store as she pointed out the items I needed. I purchased three flashlights, each with red and green filters, and batteries, including a new set of AAs for my GPS. I wanted electrical tape, but had to accept a general cloth-backed tape instead. I bought a case of bottled water and a dozen bottles of mosquito repellent plus a large backpack.

"Do you have energy bars?" I asked.

"Yes. How many?"

"A couple of boxes."

"Are you camping?"

"No, just a day trip along the river. Do you have some thin blankets? Maybe three or four? Also, I would like a straw hat like the farmers wear and a long-sleeved black shirt that will fit me."

"A big shirt," she said. "I think I can find that." She paused. "Here, you need a cart." She pulled a cart from a side aisle, and we packed everything in it.

We found the blankets and a loose linen shirt that buttoned up the front. I bought an extra-large, but it still looked small. Straw hats were displayed in the front of the store. I pulled one from a shelf and threw it into the cart. I saw a rack of flip-flop sandals and bought one adult pair, two ladies' small, and two others, smaller still.

Rebecca escorted me to the checkout stations. As I was about to pay, I stopped. "Wait. Do you have spray paint?"

"Spray paint? Like for street art?"

"Well, or for painting something."

"No, but just up from here, I'll point it out to you, there is a store where you can purchase paint."

After assisting me further as I paid with US dollars, Rebecca walked with me to Loi's waiting taxi.

Loi helped unload everything into the trunk of the cab.

Once that was done, Rebecca turned the empty cart back toward the store.

I offered her a twenty-dollar bill. "This is for you, Rebecca."

"No. We don't accept tips."

"But you've been so helpful." I persisted.

"Thank you, but this is our strict policy. This store is owned by the people. We are here to serve the public."

I nodded and thanked her again. Then I explained to Loi that I needed to walk to the nearby paint store. The clerk inside was helpful, but I still had some difficulty explaining what I wanted to buy. Eventually, I walked out with two cans of white spray paint.

I asked Loi to reopen the trunk. I opened the package of batteries I needed for the GPS so I could put them into the device as we rode to our next stop.

"Where go now?" Loi asked as I settled in the back seat.

"The waterfront."

"Waterfront?"

"The river. I want to rent a boat."

I could see a quizzical look on his face in the rearview mirror. "You want a boat? Why you want a boat?"

"I'm going up the river."

Loi drove to an area near Saigon Port in the heart of the city. He stopped and parked the taxi. "I go with you," he said. "This my nephew's place."

I followed him toward some docks. At the end of one branch of a series of floating wooden platforms was what appeared to be a young family sitting in a semicircle, mending fishing nets.

As we approached, a young man stood and spoke to Loi.

Loi said something back and then turned and pointed to me. "My friend, Marvin, needs to . . ." He couldn't recall the word. "He need boat," he finally blurted.

"What kind of boat?" the nephew said in fairly good English.

"Just a solid boat with a good motor. I'm going up river."

He held out his hand to shake hands like an American businessman. "My name is Phuong Lam. My wife is Loi's niece." He pointed to his wife, who nodded and smiled. Two young children, a boy and a girl, giggled and moved closer to their mother.

"Your English is very good."

"I learned some English from grandfather, who fought the communists in war. He in prison and communist education camp several years after war, but lived good life after release. He told me English would help me someday. Now I have export business plus fishing business. My grandfather very wise man."

"I need a boat large enough to carry six people comfortably and safely."

"Where go?" Lam asked. "I can take you."

"I want to go alone. Are there boats for rent or for sale?"

"For sale. Sure. Follow me."

I followed him down the docks. We reached a cluttered area where a number of boats were tied up. Lam began an animated conversation with a stooped man who was about my age—in other words, old. His face was weathered, and his hair completely white. Occasionally he looked over Lam's shoulder at me with a suspicious eye.

Finally, Lam turned to me.

"He has sixteen-foot deep-hull fishing boat. Old, but good outboard motor. He wants two hundred American dollars."

"How fast will it travel?"

"Pretty fast. Six or seven knots. But not very far. Small fuel tank."

"Okay. Tell him I need four large cans filled with gas, plus fill up the boat's fuel tank. I'll give him four hundred dollars for the boat, the cans, and the gas."

Lam spoke to the old fisherman. He smiled. Like Loi, he was missing a few teeth. He offered to shake hands with me. Then he began giving orders. Lam told me that they would deliver the boat to his dock in about twenty minutes.

I counted out the money and completed the transaction.

A few minutes later, Loi was confused and conflicted as he helped me load the boat with all the items I had purchased at the store, including the backpack and my rain jacket. Once everything was in the boat, I reviewed my plan with him. I had selected a specific point where the road from Saigon to Cambodia crossed an offshoot of the Saigon River, or, more accurately, the Ben Cat River. I asked Loi to meet me there in eight hours. If I wasn't there when he arrived, I told him to wait no more than two hours, then leave.

I unfolded the map and circled the spot for him. "Here, Loi. Meet me here. This is about thirty miles northwest of the city."

"Why not bring boat back to dock?"

"It will take too long. I will need to get back quickly. You'll understand when you pick me up."

"I will come," Loi said as he looked at his watch. "Eight hours from now." He touched the dial of the watch as though he were counting the hours. "Then wait two hours. Okey dokey."

I gave him a roll of bills.

He held up his right palm as though I was about to strike him. "Too much."

"Not too much," I said. "This is very important. You are doing me a great service."

Loi bowed and put the money in his pocket without counting it. He took the map from me and held it in his right hand. With his left hand, he touched the map. "I come in eight hours and wait two hours by bridge."

~~~

It was 3:00 p.m. when I left the dock and headed out into the main channel of the river. I drove slowly. After a few minutes, when I was out of sight of the docks, I put on the large black shirt and buttoned it up. Then I put the straw hat on and slumped down in the boat. The sun was high and hot, certainly more than one hundred degrees. The straw hat felt good, but the long-sleeved shirt added to my discomfort.

I pulled out the GPS, turned it on, and waited for it to fix on three or more satellite receivers. Once I could see the satellite positions in place, I programmed in the coordinates, 11.530982/106.463013. The GPS pointed in the direction of my destination and told me it was thirty-nine miles northwest and that I would be there in approximately five hours. However, this didn't account for the meandering river. I accelerated the engine of the boat, and soon the GPS told me I could make it in just over four hours, but I still wasn't convinced.

Chapter 29

BRAD AND ERIN WOULD LAND at Tan Son Nhat International airport in two hours . Brad was nervous and agitated. "So we go first to the consulate?" he asked, looking past Erin through the window of the plane.

"I think that's the best approach," Erin said. "Then we ask somebody from the consulate to go with us to confront Minh."

Brad turned his eyes to Erin. He wondered how a person as attractive and successful as she had stayed single. "I told you about my high school friend, Tommy. Based on my conversations with his parents, he seems to have some influence with local officials. I'd like to meet with him and see if he knows anything about Minh. Though it will be late, let's try to contact Tommy at the Majestic first, then go to the consulate."

"Sure. We have no luggage. When the plane lands, we'll go through customs and catch a cab to the Majestic and try to find your friend."

Brad nodded. If anybody could help him, it would be Tommy.

~~~

It was getting dark in the jungle. Another night without Minh. Jen was worried. Chinh had stayed in his tent most of the day, leaving it briefly to get some water and something to eat, then to the outdoor toilet. He nodded at her as he returned to his tent, but his face showed no emotion.

She gathered the children and got them into their tent. She checked LB's blood sugar: 340, far too high. She took him outside and did a urine test to check his keytones. Keytones are fats that build up in the body due to a lack of sugar or carbohydrates, the opposite of what Jen would have expected. They were negative. She was less concerned than usual that his readings would drop dramatically during the night, as they sometimes did, but she still checked him every three hours during his sleep. High numbers, especially over two hundred, were not good. She tried to keep him between 100 and 150, but this environment and diet, plus the confined space and stress, were making it very difficult.

Megan was a godsend. The sulking, sometimes difficult teenager she had been before their ordeal began had been replaced by a responsible and caring person. She had taken charge of the twins. Both of her teenage daughters had been very helpful. Jackie was an athlete and more physical than her older sister. She did the grunt work, gathering food and wood for the fire, and doing anything that required physical labor. Megan was the nurturer, making sure the emotional needs of her siblings were met.

The boys were just boys. They had handheld digital games to occupy their time. They wrestled with one another and ran around the camp, but in a limited space. Jackie played with them.

Jen took one last look at the guards. One was asleep in his tent. She could see his prone body through the open flap. The other was walking the perimeter diligently, as though Minh had security cameras monitoring his movements. She noticed that he looked in her direction as she closed the flap to her tent.

~~~

I opened a bottle of mosquito repellent and rubbed it liberally on my hands, face, and neck, then sprinkled it on the arms of the black peasant shirt. On a long, straight stretch of the river, I began wrapping tape around the handle and lower part of the eight-inch butcher's knife I had stolen from the kitchen of the Majestic. I did this slowly, ensuring that the tape was tight and thick around the handle. I did the same with the handle of the machete. I put batteries in the flashlights and laid out all of my gear on the floor of the boat in an organized fashion. I ate one of the energy bars, swallowed a malaria pill, and drank a bottle of water. Then I concentrated on piloting the boat and making the necessary turns upriver.

Fishing boats were scattered at various intervals near the banks of the river. I wondered if the fish were edible. The US had poisoned the rivers of Vietnam with Agent Orange during the fighting here forty years ago. Now the Vietnamese people appeared to be poisoning the rivers with industrial pollution. The same textile dye houses that once lined the South Fork and Catawba rivers in North Carolina now pumped toxic chemicals into the Saigon River. The river was dying, if not dead.

Nearly three hours later, I found the bridge where I had asked Loi to meet me. It would only be a thirty-minute drive from Saigon in his cab. I programmed in the coordinates as a waypoint on the GPS so I could easily backtrack to this specific location. I wasn't sure if I was still on the Saigon River or the Ben Cat, but the GPS told me that I was within fifteen miles and about an hour and forty-five minutes of my target. I kept the boat in the middle of the channel and avoided looking directly at the fishing boats along the way.

Sometime later, I looked at my watch. It registered 8:30 p.m. I soon lost the sun in the tall jungle canopy over my left shoulder. I continued north on the river. The moon rose in the south, as large and as orange as a pumpkin. As long as I stayed in the middle of the river's channel, I could see as well as if I had headlights on the boat. Mosquitoes were buzzing all around me. I poured more repellent into my hands and rubbed it on my exposed skin, then poured it on my shirt and pants. I even doused my straw hat with the repellent.

Twenty minutes later, the GPS told me I was within a mile of my destination. I pulled out the largest flashlight I had purchased and directed it toward the shoreline. I soon found a place to dock the boat along the west side of the river. The brush was thick, but there was a break in the undergrowth that indicated a path—human or animal, it didn't matter. I got out of the boat, quiet in the shallow water, and pulled the hull onshore. I put a red filter on a small flashlight and pointed it down to see if I could make my way through the undergrowth and read the GPS. I could. I picked up the backpack, fished out the knife, and stuck its handle in my back left pocket. I left the straw hat in the boat. I put one can of white spray paint in the backpack and held the other can in my left hand. I pulled the backpack on over my shoulders and stuck the machete, which was encased in a leather sheath, between the pack and my body, the handle at my left shoulder. I hoped the path would take me to the campsite, if it was there at all. But I knew enough about the jungle to know that you could not advance at times without chopping your way through.

I started toward my objective, pausing every few feet to spray the ground or a tree trunk liberally with the white paint to mark my trail, like Hansel and Gretel had done with bread crumbs. Unlike them, I didn't have to worry about birds eating my white paint.

Within fifteen minutes, I found the campsite. One guard was walking the perimeter around four tents. A large fire burned in the center of an open area, and something was cooking, probably rice, in a black pot suspended on a tripod. I could smell the food. As I approached the lighted area, I closed my left eye to maintain my night vision.

A large linen tent sat in the middle of the campsite. Two somewhat smaller tents sat near it, and across the open area was a tent that looked large enough for two or three men. I guessed that, if Jen and the children were here, they were in one of the larger tents, probably the largest. The others would likely be for Minh, the guards, or workers.

I removed the backpack, laid the machete on it, took the knife out of my pocket, and low-crawled closer to the fire. I kept my left eye closed as I got closer to the lighted area around the campfire.

One guard was walking the perimeter. I watched and waited, trying to think of a way to neutralize him without employing lethal force. Though I would certainly kill anyone to save my family, I had lost my appetite for killing. I had decided that there was only one more person I would kill in my lifetime, if possible—and that was Nguyen Li Minh.

I knew the five points of vulnerability of a man—the bridge of the nose, the Adam's apple, the solar plexus, the groin, and the knee. Problem was, if I attacked the guard in any of these areas, he might still be able to call out or make noise.

I could, of course, simply slit his throat. But I knew well how to put a person to sleep without killing him. I had practiced it many times in simulated situations in special classes at Fort Bragg. In fact, I had done this very drill to subdue a guard walking the perimeter of a POW camp. That was forty years ago, but I knew I could do it still if I could get close enough. If I did it properly, the guard would sleep long enough for me to gain the upper hand.

I folded myself into the jungle flora and waited for the right moment.

~~~

Jen lay on her left side on her cot, her right hand clutching the paring knife. She was ready to spring into action at the first sound of an intruder. Tears ran down her face as she listened to the rhythmic sounds of her sleeping children. She had now lost all hope of rescue and was certain that Minh would leave them in the jungle indefinitely.

~~~

I lay as quietly as I could, waiting for the guard to walk past me. I controlled my breathing and thus my heart rate. But the guard did not come.

I low-crawled to a place where I could see what was going on. The guard had stopped patrolling. He appeared to be urinating into the brush. Then he leaned against a tree and lit a cigarette. I could see the end of the cigarette grow brighter as he sucked in each drag.

I low-crawled back to the position I had selected near the path that he, and perhaps other guards, had made as they circled the camp. I needed the guard to walk past me and turn slightly toward the campsite. That was when I would attack. But he didn't seem to be in a hurry to make his rounds. There was nothing I could do now but wait.

Crouched and ready, I was afraid to crawl to take another look. My legs were cramping. I was about to relax when I heard his footsteps coming in my direction.

Just as the guard passed, actually within inches, I lunged from behind, hitting him with the full force of my body while wrapping my left arm around his throat, my elbow pointing straight in front of him like a three-cornered hat. I tightened my wrist and bicep in a vise and pressed hard against both of his carotid arteries. I used my right arm to cover his mouth like a muzzle and to press against my left arm to provide more force against both sides of his neck. I had hit him hard enough to drive him to the ground and knock the wind out of him. His rifle had fallen to the side. He thrashed around in the dirt like a dying fish on a pier. He was asleep within a short time.

Once he wasn't moving at all and I was certain that he was unconscious, I dragged him back into the brush. I rushed back to my backpack and got the roll of tape. I taped his mouth closed, then taped his hands behind his back and his ankles together.

I found the AK-47 within a few feet of where I had tackled him and racked a round into the firing chamber, sending an unspent shell into the undergrowth.

I stood and was about to proceed into the camp with the weapon when I saw another guard look in my direction. He could not see me from his position. I guessed that his shift was beginning and he was looking for his partner.

I pulled back into the jungle with the AK ready to fire.

The guard appeared confused, and maybe concerned. He began to walk the perimeter, looking for his associate. He was on full alert. His weapon was ready to fire as he proceeded cautiously.

My options were limited. I could hide and kill him, but if I used the rifle, it would be noisy. I did not know who was in the other tents, how many guards there were, or how they were armed.

If I used the knife, I could kill the guard, perhaps without noise, but maybe not.

I squatted, ready to move, but making myself as small as possible. I quietly pulled the magazine of ammunition from the AK-47 and very slowly cranked the bullet that was in the chamber out and into the palm of my hand. I put the bullet back into the magazine and laid it down beside me.

The Russian-made AK-47 is a sturdy weapon. Unlike the American M-16, with its plastic stock and casings, the AK is built from solid wood. It is heavy and formidable. All things equal, I would rather have an AK in a bayonet fight than an M-16. But I had no bayonet.

On the other hand, I had been a pretty good baseball player in my youth. I reversed the AK, holding it by the narrow barrel, like a batter tensed for a ninety-mile-per-hour fastball. I waited.

The guard walked an erratic route in and out of the jungle, looking for his comrade, who lay a few feet from me, gagged and hog-tied.

I waited. The patience, mental and physical toughness I had learned in my six-year Army enlistment had never left me. They had served me well in the four decades since, in life and in business. I knew how to wait. I knew how to act, and I knew when to act.

As the guard neared, I slowed my breathing and increased my grip on the barrel of the rifle.

He stepped past me.

I stood slowly and swung the AK hard right-to-left, connecting on the side of his head. He went down like an empty sack, limp and loose. Blood shot from his right ear as he lay on the ground. The rifle he carried had fallen to the ground nearby.

I picked up his weapon and threw the shattered rifle I was still holding into the jungle. I returned to my backpack, pulled out another roll of tape, and laid a strip across the guard's mouth, unsure if he was alive or dead. I taped his hands and ankles together and left him on the trail.

I walked quietly to the largest tent and opened the flap.

A cot blocked the opening. Jen jumped to her feet, a small knife in her right hand. I held up my arm to block the blow, but she immediately recognized me and lowered the knife.

I held my finger to my nose to indicate that she should be quiet.

Tears burst from her eyes. She hugged me so tightly that I couldn't catch my breath.

I kissed her on her forehead. "Are you okay?" I whispered.

"Yes." She looked at the rifle I was carrying. "The guards?"

"Two are tied up and gagged. Are there others in the tents?"

"Just Chinh," she said. "I think he's okay."

"Think?"

"He's Minh's driver, but he has helped us and kept the guards away from us."

"Where is Minh?"

"Don't know. He left a couple days ago."

"Okay, let's go. Does everybody have shoes? I brought some sandals."

"We have shoes."

"Food? Mosquito repellent? Malaria pills?" I asked. "How is LB? Do you have insulin?"

"He's doing okay, but not great. His kit is in good shape. We've eaten reasonably well. Don't have malaria pills. Probably a good idea, though. Let's wake the kids, one at a time." She knelt by Megan first and gently rocked her on her cot.

Megan's eyes opened, and she immediately saw me. She sprang to her feet and hugged me.

"Quiet," I whispered.

We woke each child, one at a time. They were smiling and happy. I gathered them in a small circle. "Okay, be very quiet. I have a boat nearby. We'll escape down the river. A cab is waiting for us, not too far away, maybe an hour or so on the river."

Tears dripped down Jen's face. Then all four children cried as they clung to me and to each other.

We walked out of the tent and right into a very large man holding a small pistol.

Chapter 30

BRAD AND ERIN SAT PATIENTLY in the ornate lobby of the Majestic Hotel. It was the middle of the night. Tommy had an apartment on the top floor of the hotel, a perk for taking the job here. The desk clerk had been reluctant to disturb him, but Brad had insisted that it was an emergency. When he spoke to him, Tommy had told Brad he had a message from Travis.

Soon, his old friend burst from the elevator of the hotel, and Brad stood to greet him.

"Brad," he said as the two men embraced. "I can't believe it's you. And I just saw your father yesterday morning." He noticed Erin.

"Tommy, this is Homeland Security Deputy Director Erin Stephens. Erin, this is my best friend from high school, Tommy Van."

Erin offered her hand, and Tommy shook it.

"What's happening with Jen?" Tommy asked. "Please sit." He gestured toward a table with four chairs.

They sat down.

Brad leaned toward Tommy. "Jen and the children were abducted by a Vietnamese man named Nguyen Li Minh. Minh brought them here from North Carolina, we think. A number of people were killed in the

States relating to this, including an Undersecretary of Homeland Security, General Walt Bradley. Bradley was my father's company commander in Vietnam. It's a long and complicated story, but right now, we're just trying to find Jen and the children."

"I know Nguyen Li Minh. He's sort of a big shot in Saigon, one of the wealthiest members of the Communist party. I have never liked him, nor do I know anyone who does, including party members." He paused and placed a piece of paper on the table. "Your father gave me this. He said to give it to you if I saw you."

Brad picked it up and held it so that Erin could see it as well. It had coordinates on it and a message from Travis: *Go to consulate first!*

"What does it mean?" Tommy asked.

"These are coordinates, latitude and longitude," Erin said. "Minh says this is the location where his father was killed by Travis in February 1969. Travis must think his family will be there."

"My guess is that he went to get them," Brad said. "That's what he told me he would do. Just go get them back, end of story, as he would say. If he's successful, he'll bring them back to the consulate."

"Okay, let's go to the consulate now," Erin said. "We'll see if they will help us."

"I'll drive you," Tommy said as they left together.

~~~

I had neither room nor time to react with the AK-47 as I came chest-to-chest with the big man. Jen immediately put herself between us. "Chinh," she said, staring up at him, "this is my father, Travis Kelly." She turned to me. "Dad, this is my friend, Chinh."

Chinh held the .38-caliber snub-nosed revolver pointed at the ground. His huge fingers appeared too large to go through the trigger guard. He nodded to me and put the pistol in his pocket.

"My father has a boat and is going to take us to the US consulate in Saigon," Jen said to Chinh.

The big man nodded and stepped aside.

As I led the children past Chinh and toward the trail, Jen held back. I heard her say, "Why don't you go with us, Chinh? It might not go well for you with Minh."

I turned and saw him nod. He seemed conflicted as he looked at the tent where the guards slept.

"Go with us, Chinh." Jen said. "I will speak to the people at the US consulate and tell them that you helped us. Do you want to continue working for Minh, knowing that he is a kidnapper of women and children?"

He reached in his pocket, pulled out the revolver, and gave it to Jen. She opened it expertly, spun the cylinder, and let the bullets fall to the ground. Then both she and Chinh followed the children and me toward the boat.

I made a game out of finding the white paint. Once we were beyond the perimeter, I told Jen that I needed to do something and to wait for me. I asked her if she still had the small knife, and she handed it to me. I handed her the AK-47 I still carried. By this time, I had figured out that Chinh was mute. I walked back to the place where I had left the guards tied up. Both were awake. Fear struck their eyes when they saw me. I reached down and grabbed both of them by the collars of their shirts. I pulled them on their backs toward the fire pit and sat them together, back to back. I laid the small paring knife in the lap of the first guard I had subdued. I was certain that it would take them hours to escape, but at least they would not die in the jungle with no hope.

I looked up and saw Chinh standing over me. He nodded. I took it as a gesture indicating that he appreciated my concern for the guards. We turned and caught up with my family.

The boat was large, with four plank rows. I pointed Chinh toward the third row, which centered the weight. He sat alone, facing me. The children and Jen took the front two rows, also facing me, looking toward the back of the boat. I had to push hard to obtain buoyancy with all the weight in the boat. Once we were fully in the water, I stepped over the side and sat on the back row. I pulled hard on a detachable rope that started the motor. It sputtered, but caught on the first pull. I steered the boat out into the channel and down the river toward Saigon.

It was now completely dark. I had to drive slowly. The moon that had helped on my trip up the river was now completely obscured by the tall trees in the triple-canopy jungle. I pulled energy bars and mosquito repellent from my backpack. I gave everybody, including Chinh, a malaria pill—children's doses for the boys and adult doses for the rest of us.

As we powered slowly forward, Joe moved from his seat beside his mother and sat beside Chinh, perhaps concerned that the big man was sitting all by himself. Chinh looked at the small boy and at me. He nodded and seemed to smile.

We had travelled a few minutes when I dumped the AK-47 into the river. Jen threw the revolver into the muddy water and smiled at me. I pulled Marvin's passport and driver's license out of my back pocket and dropped them over the side of the boat. It felt good to be Travis Kelly again.

Given the slow pace of the boat in the dark river, it took longer to get back to the bridge where I had asked Loi to wait than I had anticipated. I hoped he would still be there.

Nearing the bridge, I turned the boat toward the shore, gave the motor a little extra power, and ran us aground on the gentle slope. This pushed the bow of the boat well ashore. Jen, who was at the front, got out and helped the children, one at a time. Big Chinh stepped out of the boat and lifted Joe to shore as though he were a small toy. I pointed up the hill. They all started climbing toward the road. I followed closely behind.

The cab was there. Loi was sleeping in the driver's seat with the windows up, probably to keep mosquitoes out.

I tapped on the window. Loi awoke with a start. He smiled his big, nearly toothless smile and rolled the window down.

"Marvin," he said as he opened his door and got out of the taxi.

"Loi," I said, "this is my daughter, Jen, my four grandchildren, and our friend, Chinh."

Loi nodded. He seemed both pleased and worried. He looked at the cab, then back at all of us. "Okey dokey."

We had to think about how we would all get into the cab, which was a mid-sized sedan. An old Peugeot, I thought.

"I think I can sit in the front seat with the twins," I said, more to Jen than to anyone else. "Chinh and Jen in the back seat." I looked at Jackie, who, though younger than her sister, was bigger. "Why don't we let Megan sit between your mother and Chinh, and you sit on the floorboard in front of your mother. It's a relatively short trip."

Everyone agreed, and we piled into the cab.

Once we had settled in, Loi started the engine, looked at me, and smiled. "Okey dokey, where now?"

"United States consulate in Saigon," I said.

We were all smiling as we got underway. Jen handed me LB's insulin kit, and I checked his blood sugar. He was 115, a good reading. We were on our way, in pretty good shape.

As I sat in the seat with my twin grandsons on my lap, my daughter and two granddaughters in the back, safe now, it occurred to me that I had not had a headache in a long time. Then I remembered the prayer in the parking lot somewhere in South Carolina or Georgia. I had prayed that whatever was going on in my body would not prevent me from getting my family back. I felt cold chills run down my spine, and I said a silent prayer of thanks.

About fifteen minutes into the drive, I heard Jen talking and realized that she was speaking to Chinh. She had kept one of the flashlights and was looking at something. I turned in my seat, and she handed me two photographs.

"These are pictures of Chinh's parents," she said.

I twisted further to look at Chinh, and he nodded. I turned on a small light on the sun visor of the sedan and looked carefully at the pictures. They were old black-and-white pictures. The first was of a very pretty young Vietnamese woman, maybe in her early twenties, wearing a traditional silk gown elaborately woven with a decorative design.

The second picture was of the same woman, in the same gown, standing with a tall African American soldier, an E-8, first sergeant, in his Class A uniform. He was highly decorated. I turned the pictures over. Nothing was written on the back of the first picture, but on the back of the second, in black ink, were the words, *First Sergeant and Mrs. Abraham P. Matthews, Magnolia Springs, Alabama, June 11, 1974*. This would have been about one year before the fall of Saigon to the North Vietnamese Army. I turned the picture over and studied the background. I had been to Magnolia Springs, a very small town near the Gulf of Mexico in southern Alabama. The pictures, both of them, seemed to have been taken there.

I turned and gave the pictures back to Chinh. "Are these your parents, Chinh?"

He nodded.

"So they came back to Vietnam, and you were born here?"

He shook his head.

"Just your mother came back?" I asked.

Again he indicated no.

"Chinh, were you born in America?"

He nodded in the affirmative.

I looked at Jen, who smiled through moist eyes. "He's an American citizen," she said.

~~~

Brad's stomach churned as he stood outside the US consulate in Saigon with Erin and Tommy. This was the building made famous in photographs and film on April 30, 1975, the day Saigon fell to the NVA. The three of them had successfully convinced one Marine, a lance corporal, to permit them to speak to his superior, a gunnery sergeant.

Brad stood close and let Erin take the lead as she did the talking for the group.

"This is ridiculous," Erin said to the sergeant once he had arrived. "Will you please tell someone in the consulate that I'm an officer with the Department of Homeland Security and that we, all three of us, are American citizens? We desperately need to see someone relating to a crime that has been committed against an American family by a Vietnamese national."

"Ma'am, I apologize, but it's very late, or early, I guess. We are short-handed. There's just one civilian State Department person on staff in the building right now, and we're waking her. I have also sent word to an FBI agent stationed in Saigon, but he's on assignment and is in another town right now."

"I understand," Erin said. "I'm sorry, Gunny. It's been a long day."

"No apology necessary, ma'am. Stressful situations are the norm around here." He held a phone to his ear. "Yes," he said into the phone. "Yes, ma'am. I'll take them there." He directed them toward an entrance to the consulate.

Just as they were about to enter the building, a cab pulled up at the guard station about twenty-five yards away.

Brad turned toward the cab and thought he recognized his father sitting in the front seat with his nephews on his lap. He said, "Wait!" and he ran toward the cab.

The back left door opened, and his sister got out.

Brad embraced her as the other occupants, his nieces, nephews, father, and a big, dark-skinned man, poured out of the vehicle.

"Uncle Brad!" Jackie yelled, and all the children started running toward their uncle.

~~~

I stretched and rubbed my thighs where LB and Joe had been sitting patiently for nearly thirty minutes as Loi drove us to the US consulate in Saigon.

Jen and the children were embracing Brad. Erin stood near a Marine gunnery sergeant, but started walking toward me.

I heard three short, loud blasts on a whistle. I turned toward the street. Two Vietnamese men in business clothes, coats, and ties were approaching us. Behind them were two uniformed policemen.

A small military vehicle rushed toward us at high speed. It stopped abruptly near the guard station. Six uniformed soldiers with AK-47s jumped from the truck and surrounded us in a semicircle that also included the men in suits and the uniformed police officers.

The Marine gunnery sergeant drew his service weapon and yelled something to the guards at the guard station. One of the Marines got on the telephone. The other Marine, a lance corporal, rushed toward us, cranking a round of ammunition into his M4 carbine.

Damn, I thought. *To get this far and then have Minh's political contacts prevent my family from getting to a safe place. I won't let it happen. Damn it! I will not let it happen!*

Chapter 31

CONSULATE OFFICER PENNY STAFFORD, a fifty-something career diplomat with short blond hair and a slightly rumpled look from being rousted out of bed at five o'clock in the morning, stood nose-to-nose with the chief of police of Ho Chi Minh City, Nghiem Van Thi. Nghiem, also somewhere north of fifty, wore a business suit. His dark hair was perfectly combed straight back and slick, which accentuated his sharp facial features. He wore thick, round glasses like John Lennon, but he resembled Yoko Ono more than John. Stafford and Nghiem spoke alternately in English and Vietnamese. I was tracking the conversation fairly well, catching a few words and phrases of the Vietnamese.

Nghiem, in a high tonal voice, said, "How do you know these people are American citizens?"

"We do not have to know or prove that they are or that they are not American citizens," Stafford responded. "They are on American soil. If they claim to be citizens, we can and will take them into the consulate and determine their status. *Đó là đối với chúng tôi để xác định,*" she said, the last phrase meaning something like, *We determine that, not you.* Stafford was short, square, and one weight class heavier than Nghiem.

It was an extremely tense situation. The sun was now lighting the early morning sky, and street lights were blinking off. A dozen armed Marines, weapons at the ready, now faced the two armed plainclothes police officers, six Vietnamese soldiers, and the chief of police, who had been summoned by the officers and rousted from sleep at his home, extending the standoff an awkward thirty minutes.

"We only need to arrest Travis Paul Kelly," the chief said, gesturing toward me. "The others may go, except for this man." He pointed at Chinh.

"You will arrest no one standing on American soil," Penny Stafford nearly screamed. "We have an agreement with your government that this consulate has the same status as similar buildings and grounds throughout the world. You have no authority here."

As she was speaking, I heard more vehicles arriving and turned to see two additional truckloads of soldiers, who sprang from their trucks and joined their comrades, surrounding us. Now we were seriously outnumbered.

Jen, Brad, and Erin wrapped their arms around the children, who were crying and shaking with fear.

I raised my hand and spoke. Stafford and Nghiem turned to me, whom they had been generally ignoring. "If I surrender and am arrested, can my family go into the consulate?"

"That's not an option, Mr. Kelly," Stafford responded.

"Yes," Nghiem said. "We only want you for the murder of Tran Duc Manh, Ho Chi Minh's son."

"Fine," I said. I turned to Loi and tossed him the rain jacket in which I had stuffed about four thousand dollars. "Loi, please accept this jacket and anything you find in it for the great service you have done for my family. This will get you through the next monsoon season." I walked over to my family and hugged and kissed them all, including Brad, and then walked quickly off the consulate grounds and into the street. I was immediately accosted and handcuffed by the uniformed police officers. As they pushed me toward their cruiser, I looked back at my family. Jen and the children were sobbing, but they were safe, I thought. I settled into the back of the police car, and it immediately drove away at a relatively high rate of speed.

I assumed that the policemen spoke no English. They were quiet as we drove through the streets of Saigon. I was alone in the back seat. There were no handles on the doors, and my hands were cuffed behind my back.

I thought through the words I needed to say and said, "*Tôi có một con dao trong túi của tôi trở lại,*" telling them, I hoped, that I had a knife in my pocket. I had two reasons for telling them. First, I didn't want them to think I was trying to sneak a knife into jail. Second, the damn thing was cutting into my butt.

"Knife?" the officer in the passenger's seat said to me in English.

"Yes," I said, trying to turn to show him the knife sticking out of my pants pocket.

He nodded, but they didn't stop the cruiser.

~~~

The police station and jail looked like something out of 1950s Hollywood, more like Mexico than Vietnam: a concrete building, thick, square, and well-lit. As the police officers pulled me out of the squad car, they withdrew the knife from my back pocket, revealing blood on the blade—my blood.

I was pushed and prodded like an uncooperative animal into a large room where several policemen were suffering through the last hour of the graveyard shift. My arrival caused some excitement.

The interior looked like the jail that Andy Taylor and Barney Fife managed on *The Andy Griffith Show*. I was certain, however, that I would not be receiving any cakes baked by Aunt Bea, and that Otis would not be sleeping off a bottle in the next cell. The cells, located in plain sight of the jailers, were occupied by nine young men and women—I counted—all of whom found me quite a curiosity.

The officers removed my handcuffs and pushed me unceremoniously through the open doors of a cell, which were then closed behind me, the metal clanging with an echo.

I nodded to my three cellmates and to the others in nearby cells. Then I turned and looked back at the office, holding the bars as though I intended to pull them apart.

A fellow prisoner in my cell, a young man of about twenty, walked slowly toward me and stood quietly, close beside me. "American?" he whispered.

"Yes," I said quietly.

He was still and quiet for a minute. "Not supposed to speak, so be careful."

I nodded.

"Your crime?"

"Murder," I said.

He looked stunned and widened the separation between us by a few inches.

I turned so he could see my face. "Not guilty," I said. "Your crime?"

"Talking. All of us." He waved his hand around the three cells. "We are guilty, I am afraid."

I nodded, but said nothing further.

One of the plainclothes detectives who had been at the consulate burst through the front door of the jail, followed by consulate officer Penny Stafford, the police chief, and another well-dressed Asian man I didn't know. They walked straight toward me.

"Mr. Kelly," said the well-dressed, handsome man in perfect English, "my name is Tran Le. I am consul general at the US consulate. Have you been mistreated?" He nodded toward my slacks, which were bloody.

I shook my head. "No, sir. That is a self-inflicted wound. I have been treated reasonably well."

"Ms. Stafford is going to arrange a local attorney to represent you. We, of course, will work diplomatic channels to see if we can expedite your release. In the meantime, I am afraid you will have to remain incarcerated."

Stafford and Nghiem Van Thi, the police chief, stood close by. They said nothing.

"I understand. How are my daughter and grandchildren?"

"They are fine. We are researching the situation and interviewing your daughter. Also, there is an officer from the Department of Homeland Security who is validating the information. This is very complicated. Unbelievable, actually."

"Yes, sir. It is unbelievable, but my only goal here was to rescue my family. I don't care what happens from this point on."

"Well, we do. It is clear that you have been the victim of an international crime. US citizens have been kidnapped, and US officials, Homeland Security and the FBI, have been killed. Plus, we know that an undersecretary of Homeland Security was assassinated, along with his wife. These are facts on the ground. Ms. Stafford will immediately take your case on a full-time basis, and we will get this resolved."

Stafford nodded at me, but said nothing.

"This man is a murderer and is in our country illegally," Nghiem said to the consul general. "He will be tried in the People's court for his crime, and punishment will be swift and just."

Tran Le turned to Nghiem. "So he will be tried, and punishment will be swift and just, Nghiem. What if this man is innocent?"

"He is not innocent of entering our country illegally. We have pictures of him at the airport. We believe also he killed the son of Ho Chi Minh."

The consul general shook his head and turned back to me. "Expect to hear from us in a couple of hours. They may move you to a prison, but they are obligated to provide access to you, and they like our money more than they want to make a point, I think. Just be patient, and we'll get through this."

I nodded.

The three officials turned in unison and left the jail.

My fellow prisoner walked back up to me. "Prison is not good. Not good at all," he said.

"Well, I guess I just go where they take me."

He looked me in the eye and said, "Sorry."

Chapter 32

BRAD WALKED INTO THE COMFORTABLE sitting area where Jen and Erin waited in the US consulate. He had just returned from standing at the children's bedroom door and staring through the glass window at his nieces and nephews, curled together and sleeping soundly. Two separate bedrooms had been offered to them, one for the boys and one for the girls, but they had asked to stay together.

"They're sleeping soundly," he said as he sat down in a cloth chair. "With all they've been through, I can't believe they can go to sleep so fast and sleep so well."

Jen nodded as she sipped on a cup of coffee. "I am so proud of them. They all were just remarkable, taking care of each other, and even me."

"How are you doing?" Brad asked his sister.

"I'm okay, I think. Worried about Dad."

"Yeah. Me, too."

Erin broke the silence that followed. "Let me tell you what I learned about Chinh."

Jen moved to the edge of her seat. "What?"

"Turns out, he's an American citizen. He knew his date of birth, his birth name, his father, and his mother. He was born in Huntsville,

Alabama. We think he came back to Vietnam with his father and mother when he was less than a year old. The father is listed as 'killed in action' in 1974, one of the last casualties of the Vietnam War. The mother and Chinh ended up in a refugee camp, where the mother died when he was about ten. Chinh somehow survived on the streets of Saigon and got a job in Minh's factory, doing maintenance on textile equipment when he was in his late twenties. Minh made him his driver, just two years ago."

"How did he tell you this?" Brad asked.

"He wrote it down," Erin said. "He's actually very intelligent and self-educated. He understands English, but he wrote all of this in Vietnamese. With a little coaching and encouragement from Penny Stafford, he has asked to go to the States."

Jen cried softly through a smile.

Brad nodded. "That's good." He looked out the window and asked Erin, "Now, what about Dad? I'm worried about him. Is there anything we can or should be doing? I know we need to work with the officials here, but I feel like we're just sitting here waiting for Minh to take his revenge."

"Not much we can do," Erin responded. "We just have to wait."

"Have you heard anything from Duff?"

Erin shook her head. "No, but I haven't been able to get online. I'll find a computer and e-mail him in a few minutes."

"What will happen to Dad?" Jen asked.

Brad reached out and held his sister's hand.

Erin sighed. "Hard to say. Sounds like Nguyen Li Minh is well connected. They have Travis in custody. I'm thinking they'll do a show trial, find him guilty, and sentence him to a long prison term."

"How can they do that?" Jen said. "That would mean that any soldier who fought in the war and came back to Vietnam as a tourist would be subject to possible arrest and imprisonment, assuming they killed enemy combatants."

"But they're not accusing him of killing just any enemy combatant," Erin said. "They have arrested him for killing the son of Ho Chi Minh."

"Not likely," Brad said. He stood and walked toward the window, thinking about his father and how little he knew about him, especially his military history. "Ho may have had a daughter, but that isn't certain. For much of his life, he claimed to be celibate. I think this is all bogus."

Jen stood and walked to Brad. She put her arm around his waist. "It doesn't matter. Dad is sitting in a Vietnamese jail, and there seems to be nothing we can do about it."

~~~

"I need to go to the bathroom," I whispered to my new friend and cellmate, whose name was Pham Dinh.

"Just ask the guard," Dinh said. "That one is okay." He pointed him out.

"'Toilet' is '*nhà vệ sinh?*'"

Dinh nodded.

I stood as close as possible to the guard of whom Dinh approved, and said in my best tonal Vietnamese, "*Nhà vệ sinh?*"

The guard turned to me. He seemed pleased that I had attempted to communicate with him in his language. He nodded and unlocked the cell, then pointed me toward a small door a few feet away.

I walked in front of him, opened the door, and stepped inside. Though I closed it, the door could not be locked. I could tell that the guard stood nearby. As I relieved myself in the toilet, a headache hit me like a sledgehammer to the front of my skull. It nearly knocked me to my knees. I braced myself against the wall.

I washed my hands in a sink on the facing wall and rubbed them over my face. My reflection in the small mirror over the sink was blurred, as if I were "looking through a glass darkly," as Paul wrote in the Bible. But it was clear enough that I could see my gray beard, sunken eyes, and disheveled hair. I looked like hell and felt worse.

I stumbled out of the bathroom into the surprised guard. He backed a step and looked at me, then directed me to the cell.

When I was back inside, I slid to the floor and braced my head in my hands.

Dinh knelt beside me. "Travis, are you okay?" he asked.

"Headache. Bad. Just need to be quiet and still."

"Okay," he said as he gently touched my shoulder.

~~~

The prison was on a hill on the outskirts of Saigon. Based on the one-hour drive through the cluttered, clanging streets of the city, where we inched forward from one stop to another, it was about fifteen miles from the jail. The smell hit me in the face when they pushed me through dark doors that led to narrow passages. It was urine, human feces, and fear, the latter almost palpable. Human skeletons in cotton pajamas and sandals stood quietly behind steel bars as I was hustled past their cells. They didn't make eye contact with me or with the guards.

I was placed in a large room with four guards. They each held a collapsible, lightweight hard nylon baton called an "ASP" for the Wisconsin company that manufactures them. They watched me carefully, their ASPs fully extended, looking, I assumed, for an opportunity to deploy a stinging blow to my body.

But I was passive. I did exactly what they required. In Vietnamese, they told me to strip naked. I think they were surprised when I immediately complied without protest. Standing before them completely naked, I stared straight ahead.

They directed me toward a shower in an adjoining room where the water had been turned on full force. They gave me a bar of soap. The water was cold. I applied the soap and washed thoroughly, thankful that they had not used a fire hose, as I had anticipated. I urinated as I washed myself, just in case I didn't get toilet privileges. The smell that had met me when I first entered the facility made me think this was a distinct possibility.

I was shaking when I finished the shower, goose bumps covering my exposed skin. A guard handed me a small towel, not much larger than a washcloth. I dried myself as well as possible. Another guard gave me striped pajamas and sandals, both of which were far too small. My heels hung over the ends of the sandals.

Two guards led me to my cell, a small room constructed of concrete blocks, with no windows and bare hardwood floors. The stench of urine was so strong that I nearly vomited.

They shoved me inside and locked the thick steel door behind me. Although it was mid-morning, maybe ten o'clock, the cell was dark. There was no lighting fixture and maybe no electricity. A small cot with a thin blanket folded on top was pushed against one wall. There was no pillow, no toilet, and no sink.

I walked to the steel door and looked through a thin slot. I could see light, but nothing else, neither prisoners nor guards. I thought that they had placed me far away from the general population, but they hadn't. There were prisoners all around me, as I would soon learn.

I sat on the cot and covered my nose with my forearm and elbow. The smell of the soap from the shower helped dull the stench in the air. But it was hot, very hot. I began perspiring. I thought that maybe I would get used to the smell eventually. I was wrong.

As I lay on my back with my arm covering my nose and my eyes closed, I heard a faint sound like a slap against the wall. It was barely audible. My first thought was an animal, perhaps a rat. I sat up and squinted in the darkness. No rats, not yet, anyway. Another slap. Then on the opposite wall, two slaps. I walked to one wall and slapped my palm against the cold concrete block. I was rewarded by a replying slap on the same wall. I walked to the opposite wall and slapped my hand twice and got two slaps in response.

I walked back to the slot in the steel door and looked out into the dim hallway. "Anyone there?" I asked.

No response, but I immediately heard footsteps approaching rapidly. I heard keys jangling, and my door opened. Three guards holding extended ASPs burst into the room and thrashed me on the neck, shoulders, and back. I fell to the floor and wrapped my arms around my head to protect myself as much as possible.

"No talking," they ordered as they continued beating me for a minute or more, though it seemed like an eternity. Blow after blow rained down on my body, mostly my back. Then they were gone.

I lay on the floor, the beating stinging more than hurting, but the pain was intense. Then, of course, a headache hit me, and my misery was complete. I crawled to the corner of the cell and vomited, wiping my mouth with the sleeve of my pajamas. I may have passed out, but sometime later I heard a slap on the wall from the one-slap prisoner, followed by two slaps on the other wall.

I pulled myself to my feet and staggered to One-Slap's wall to return the greeting, then did the same with Two-Slap. "Yes, I'm still alive," I whispered.

I returned to the cot, but could not lie on my back because of the pain. The wounds may have been bleeding. I curled on my side and pulled my knees up to my stomach in a fetal position. I thought about Claire. She had always been cold, while I had always been hot. I slept under a thin sheet in loose boxer shorts and a thin T-shirt, while she slept under a mountain of blankets in long pajamas. She was so small that sometimes I wasn't sure that a female human being was under all those covers. I would curl up to her in a spooning position, kiss her on the back of the neck, and wrap my left arm around her, pulling her to me. She would take my hand, kiss it, and say, "I love you." Sweet thoughts of her had always helped me get through tough times. Every night I spent in Vietnam, no matter how bad the day had been, I went to sleep thinking about being with Claire. So this was a lot like that, I thought. I was back in Vietnam, dreaming about Claire.

After some time, I was able to sit up on my cot as I recovered from the shock and the sting of the beating. I activated the clock that the Army had put in my head more than forty years ago. I figured it was about ten o'clock when they had first put me in the cell. I had violated the no-talking rule and taken a beating. Then I had tried to recover on the cot. Must have been two hours, I thought. So it was noon.

I heard activity outside the cell and crept to the steel door and peeked through the slot. The guards were delivering bowls of food to the adjoining cells, probably rice. They didn't deliver one to me. I assumed this was more punishment for talking. No problem. I wasn't hungry anyway.

I returned to the cot, found a comfortable position, and began daydreaming.

Claire walks toward me as I sit on the screened porch of our home in North Carolina. She wears a long, casual dress. She is tall and thin and graceful. She lost about fifteen pounds with her first round of chemotherapy when she was forty years old. Though she looks healthy now, she has not regained her weight. She never will. She pours me a glass of iced tea and bends down to kiss me on the cheek. I stand and take her in my arms. We kiss each other on the lips.

"What are you doing?" she asks.

"Working on payroll," I say.

"Are we going to get paid this month?" She laughs, but it's strained.

"No. It's getting better, though. Orders are picking up again. We'll be fine."

She nods and walks back to the kitchen to start our dinner.

The cell door opened. I sat up on my cot. Two guards walked in and told me to stand. They pulled my hands behind my back and cuffed my wrists tightly in metal handcuffs. One walked in front of me and the other in back as they led me out of the cell and down the narrow corridor outside. I tried to see my fellow prisoners as I passed them. Their cells were not enclosed like mine. Still, I could not see them and assumed they stayed as far away from the guards as possible. *Not a bad decision*, I thought.

We walked down several corridors, like mice finding their way through a maze in search of cheese. But it was an office area, not cheese, that we eventually found. Locked doors were opened, and the guards escorted me into a small room with a table and two wooden, straight-backed chairs. One guard remained by the door while the other left the room.

I asked to go to the bathroom and received no response. I asked for a drink of water with the same result.

A small man in an expensive business suit walked into the room. He wore glasses perched on a straight nose. His thinning hair was combed straight back. His fingernails were clean and, like the rest of him, perfectly groomed. His white shirt was starched. An expensive wristwatch hung loosely on his left wrist. I knew immediately who he was.

"You don't look so good, Travis," Nguyen Li Minh said.

I stared at him.

"Do you need anything?"

I said nothing.

Another man walked into the room. It was the first guard I had attacked at the campsite. The other guard followed. He wore a thick bandage on the right side of his head, covering his right ear.

Minh stood and nodded toward the two guards. "You have been released into my custody. Time to go."

The guards grabbed me roughly by my forearms and forced me to my feet. They pushed me out of the room, Minh leading the way.

A black Mercedes was parked in an alley outside the prison. The trunk was open. The guards pushed and shoved me into the trunk and slammed it shut. I lay on my side and urinated in the thin pajamas as the car bounced along at a slow rate of speed. I knew where we were going, and I assumed it was near the end for me. It didn't matter. At this point I didn't care about anything, not even getting even with Minh. I was just ready for it to end.

Chapter 33

JEN WAS IN THE MIDDLE of the entourage that descended on the prison. She was extremely impressed with Tran Le, the Saigon Consul General for the United States, who had taken charge of and led the group. Equally impressive was his first assistant, Penny Stafford, who walked a couple of paces behind Tran Le.

The group also included a Marine Colonel by the name of Stuart Foster, two Marine sergeants, Homeland Security officer Erin Stephens, and Jen's brother, Brad.

Tran Le spoke in Vietnamese while Penny Stafford interpreted so that Jen, Brad, and Erin could understand what was happening.

"Where is he?" Stafford said softly, indicating what the consul general had demanded of the prison warden, a short, fat man with lazy eyes. Stafford paused to listen. "He says they released him."

"Released him?" Jen said.

Stafford raised her hand, indicating that she needed to listen to the conversation.

"Released him to whom?" Tran Le asked in Vietnamese.

"To a friend, I assume," the warden said in a dry monotone.

"An American friend, or a Vietnamese friend?" Tran Le demanded.

Jen squeezed as close to Stafford as possible to hear her interpretation of the conversation.

"Vietnamese," the warden said. "They left one hour ago. All charges have been dropped." A smile was encased in his fat cheeks.

Tran Le turned to the group huddled in the receiving area of the prison. "Minh has him," he said. "Let's go!"

"Where are we going?" Jen asked as they rushed back to their vehicles.

"To the residence of Nguyen Li Minh," Penny Stafford said as she strode step-for-step with the consul general.

Jen tried to keep pace with the group and control her emotions. But now anger boiled out of her like lava from a volcano. She looked at Brad and saw the anger in his eyes, also. She was sure that it would take more than a few Marines to keep her brother and her from tearing Minh limb from limb if they found him.

~~~

The ride in the trunk of the Mercedes was long and unpleasant in the damp pajamas. When the vehicle stopped and the trunk swung open, I was relieved to be pulled out by the guards. Bright sunlight hit me like a lightning strike in a summer storm.

Without discussion, the two guards pulled and pushed me through the thick flora of the jungle. I squinted into the light that penetrated the canopy. Soon I saw Minh, who was ahead of us, reach down to pull up a trap door on the jungle floor. He pointed to the opening and said something in Vietnamese which I didn't understand. One guard descended a ladder into the dark tunnel, and the other pushed me down the shaft after him. I tried to find my footing, but I mostly fell ten feet to the dirt floor below. The guards picked me up as Minh followed down the ladder, a flashlight in hand.

Minh pointed the flashlight down a corridor of the tunnel. The walls had been raised and widened to allow tourists to experience the war from the perspective of the Viet Cong and North Vietnamese Army soldiers who had used the tunnels to hide and recover from battles with the Americans.

I had been in the tunnels near the Cambodian border many times. They were called the Cu Chi tunnels. Sadly, I had killed a female nurse in black pajamas when she darted across an opening in front of me during one scary mission. I still remember creeping slowly to her body, shocked to see that she was an unarmed woman whose back I had blown away with my forty-five. I knelt beside her and cried until my radio operator pulled me to my feet and pointed me farther down the tunnel, where we found four enemy combatants who were willing and able to fight from their fortified positions. The sound of the weapons firing on semi-automatic inside the tunnels was something I would never forget. That, plus the face of the young Vietnamese woman, had often been a part of my flashback dreams since the war. Over time it had gotten better, but now it was all coming back.

Minh used his flashlight to find three kerosene lanterns, which he lit with matches he carried in his pocket. The guards pulled a wooden chair into the center of the room and forced me to sit in it.

Minh pulled up a similar chair and sat in front of me. "To simply put a bullet in your chest as you did to my father seems too simple, and even too kind. I prefer a slow process that will permit you to think about what you did to me and to so many young people when you were here. So many fathers and mothers were taken from their children. So much grief. So much devastation. It will give me great pleasure to know that you are here alone in the dark, dying from starvation and thirst."

I had decided that I would not speak to him. I would not plead for my life. I would show as little emotion as possible. Given my condition at the time, this wasn't difficult. I was so thirsty that my tongue stuck to the roof of my mouth, and the pain from the prison beating lingered. I had no emotion left inside me, nor the energy to express it. I simply stared into the darkness beyond the lanterns and prayed that I would die more quickly than Minh might have wished.

Getting no response from me, Minh finally stood. He extinguished the lanterns. Pointing his flashlight down a corridor, he said something to the guards.

They walked into the darkening tunnel. I heard them climbing up the ladder. The trap door closed with a loud thud like a nearby artillery round smacking the jungle floor. The darkness that engulfed me was black and deep, a complete absence of light. My hands remained painfully cuffed behind my back. Had I been able to place one in front of my face, however, I could not have seen it. I remembered being in caverns in the mountains of North Carolina when a guide extinguished all light, creating a darkness very close to what I now experienced. The fish that lived in the streams flowing through the caverns were blind, she explained. Living in total darkness twenty-four hours every day of the year had stripped them of their ability to see. I wondered if I would live long enough to know that I had lost my eyesight, or if I would even know. I closed my eyes and tried to regain some strength by resting and maybe even sleeping.

~~~

Brad sat as close to Consul General Tran Le as possible. His heart was thumping in his chest. He felt they were on the trail of his father, but he also felt that the odds were against them. He looked with great interest at the wife of Nguyen Li Minh. Tran Le had said that her name was Tran Thi Lam. She sat politely on a sofa facing them. Brad tried to assess her circumstances. She seemed to be an elegant woman of cultured upbringing. She had offered tea and hospitality to the large group of visitors that descended on her home unannounced. She was nervous, but understandably so. It was clear to him that she didn't speak English.

Consul General Tran Le introduced Brad and Jen as the children of Travis Kelly. He spoke in Vietnamese, but Brad understood the nods and heard his and Jen's names spoken, along with their father's. Lam nodded to them. She recognized Jen, and her eyes widened. She didn't seem to understand what was happening.

Tran Le then turned to Brad, and in the direction of Jen and Erin, who stood behind the sofa where he was sitting. "I am going to let Penny ask her some questions," he said. "I think she will respond better to a woman. We will try to determine where Minh is and where we go next."

Brad listened as Penny Stafford leaned close to the woman and spoke softly. The conversation lasted several minutes. Stafford's gentle tone seemed to relax Minh's wife. At one point, she looked at Jen and Brad, bowed her head slowly, and said, "I am sorry," in halting English. Tears sprang from her eyes.

Stafford spoke with her for a long time. Brad became frustrated, unable to tell whether Stafford was making any progress. Perhaps the wife truly knew nothing. She didn't seem to be an evil person like her husband.

After several minutes, she pulled a drawer out from the table beside her and took out what looked to be a business card. She handed it to Stafford, who examined it and passed it to Tran Le. The consul general nodded to Minh's wife and stood.

Brad took this as a sign to stand, as well. Stafford nodded to Minh's wife and said something in Vietnamese, then looked at Brad and the others and said, "Let's go!"

Brad walked closely beside Stafford as she hurried to the exit. "What did she say?" he asked. "Where are we going?"

"She has no idea where Minh is," Stafford said. They stepped outside into the warm, moist air. "But there is a brother in Hanoi, a professor. It was his business card that she gave us. She says that Minh told her he would visit his brother today. We're going to get a helicopter and fly to Hanoi."

Brad's heart rate increased another notch. He stepped aside and let Jen and Erin catch up with him. He told them what Stafford had said as they ran toward the waiting staff car.

~~~

Claire was a great money manager. She saved nearly eighty percent of our military pay the last two years I was in the Army. That twenty thousand dollars, plus the GI Bill and a couple of part-time jobs, put me through college and graduate school. We moved to Chapel Hill, North Carolina, the year after I got home from Vietnam. I enrolled in the University of North Carolina as a sophomore, majoring in business and economics. I made nearly perfect grades the first semester and was cruising through the second when the dreams started.

It was about three o'clock in the morning on a Wednesday in March. We had to get up early so Claire could get ready for her job in the accounting office at the university, and so I would have plenty of time to take Jen to daycare before my first class. But three o'clock was too early.

Dressed only in boxer shorts, I somehow found my way to the front porch of our little house on Purefoy Road. I was sitting in a swing, crying and shivering in the cold air, when Claire found me. She sat down beside me and put her arm around my shoulders.

She said nothing. She just held me as close as she could. I put my head against her neck and sobbed, shaking as though my best friend had died. In fact, he had. When I closed my eyes, I saw the lifeless body of Marvin Evans, half of his throat blown away by a heavy .30-caliber bullet fired from an enemy soldier's AK-47.

The dream had brought it all back: pulling Pep out of the bunker, cradling his lifeless body in my arms. A young private ran to another trooper who had died and did the same. We sat side-by-side, holding our friends, both of us crying uncontrollably. A dozen men stood around us, some of them crying, some with expressions of profound grief and fear. Every time someone was killed, it was both a painful loss and a reminder that any one of us could be next. I had long decided that I would not make it, but the thought of losing Pep had somehow not entered my mind. Not Pep. He was so kind, so competent, so tolerant of the bigotry of others. In short, he was everything I wanted to be.

That's what eventually got me back on my feet. I decided that I would keep some of Pep inside of me and that I would try to be more like him.

That thought gave me the strength to tie his dog tags into the laces of his jungle boots and zip his lifeless form into a body bag.

Claire kissed me on the top of the head.

The screen door opened, and little Jen walked out carrying Flop Head, a bald-headed doll with a limp neck. The doll's head flopped from side to side as Jen cradled it in the crook of her arm. She wore wool pajamas that covered her tiny feet. She toddled up to the swing and crawled up in my lap. I held her close while Claire held me close. I shut my eyes. Pep was gone.

~~~

Jen sat beside the consul general and a Marine colonel in a powerful Marine helicopter, flying from Saigon to Hanoi. Brad, Erin, and Peggy Stafford sat across from them. The pilot had told them the seven-hundred-mile trip would take about four hours.

Jen fought nausea as the noisy aircraft flew hard toward the north. Directly beside them, another helicopter, filled with high-ranking Vietnamese civilian and military officials, flew nearly in lock-step. She could see it clearly over Tran Le's head.

The consul general seemed distracted as he gazed out the window.

Jen spoke into her headset, directing her question to Penny Stafford. "Do you know anything about Minh's brother?"

"No," Stafford responded, "but his name is Trinh Dinh Hai. It seems odd that he wouldn't share his brother's Nguyen surname."

"The first name is the surname?" Jen said.

"Yes. Ho Chi Minh, in the US, would have been Minh Chi Ho. Your father, in Vietnam, would be called Kelly Paul Travis."

"I see." Jen fell quiet for a minute. "So what do you mean about the brother?"

"Nothing. It just seems odd," Stafford said as she turned to the window and stared at the accompanying Vietnamese officials' helicopter.

"Why are they following us?" Jen asked.

"It's protocol. We can't just fly around Vietnam willy-nilly. We had to notify them about what we're doing and give them the opportunity to participate."

Jen settled back in her thoughts and concentrated on keeping her stomach settled for the balance of trip.

Four hours later, at about five o'clock in the afternoon, Jen stood beside her brother at the back of a large lecture hall at the University of Science and Technology in Hanoi. Professor Trinh Dinh Hai lectured to nearly one hundred students, who took copious notes, their heads down, their attention focused intently on the honored professor's words.

A myriad of formulae, charts, and graphs covered a large screen behind the professor. Jen couldn't tell if it was a course in advanced mathematics, physics, or econometrics. But it was clear that the professor was highly engaged and enthusiastic about his subject and his students. Jen thought, *He looks just like Minh. Must be his brother.*

When the lecture ended and the last student politely thanked the professor and left the classroom, the consul general made his way to the front of the classroom, with Jen and the others close behind.

"Professor Trinh," Tran Le said in English, to Jen's surprise and relief. "I am Tran Le, consul general of the US consulate in Ho Chi Minh City."

"You mean, Saigon?" the professor said with a broad smile, extending his hand for a handshake.

Jen noticed that he spoke with a British accent and that, when he smiled, he looked nothing like Minh. Minh's smile was devious and contrived. The professor's smile was genuine, bordering on laughter.

The professor scanned the others, who stood in a semicircle around him. "How may I help you?"

"We are looking for your brother, Nguyen Li Minh," said Tran Le.

"Well, he is not exactly my brother," the professor said. "But I have not seen him today, nor lately."

Jen spoke without thinking: "Not your brother?" Then she turned to Tran Le and stuttered, "Excuse me, sir."

"This is Jen Phillips from America," Tran Le said to the professor. "Your brother kidnapped Ms. Phillips and her children and brought them to Vietnam."

Jen spoke again, "We thought you were his brother."

The professor nodded. "Well, we are related. My mother and Minh's father were siblings. When my father was killed in the war, we went to live with Minh's family. We are about the same age, and if you have seen him, you would know that we do look somewhat alike. We are actually cousins."

Tran Le considered this. "When was the last time you saw or spoke to him, if I may ask?"

"Certainly, you may ask. Well, it has been more than a year since I have seen him, but I spoke to him not so long ago. He asked that I sit in on the annual meeting of the Communist Party here in Hanoi, pretending to be him." He laughed. "I felt a little guilty doing this, but I did it because I wanted to understand more about the Party. I had to walk on eggshells for four days, not knowing who might know Minh well, or might know me, for that matter, but I found that no one really wanted to speak to him, or me." He shrugged. "I am not engaged in politics like my cousin. I am simply a teacher. Is Sang in trouble?"

"Sang?" Jen asked.

"Yes. His given name is Sang. He changed it to Minh when he moved into business and up in the party."

Jen noticed a sharp look from Tran Le. She forced herself to remain quiet and allow the consul general to carry the conversation, but she wanted to say that not only was Minh in trouble, but if she could get her hands on him, with an assist from her brother, she would like to choke the life out of him. She bit her tongue and listened closely to the conversation.

"Well, this is complicated," Tran Le began. "We are looking for an American, a former soldier, whom your brother accuses of killing his father. He says further that his father was the son of Ho Chi Minh."

Trinh laughed. "Well, that sounds like my cousin. His father was *not* the son of Ho Chi Minh. I'm quite certain that Ho did not have a son. Sang's father, my uncle, my aunt, and my mother all died a few years ago, my uncle from heart problems, my aunt and mother from cancer. They were farmers, all three, and prolific smokers." He sat on the edge of his desk, perfectly comfortably. "I am not so close with my cousin. We disagree on many matters, especially politics. I see the Communists as taking advantage of the people. I'm an outspoken democrat and have paid the price by remaining an entry-level professor for more than twenty years while others, more willing to kiss Communist asses, have advanced. But I like it that way. I like to teach." He smiled.

Tran Le responded, "The man we are looking for says he killed a young NVA officer in 1969 who was traveling with a small boy. He let the boy go, rather than turning him over to the ARVN."

"That was me," Trinh said. "I told my cousin that story. The man I was traveling with was my father, Sang's uncle. Many years later, as I reflected on what happened, I realized that the American soldier probably saved my life. I loved my father, but I know that he was killed as an act of war and that I was saved by the man who killed him."

"Why would your cousin do what he has done, claiming to seek revenge for his father's murder?" Tran Le asked. "Why does he claim to be the grandson of Ho Chi Minh?"

"It's just the way he is," Trinh said. "He believes the world revolves around him. In my psychology courses at Oxford, the professors would have called him a sociopath. He doesn't believe that the ordinary rules of society apply to him. I'm sure he just woke up one morning, concocted this story, and went with it. Unfortunately, he has the resources to fulfill his fantasies, regardless of their impact on others."

Jen spoke again, aware that she was stepping on Tran Le's authority. "Knowing him, where do you think he would take my father, who is his prisoner? What do you think he would do?"

"It would be something to do with the war. He is obsessed with the war, with the injustices done to the Vietnamese people by the American soldiers. He would go to where the war was fought, maybe close to where my father was killed, near the Parrot's Beak on the border of Cambodia."

Tran Le nodded. "Thank you, Professor. Here is my card. If your cousin contacts you, will you call me?"

Trinh nodded.

Jen followed the consul general and the others as they walked out of the lecture hall.

"Where now?" she asked as she caught up with Penny Stafford.

"Parrot's Beak," Stafford said. "The jungle near Cambodia. But we'll have to start the search in the morning. We'll fly back to Saigon tonight, and tomorrow we'll fly up and down the Cambodian border in the Parrot's Beak area. Unfortunately, it will be like looking for a needle in a haystack."

Jen's heart sank.

Chapter 34

MARTHA ACCEPTED EARPLUGS FROM ONE of the tour guides, but chose to walk as far away from the firing range as possible. She found a bench near the opening to one of the tunnels and sat patiently as the men played with the tools of war. Most of the veterans were excited about firing the AK-47s and M-16s from the bunkers into the jungle ahead.

She adjusted her yellow, wide-brimmed hat to block the sun. She had applied sunscreen and mosquito repellent to any skin not covered by the khaki slacks, comfortable cotton blouse, and boots she wore for the jungle adventure. The hot air, heavy with moisture, didn't stir. She fanned herself with a fan provided by the tour bus driver.

As the firing continued, she noticed that two uniformed police officers were providing the weapons to the veterans. They stood nearby, wearing ear protection.

One of the female guides, who had introduced herself as An, pronounced like the American name, Ann, approached her. "Would you like to join the other women and two men who are not interested in the guns? We are going to do a tour of the tunnels."

"Oh, yes," Martha said. "Anything to get away from this noise." She stood and followed An and the others deeper into the tunnels.

~~~

I'm not sure how long I sat in the chair after Minh and the guards left, but I soon came to realize that I could stand and walk around the room, even though I was in total darkness and could see nothing. My hands were cuffed behind my back. I returned to the chair and tried to orient myself in the direction in which Minh had left. I reasoned that if I could get to the ladder, I could climb up and perhaps force the trap door open with my head.

Totally blind, I stumbled down a corridor in the bunker. My bare feet tripped over vines and other objects. I had no concept of time in the total darkness, but it seemed that I had stumbled around an hour or more when I realized it was hopeless.

Having slept so little in the past four days, I was exhausted. I slid down against the dirt wall and sat miserably on the damp floor of the tunnel. I could see nothing. It was as though the darkness that surrounded me had become a living thing and had stolen my eyes. The musty smell of the dirt floor and walls filled my nostrils. I heard small animals scurrying in the dark. *Rats.* They brushed my bare feet. "Get away! Get away!" I screamed. The echo of my voice bounced down the narrow corridors of the tunnel and back to me, as though an invisible twin stood nearby, crying softly, "Get away. Get away."

Tears flowed down my cheeks. I started to laugh. *My eyes have not been stolen,* I thought. *Otherwise I couldn't cry like a baby.* I relaxed and let sleep take me away.

~~~

I felt that I had been asleep a long time when I realized that I was dreaming of a military firefight. I could distinctly hear the enemy's AK-

47s firing, and our return fire with our M-16s. I opened my eyes and could still hear the gunfire. I wasn't sure if I was asleep or awake in the total darkness. I rose to my feet, whether in my dream or reality, and stumbled in the general direction of the gunfire.

~~~

Martha and the others followed An into one of the tunnels. An was very pretty, quite young, and spoke perfect English in a cultured British accent. She wore Western clothes: khaki slacks, lightweight canvas-topped boots for the jungle hike, and a thin red blouse.

She stopped the group by raising a red umbrella. Although there had been no rain or even dark clouds, red umbrellas were constant companions to all of the tour guides in her group. The two men and six women gathered around An in a semicircle. Martha stood next to her.

"The North Vietnamese Army and the Viet Cong both used the tunnels here," An said, pointing with the umbrella. She also carried a bright flashlight, which she pointed down the tunnel as they walked together. Occasionally, she found and lit kerosene lanterns in wide areas of the tunnels. "The soldiers gathered in these somewhat wider areas of the tunnels, which they called 'rooms.'"

Martha and the others gathered into a semicircle in one of the rooms.

"In this room," An said, "you can see these sleeping mats. These are not the actual mats, but replacements. This would have been a place where soldiers could come before or after battles to sleep or rest. Farther down this way"—she pointed with the umbrella—"you will see an actual field hospital."

Martha and the others followed An deeper into the dark tunnel like schoolchildren in line for recess, one person walking behind the other. Martha was midway in the short line. She nearly fainted when An screamed.

A tall man, who had told Martha that he was a retired urologist, stepped past her. "What is it?" he asked An.

An's face looked frightened in the dim light. "A dead man."

Martha nudged her way forward as the line collapsed into a crowd, with each person trying to see what, or who, lay on the floor in front of An.

The man wore thin pajamas and the pungent smell of urine and perspiration. He had a short, gray beard and graying brown hair that was matted to his skull. He was barefoot, and his hands were handcuffed behind his back.

The retired doctor knelt beside him and pressed two fingers to the carotid artery on the side of his neck. "He's alive. Come, help me."

Another man, short, stocky, and strong-looking, helped pick up the man, who opened his eyes. He tried to stand. The two men in the tour group supported his weight as they stumbled toward the gunfire and the opening of the tunnel.

Martha trailed just behind them. She watched as they put the injured man down on a wooden bench. The gunfire stopped, and everyone gathered around to see what was happening.

One of the policemen offered to remove the handcuffs. Martha saw that the man's hands were blue and swollen. The doctor asked for water. He turned the man's head to the side and slowly poured water into the corner of his mouth.

Martha stepped closer. She knelt beside the man, whose eyes were barely open. "I know him," she said, to the shock of all her traveling companions and the others gathered around the man on the bench. "Travis," she murmured. To her traveling companions, she said, "This is Travis Kelly from North Carolina." She put her hand on his forehead. "Travis," she repeated.

~~~

Brad knelt at the window of the helicopter as it rode up and down the border of Cambodia. They had been searching since early morning for any civilian vehicles near the Parrot's Beak, according to the pilot. There was nothing below but dense jungle. He thought about the American soldiers of a prior generation riding helicopters into battle at this very spot, their hearts thumping in rhythm with the chop of the blades and the staccato clap of the door gunner's M-60 machine guns.

Suddenly the helicopter, accompanied by its Vietnamese shadow, turned sharply and began to descend toward the tall trees. Brad could not see where they were going from his perspective, but soon they were landing on a straight road.

Tran Le and Penny Stafford opened the door, and the entire entourage spilled out of the chopper. Brad followed his sister and Erin Stephens.

Brad noticed immediately that the helicopter had landed behind a large tour bus. A small crowd, presumably tourists and guides, were gathered around a man lying on a wooden bench. He grabbed Jen's hand. "Is that Dad?" he asked loudly. They both started running toward the man who resembled their father. Brad held his sister's hand tightly as their pace quickened.

Brad and Jen slid to their knees in front of the bench.

"It's Dad!" Brad said.

They both pulled their father to them, but his eyes were closed and he didn't respond.

"Is he alive?" Jen asked the people near her father.

"Yes," said a tall, dark-haired man, "but we should get him to a hospital. He's dehydrated and has been severely beaten."

~~~

Nguyen Li Minh had not gone home the prior night. Neither had he visited his cousin in Hanoi. He had stayed at his plant in Saigon once again, as he often did when his business required his presence or he wanted to spend time with his mistress. He had called his wife early in the morning and learned about the visit of Tran Le and others. He immediately called his cousin in Hanoi as well, but had not been able to get in touch with him. Based on what his wife had said, Minh had decided to return to the tunnel that morning and finish the job on Travis.

He was in the passenger's seat of the Mercedes sedan, nearing the Cu Chi Tunnels, when two large helicopters landed in front of his car just behind a large tour bus.

"Stop the car," Minh said to his driver. He got out of the vehicle, his bodyguards following, and circled through the jungle to try to see what was happening. As he came to a clearing, he saw a large group of people, including a few Vietnamese military and police in uniform. This gave him confidence. He walked directly toward the group.

~~~

Brad cradled his father's limp body as Jen brushed his matted hair away from his face. Something caught her attention, and she looked up from her father to see three men walking in her direction, perhaps fifty yards away. She stood.

"What is it?" Brad asked.

"That's Minh!" she exclaimed.

Brad stood. "Are you sure?"

"Yes," Jen said emphatically. "That man in the coat and tie. That is Minh!"

Brad leapt to his feet and ran toward Minh like a defensive safety running toward an opposing team's tailback. He slammed into Minh and knocked him down. Erin intervened and rolled Minh over on his stomach. She pulled his hands behind him and put her knee in the center of his back, pinning him painfully to the ground.

Four US Marines tackled and neutralized the bodyguards. The two Vietnamese policemen and the Vietnamese government officials who had ridden in the other helicopter arrived on the scene about the same time as Tran Le and Penny Stafford.

"What is this?" one of the Vietnamese officials asked.

Erin sat up, breathing deeply and clutching the wound on her chest. Brad assumed the role of holding Minh down.

Brad looked across the bodyguards and the Marines to Tran Le and Penny Stafford, who stood nearby. They were engaged in an animated conversation with the Vietnamese officials and the policemen. Brad didn't know what was said, but the result was that Minh and his men were placed in handcuffs and roughly dragged to a police vehicle nearby.

~~~

I came to as two soldiers carried me to the medevac. They laid me on the floor of the helicopter, and we lifted away from the battlefield. My arms felt strange; I couldn't move my hands. A nurse who looked a lot like my daughter, Jen, sat beside me and propped up my head. She gave me water and told me to just sip it slowly. She was beautiful.

The brigade commander looked a lot like my son, Brad. A Chieu Hoi in a white shirt and blue trousers sat nearby, smiling and talking to his wife.

My memory began to come back. I didn't recall being hit, but I remembered a medic checking me out before he and another trooper helped me out of the tunnel to safety. I had seen Martha as they led me past the squad. That was odd. What was Martha doing on the battlefield?

I couldn't tell where I was hit. Maybe it was the million-dollar wound, bad enough to get me home to Claire and Jen, but not bad enough to ruin the rest of my life. No way to know until I reached the field hospital. I tried to relax and follow orders. That's what soldiers do—follow orders.

Chapter 35

JEN SAT IN THE WAITING room of a hospital in Ho Chi Minh City. She felt relaxed for the first time in a long time. But her Dad was still in trouble. She knew that.

Dr. Hoang Tri Lam sat on a high stool in front of her. Penny Stafford, Erin Stephens, and Brad sat on sofas, their full attention given to the Vietnamese doctor.

"The MRI shows a mass in the visual cortex of the brain," Dr. Hoang said, directing his comments to Jen and Brad, as family members of the patient. "This is in the optical lobe, at the back of the skull." He touched the back of his head. "I fear that there could be some bleeding, very slight, but it would account for some of his symptoms—confusion, headaches, and visual impairment."

Jen turned to Penny Stafford and asked, "Can we get him home to an American hospital?"

Dr. Hoang answered before Stafford could respond. "I would not advise travel."

"This is a highly respected hospital," Stafford added. "Dr. Hoang is a trained and experienced neurosurgeon."

Jen nodded. "So what should we do, Dr. Hoang?"

"Operate immediately," he said. "These tumors are often benign. But his is large, very large. My guess is that it has been there a long time. It will be a delicate surgery. By pure luck, an American colleague is here helping me train physicians. His name is Dr. Blanton. We studied together at Duke. He can assist me with the surgery. He is on his way to the hospital now."

"Have you done this surgery before?" Jen asked.

"Just a few times," Dr. Hoang answered. "Fortunately, this is a rare condition. It usually affects women and is very rare in men. Dr. Blanton has also done the surgery a handful of times, so together we have some experience. On the other hand, it is not dissimilar to other brain surgeries with which we both have extensive experience. We will do our best for him. I promise you there is no other option."

"Okay," Jen said. She looked at Brad.

Brad nodded. "Yes. I agree. Thank you, Doctor."

~~~

When I graduated from high school, I wanted to join the Army or Marines like just about every other boy in my class of one hundred students. My parents were opposed, and I was just seventeen. So I had to wait until my eighteenth birthday to volunteer for military service. In the meantime, I took courses at the community college and worked a couple of part-time jobs.

Two months before I was scheduled to go to Fort Bragg for basic training, I dramatically cranked up my physical conditioning program. I ran six miles every day and did dozens of pushups, pull-ups, and sit-ups. By my eighteenth birthday, I was in top physical shape. This turned out to be a blessing and a curse.

In 1962, the Beatles invaded the US with good music and long hair. When I graduated from high school a couple of years later, the music was still good, and just about every boy my age had let his hair grow over his ears like John, Paul, George, and Ringo. This was the era of the draft. Any young man between the ages of eighteen and twenty-five who wasn't in college or in a vital job, such as teaching, was subject to being drafted into the military. On the first day of basic training, Army barbers took great joy in shearing off the long locks of Beatle look-alikes, both draftees and volunteers.

The day before I left for basic training at Fort Bragg, I got a buzz cut. My hair was barely visible, but it was visible. This also turned out to be a blessing and a curse. On my first day of basic training, the barbers were offended that I didn't have long locks for them to shear. So they shaved my head, leaving my skull as slick as a cue ball. I looked like Telly Savalas in *Kojak*, minus the lollipop.

That same day, my drill sergeants were equally offended by my superior physical condition. So when they ordered my platoon to do twenty pushups, they required me to do forty. When my contemporaries did thirty sit-ups, I had to do sixty. Five pull-ups for the platoon got me ten. But the result was that I had the highest score ever on the final physical training test, a 498 out of a possible 500.

Now, however, as I lay on a hospital bed, I wasn't thinking about the PT test. I was thinking about hair—specifically, my hair. Somehow I felt as bald as a cue ball once again, and I wanted to say, "Who loves ya, baby?"

The person responsible for my baldness was my doctor, Dr. Hoang, who now walked into my room smiling, as he had every morning since my surgery. "Before your visitors arrive, I want to check you out again," he said. He held a small penlight up to my left eye and punched the end to illuminate the tip. The bright light hurt. "Look to your right without moving your head," he said. "Look up. Look down."

I did as ordered.

"Okay. Now look the other way." He moved the light to my right eye and examined it. Then he walked to the foot of my hospital bed. "Close your right eye. How many fingers?"

"Three," I responded.

He did the same with my left eye closed. "Okay. Headache?"

"Not so bad today."

"Have you taken anything for pain?"

"No. Nothing."

"Okay. It all sounds good. I will come by to see you a little later today." He touched my shoulder and left the room.

I closed my eyes and must have fallen asleep. I awoke a couple of hours later as Brad and Erin came into the room.

"You're looking a lot better," Brad said.

"Feel better, too," I said.

Erin smiled. "Jen is on her way up. She has a surprise for you."

A minute later, Jen walked in with all four grandchildren in tow. They swarmed my bed, but having been warned to be gentle, merely placed their hands on my chest and held both my hands. I had never felt better in my life than I did at that moment. They had prepared an oversized get-well card for me that they unfolded and later taped to the wall of my small room.

After just a few minutes, they all made a ceremony of kissing me on the cheek, and Jen took them back to the consulate where they were still staying. She had told me that she was getting them ready to go home. Brad and Erin planned to stay and accompany me when I was allowed to travel.

"We have another surprise for you on Friday," Erin said.

Today was Wednesday, so Friday was a couple of days away.

"Why Friday?" I asked.

"Let's let it be a surprise," Brad said.

"Okay." I noticed that they were holding hands as they left the room.

~~~

Jen and the children left the next day. I was feeling much better and stronger, virtually by the hour. My Vietnamese nurses were excellent. I was now able to walk to the bathroom without their assistance. They had told me that I would soon be allowed and encouraged to walk up and down the hallway outside of my room. My language skills were getting better and I enjoyed teasing and joking with the nurses and custodians in Vietnamese.

Friday morning came, and I noticed a level of excitement among the hospital staff. Brad and Erin had arrived early and sat comfortably in my room, engaging me in small talk. I heard noise outside of my room and sat up somewhat in my hospital bed.

Four people walked into the room. One person, whom I now knew as Tran Le, the US consul general in Saigon, led the way toward my bed and stood beside me. Two men who appeared to be Secret Service followed behind him, and then an attractive woman about my age, whom I immediately knew to be the United States secretary of state.

"Good morning, Travis," she said without ceremony.

"Good morning, Madam Secretary," I said, as though I were a congressman addressing her at a congressional hearing.

"How are you doing?" she asked with a big smile.

"I am doing well." I was very nervous, and I'm sure it showed.

"I asked the consul general to allow me to come by to see you and tell you personally that your family has gotten back to their home in North Carolina. They are safe and secure. Also, especially, I wanted to tell you that the Socialist Republic of Vietnam has agreed to press no charges against you for entering the country illegally. Further, there will be no charges brought by the US government for falsifying passports and other documents. However, there is a legal matter in North Carolina which you will have to address when you return home." She spoke with a strong, authoritative voice.

"Yes, ma'am," I said, still at a loss for words.

"But my primary reason for dropping by to see you is to tell you that Nguyen Li Minh is going to be extradited to the United States and will be tried in Virginia for the assassination of Homeland Security Undersecretary Walt Bradley and his wife, Mia. He may be tried for other crimes in Virginia and North Carolina. But most assuredly, he will be tried for his many crimes in the United States and, if convicted, he will be properly punished." She smiled.

Relief flooded me. I nodded. "I'm glad to hear that. And thank you for personally telling me this."

She shook my hand and told me she hoped I recovered soon and got back to my life in North Carolina. Then everyone but Brad and Erin left the room, and I took a deep breath, trying to process what had just happened.

Two weeks later Brad, Erin, and I flew home together. I was happy to be leaving Vietnam once again, but it wasn't the end of my troubles.

Epilogue

I STOOD IN FRONT OF A mirror in the men's room of the federal court house in Charlotte, North Carolina. Joel Henderson had insisted that I purchase a navy-blue suit for the trial. I tightened the tie, the first one I had worn in years, and smoothed out the jacket. My hair had grown back after eight months, with more gray than brown. Jen thought I should color it. Brad said I looked distinguished. I just thought I looked old.

I walked out of the bathroom and found Joel waiting for me in the hallway. He looked like a penguin in his white shirt and dark suit that was narrow at the shoulders and wide at the hips. The recessed ceiling lights reflected off his nearly bald head.

"You look very good, Travis," he said in his strong baritone voice. "Just relax. You won't have to say anything. But I have some bad news."

"What's that?" I was anything but relaxed.

"Judge Thorpe was in an automobile accident and broke his collar-bone and left leg. His replacement is Judge Max Maples." His tone suggested I had just received the death penalty.

"What's he like?" I asked.

"Not he, *her*. Her name is Maxine Maples. Defense attorneys call her "Judge Max" because she always opts for the maximum penalty allowed by law. If the sentencing guidelines are fifteen to twenty years, and the defendant is found guilty, you can damn sure bet they're going away for twenty years. Sorry."

"But what if I'm innocent?"

Joel pushed his glasses up on his nose. He put his fat right hand on my left shoulder and stared at me with his large, dark eyes. "Travis, were you told not to leave the country by a federal judge?"

"Yes."

"Did you leave the country?"

"Yes."

"You're not innocent, Travis. But I'm going to fight like hell for you in there. I promise." With a flourish, he directed me toward the courtroom.

~~~

We walked through twelve-foot-high wooden doors and down the center aisle of the courtroom, which, to my great surprise, was filled to capacity. I saw many friends and relatives in the gallery. Florence Johnson and several members of the Johnson family were in attendance. My aging parents, stooped and frail, my sister and brothers, their spouses, and my nephews and nieces all sat together near the Johnsons. Directly behind the defendant's table sat my immediate family, Brad and Erin, now Mr. and Mrs. Bradley D. Kelly of Falls Church, Virginia, plus Jen and my four grandchildren. Erin, now six months pregnant, looked radiant in her stylish maternity clothes. Just behind them, on the second row, sat Martha Koslinski with her three daughters and two grandchildren.

I nodded and waved to everybody as I worked my way toward the defense table.

The federal prosecutor and a team of young attorneys sat at a table beside ours. Joel stopped to shake hands and speak briefly with the prosecuting attorney before we sat in our assigned chairs to wait for the judge.

Soon an officer announced, "All rise for the Honorable Judge Maxine W. Maples!"

We stood as the judge settled in at her desk high above the court.

"Please be seated," she said. With her strong chin, austere expression, and dark hair pulled back in a bun, Judge Maples looked intense. She looked important. Of course, a federal judge *is* important.

Once everybody was seated, Judge Maples leaned into a microphone and said, "I would like counsel for the state and for the defense to please approach the bench."

Joel and the federal prosecutor stood in unison, looked at each other, and walked to the front of the court, just to the right of Judge Maples. She turned and engaged in a lively presentation to the two attorneys. The federal prosecutor tried to speak, but Judge Maples raised her hand, silencing him. The speech went on for several minutes while both attorneys listened, saying nothing.

When the attorneys turned back to the courtroom, Joel was smiling so big that it seemed as if the Joker and the Penguin had occupied the same body. The federal prosecutor, on the other hand, looked like a wet puppy that had been punished for bad potty habits.

As Joel stepped beside me, I said, "What?"

He whispered, "Just wait. It's okay for you to answer the judge's questions."

Judge Maples spoke into her microphone, "Will the defendant and counsel please approach the bench."

Joel nodded to me, and we walked to the front of the judge's bench.

"Mr. Kelly," Judge Maples said, "do you know who I am?"

"Yes, ma'am. You are a federal judge, Judge Maxine Maples."

"Yes. Sometimes the defense attorneys call me 'Judge Max' because I don't go lightly on people who break federal laws." She smiled at Joel.

I nodded, but said nothing.

"My name is Maxine W. Maples," she said. "I was appointed by the president and approved in the US Senate. 'Maples' is my married name. Southern girls like me sometimes drop their middle names and use their maiden names after we're married, thus the *W.*"

"Yes, ma'am," I said, thinking I should respond in some way.

"Mr. Kelly, you know that disobeying an order issued by a federal judge is a serious matter," she said, going in another direction.

"Yes, ma'am."

"You did disobey an order of a federal judge, didn't you?"

"Yes, ma'am."

"But you did this to save your family. I'm betting you would do it again, but I'm not going to ask you to respond to that assumption." She smiled again. "So, my middle name is my maiden name. My middle name is Wendelman. Does that name mean anything to you?"

I started to respond, but nothing came out. I merely nodded as tears sprang from my eyes.

Judge Maples's chin quivered, and tears dripped down her cheeks. She pulled a box of tissues from beneath her bench and wiped her eyes. Her voice was shaky as she spoke. "My father was a Marine pilot in Vietnam in 1969. This was four years before I was born." She blew her nose loudly. "Sorry," she said. "In late August 1969, his airplane was shot down near the Cambodian border. He and his senior pilot were captured by the North Vietnamese and held in bamboo cages in Cambodia." Now she seemed to be addressing the courtroom. "My father told me this story the first time when I was about ten years old. He was a successful attorney in Huntersville, North Carolina. He said that, after being held two days in a four-by-four bamboo cage, he had resigned himself to being tortured, killed, or held captive in North Vietnam. But it was not to be, was it, Mr. Kelly?" She looked back at me.

I shook my head, my emotions still not under control.

"No," she answered her own question. "It was not to be, because four incredibly brave soldiers parachuted into Cambodia at night. They made their way to my father's bamboo cage. Their leader crawled up to my father and cut him out of the cage. Then he and the others, including my father, fought with a large force of North Vietnamese soldiers. They were rescued under intense fire by a Marine rescue helicopter."

I stood as straight as I could, not really knowing where this was going.

Joel put his hand on my shoulder in support.

"One man, Captain Travis Kelly, stood out among all the American soldiers," Judge Maples continued. "When the enemy mortars had them zeroed in, my father told me that Captain Kelly ran through a barrage of exploding rounds, found the enemy spotter, and killed him. As the North Vietnamese soldiers attacked, Captain Kelly stood, threw grenades, and charged directly into the enemy fire, driving them back. Though he was later painfully wounded by an enemy mortar round, he risked his life to save and carry a friendly Vietnamese soldier, who had been shot, to the waiting helicopter. He was the last man on the helicopter. Had he not done what he did, my father and his senior pilot, Major Ellis, would have died or been held captive in a North Vietnamese prison for years." Tears appeared once again on her cheeks. Her voice cracked as she said, "My father never, never forgot Captain Travis Kelly. As he was dying from injuries suffered in an automobile accident a few years ago, he said, 'Tell Travis I had a good life and I never forgot him.'" She pulled out more tissues and wiped both eyes.

The courtroom was silent except for some audible crying.

Tears streamed down my cheeks.

Finally, Judge Maples said, "Mr. Kelly, I have arranged with your attorney to change your plea from 'not guilty' to 'guilty,' and I hereby fine you one dollar." She pulled a dollar from beneath her desk. "And, given what you did for my father and my family, I am hereby paying your fine." She reached across her desk and handed the dollar bill to a female court officer. "You are free to go."

The courtroom burst into applause. Everybody was standing. The prosecuting attorney congratulated Joel. My family surrounded me. I knelt on one knee and hugged my two grandsons, then stood and hugged my two teenage granddaughters. Erin, Brad, and Jen hugged and kissed me.

I broke away and walked to the bench where Judge Maples was still sitting. I reached up to shake her hand.

She took my hand in both of hers and said, "Thank you for what you did for my father."

I nodded and returned to my family. Martha and her daughters and grandchildren had joined us, as had my extended family, including Florence Johnson and the Johnson family. My poor parents, barely able to walk, hugged me and cried happy tears.

Brad announced that there would be a celebration party at my farm in two hours, and everybody was invited.

~~~

It was four o'clock in the afternoon, just a few hours after Judge Maxine Maples had found me guilty of disobeying a federal judge's order and fined me one dollar. My farm was bustling with activity. Children were playing dodgeball in the pasture beside my barn. Some were cousins. Many were friends. Others were total strangers and now new friends.

A handful of toddlers and young children rode with their mothers on a flatbed trailer loaded with hay. I waved at the big tractor driver. Chinh nodded. He had accepted the job of caretaker on my farm and lived in the apartment over the barn.

The house was packed with guests. Florence Johnson directed the operation from the kitchen, ensuring there was enough food and drinks for everybody.

I sat in a rocker on the front porch, drinking a mixture of tea and lemonade. Brad sat beside me with a beer in hand.

"How are things going in Virginia?" I asked.

"Good. Erin has quit her job. I'm making a pretty good salary with Bechtel. Thanks again for the referral. Charlie Benson says hello. I'm taking the two courses I need to finish my degree online. I'll knock that out before the baby comes, I hope. The money is more than enough for us right now. Baby Claire is just three months away. Life is good."

"I'm happy for you, son," I said.

"How are Jen and the kids?"

"Jen is working more now. The school hired an assistant to work with LB, monitoring his blood sugar and administering shots. Of course, they just have one more week of school. The girls can help her with the boys during the summer. I think Jen is seeing somebody, though she doesn't like to talk about it in front of the kids. They spent a couple of weekends with Chinh and me on the farm while their mom took some 'me' time. It's great to have them over. We have a good time." I smiled as I saw them enjoying themselves with the other children in the pasture in front of us.

"How about you, Dad? Seems like Martha is around a lot."

I started to say something just as Martha walked through the front door and onto the porch.

"Travis," she said as she leaned against my chair, "my girls and I have something for you."

One of her daughters, Emily, came walking toward the porch, holding a small Beagle puppy in her arms. "We know how much Ralph meant to you, and this puppy is just old enough to leave his mother. We were praying you would be able to come home today and have been keeping him for you."

Emily put the dog in my lap.

"We think you should also call him 'Ralph,'" Martha said.

I rubbed his head between his floppy ears. He looked up at me with sad brown eyes. "No. There could only be one Ralph," I said. "I think I'll call him 'Pep.'"

He wagged his tail, and I cuddled him to my chest.

"Has to be Pep," I said. "No debate on that. It'll be Pep. End of story."

The End.

Author's Note

THIS BOOK IS A WORK of fiction. It does, however, contain an element of truth, since some of the events are based on my personal experiences. But the story and the characters, with three exceptions, are fictional. Three historical figures are presented in the book.

General Creighton Abrams

General Abrams was the commander of military operations in Vietnam from 1968 to 1972. He presided over the drawdown of American forces, a sensitive and difficult assignment given the unpopularity of the war and the political turmoil the country faced. He served in three wars. In World War II, he was twice awarded the Distinguished Service Cross, the medal just below the Medal of Honor. He served in Korea and Vietnam and ended his military career as the US Army chief of staff. General Abrams died in September 1974. He was a true American hero. Though the incidents described in this book are fictional, I did serve under his command in 1968 and 1969 as a young junior officer in the First Air Cavalry Division. I have attempted to capture the essence of this great man.

General Barry McCaffrey

General McCaffrey is mentioned several times in the book. A retired four-star general, Barry McCaffrey is one of the most highly decorated military officers still living. He was twice awarded the Distinguished Service Cross in Vietnam and received three Purple Hearts and two Silver Stars. He commanded the 24th Infantry Division in the Gulf War and was the assistant chief of staff of the Armed Forces, among other significant posts. He has worked as a professor at the United States Military Academy at West Point and served as the director of the Office of National Drug Control Policy, a position also known as "drug czar," during the administration of President Clinton. I served as a field artillery forward observer with General McCaffrey when he was a captain and company commander of Bravo Company, 2nd of the 7th Cavalry, First Air Cavalry Division from November 1968 to February 1969. General McCaffrey's name is used by permission.

First Sergeant Emerson Trainer

Like many of the senior non-commissioned officers in Vietnam, First Sergeant Emerson Trainer had served with distinction in the Korean War. He was wounded in action three times and was known to his men as a valiant and effective leader. In 1968–1969, he served as the First Sergeant of Bravo Company, 2nd of the 7th Cavalry, First Air Cavalry Division with then Captain Barry McCaffrey. I served with First Sergeant Trainer and, as a young junior officer, learned much from this seasoned veteran. First Sergeant Trainer's name is used with permission.

Acknowledgements

SPECIAL THANKS TO MY FRIENDS Don and Mary Doctor who read early versions of this book and offered good advice. Similarly, Julie Bird, a professional writer in Belmont, North Carolina, not only read the early version, but did great work helping me polish up the final edit. Bill Greenleaf with Greenleaf Literary Services offered valuable assistance and encouragement as he does for many writers. My friends, Jack Berry, Jr. and Wil Neumann, also read the book and provided valuable feedback.

About the Author

MICHAEL K. MCMAHAN IS THE author of *A Breach of Faith* (Woodland Publications, 1996) and *Confessions of a Preacher's Kid* (Xulon Press, 2002). He served six years in the United States Army: four years of active duty from 1966 to 1970, and two years of active reserve duty from 1971 to 1972. He achieved the rank of captain. He served in Vietnam from August 1968 to August 1969 and was awarded the Silver Star for gallantry in action on November 6, 1968. A paratrooper, he also served in the 82nd Airborne Division at Fort Bragg. He has a private pilot's license. He is an honors graduate of the University of North Carolina at Chapel Hill, where he also earned a master's degree. He married his high school sweetheart, Carla, in 1966, and they have two children and four grandchildren. He is a retired financial adviser and writer in North Carolina. You may contact him at: mick@mkmcmahan.com.

An excerpt from Michael K. McMahan's next book, *Saving Hope*, follows ...

Prologue

July 9, 1985

Belmont Abbey College

Eight Miles West of Charlotte, North Carolina

I was lying on my back in the shade of a Dogwood tree in the corner of All Saints Garden at Belmont Abbey College. The sweet smell of flowers and the chatter of two squirrels in a nearby oak calmed my frayed senses. The perfectly mowed and hydrated fescue, its wide blades standing straight and firm, cradled my small body like an expensive mattress. Life-sized stone statues of the beatified surrounded me. They were silent sentinels fending off my tormentors. All but one looked heavenward as though in prayer. My favorite was Saint Francis of Assisi.

He stood straight, in a hooded robe, looking out, not up, more of this world than the next. He was holding a rabbit in the crook of his left arm.

A bird was perched on his right shoulder. Other small animals gathered at his feet.

It was the middle of summer, the time of year when North Carolina morphs into a giant sauna with a heat index consistently north of one hundred degrees. The best places at the Abbey to escape the mid-day heat were the dorm rooms with their central air conditioning systems, or the student union, also air conditioned, but with ping pong and pool tables.

I had searched for a place as far as away as possible from the other players in the football camp I was attending. Two years younger than the next oldest kid, I was skinny, quiet, and shy. The other boys were beefy, loud, and aggressive. I had no friends at the camp.

One of the coaches, early on the first day, had sealed my fate as the least popular player by complimenting my ball catching ability. He said loudly to one of the quarterbacks, "Just throw it in the general direction of Brad. He can catch anything in this zip code." Getting singled out like that, given my diminutive dimensions and age, did not endear me to my fellow football campers. I was shunned and bullied by the other boys. So I stuck to myself as much as possible.

On Tuesday, July 9th, two days after my twelfth birthday, I was reading a biography of Knute Rockne in the quiet shade of All Saints Garden when I heard movement nearby and realized that I was not alone. Just to my right, a pretty girl, maybe nineteen or twenty, lay in the sunlight on a blanket, her eyes closed, her face tilted upward in the summer sun, an angel in the midst of the saints and me. She was barefoot. Her thin cotton skirt was hiked to mid-thigh. As I watched, she began to unbutton her blouse. She pulled it open, revealing a lacy bra and bare mid-riff.

I did not think she had noticed me until she said, loudly enough for me to hear, "I know you are over there, you know?"

My heart was pounding and my throat was dry. I thought I should run. But I could not take my eyes off of her.

She tossed her long, blond hair to the side, turned her head and looked straight at me. The reflecting sun on her face and hair did indeed make her look like a heavenly creature. "Come over here. I won't bite."

I stood cautiously, looked around, and walked closer.

She put her hand over her eyes as though she were doing a poorly executed salute and said, "My name is Susan Tucker, but my friends call me Suze."

I just stood there, a skinny little boy, curious, and nervous, still as a deer caught in a car's headlights on a dark country road.

She sat up a little and patted her blanket. "Come and sit with me for a while. What's your name?"

I walked cautiously toward her and sat cross-legged like a little Indian brave, my back straight, my eyes slightly averted from her bare legs and other interesting body parts.

After a pause, I finally said, "My name is Brad."

She turned her head more toward me. Her eyes were deep blue. Her eye lashes were thick and long. She was the most beautiful girl I had ever seen in person. She smiled. "Are you here for the football camp?"

I tried to speak. Nothing came out, so I nodded.

"I'm taking an English course and trying to meet a future husband." She laughed. "But you're the first boy to notice me and I think you might be a little too young."

I nodded again.

She looked at the book I was holding. "What are you reading?"

I licked my lips and said, "Knute Rockne. He was a famous football coach."

"Do you like football?"

"Yes, ma'am," I said.

"Don't *ma'am* me, Brad. I'm just a college student. How old are you?"

"Twelve."

"I'm just seven years older than you. I go to UNC-G up in Greensboro. I'm from Shelby. Where are you from?"

"Darden."

She looked at her watch, sat up a little, and began buttoning her blouse.

"Got to get to class." She stood and began gathering her books.

I stood also as she stooped to scoop up the blanket. This provided me a good view of the tops of her breasts. Her blouse was not fully buttoned.

She finished buttoning her blouse and slipped into her sandals. As she turned, she said, "Hope to see you again, Brad. Nice to meet you."

I stood there in the middle of the garden watching as she walked away. My heart was pounding and my head was spinning.

~~~

The next day was Wednesday, the third day of my five-day camp. I made it to the All Saints Garden at the same time. Suze was already there. This time she wore a two-piece bathing suit. She was on the same or a similar blanket. A cotton robe lay beside her.

She saw me walk into the garden and waived.

I walked straight to her.

"Hi, Brad," she said. "Still reading that book?"

I nodded and showed her my bookmark. I was halfway finished.

She patted the blanket again as she had done the previous day and I sat cross-legged facing her.

"How is your camp going?" She lit a cigarette and blew smoke away from me. "I would offer you a cigarette, but athletes aren't supposed to smoke, are they?"

"No. I," I was nervous. "I don't smoke. The camp is going good." I lied. It was not going so well. The coaches liked me but the other boys hated me. I was getting pushed around and beaten up pretty badly.

"Why don't you take your shirt off and get some sun?" she said. She crushed the cigarette out in the dirt. "I don't really like these things so much, but everybody smokes these days."

I pulled my tee-shirt up over my head and laid it on top of my book.

"You're going to be handsome when you grow up and fill out," she said. "Wish I could wait for you."

I nodded, but could not formulate any response.

"Do you have brothers and sisters?"

"A sister. Her name is Jennifer. We call her Jen. She's five years older."

"She's in high school?"

"Yes. Going to Chapel Hill next year."

"Good for her. I applied there, but ended up at UNC-G. Same school my mother attended, but they called it Women's College in those days."

We talked about college and football and boys my age and when she first kissed a boy, which was when she was twelve years old. She said she took the summer courses at the Abbey, hoping to meet a nice Catholic boy. Her family was Catholic and there were not many Catholics in Shelby. She was the oldest in a large family with lots of brothers and sisters. I just nodded and mostly listened. She treated me like I was someone her own age and I grew more and more comfortable with her on that second day.

Then, suddenly, she looked at her Mickey Mouse watch, showing it to me, and said, "Got to go change and get to class. See you tomorrow?"

"Okay," I said.

She walked out of the garden pulling her thin robe around her and folding her blanket.

~~~

On Thursday I walked toward the garden carrying my book as before. I parted the bushes and saw Suze was lying on a blanket with a man, a very big man.

I only saw his back. He had red hair and broad shoulders. I heard her moan, then her head moved to the side and I could see her face.

She saw me. "Run, Brad! Get help," she said in a scratchy voice.

The man turned. He held a large knife in his right hand.

I ran toward him. "Stop!" I screamed. "Stop!"

He stood and turned to face me.

Suze was nearly naked. Her skirt had been torn. Her panties were ripped and were dangling at her right ankle. Her blouse was open and her bra had been pulled down, exposing her breasts.

I ran toward the man like a little linebacker running toward a giant quarterback on an all-out blitz. "What are you doing?" I screamed.

The man was tall, taller than my father, and big. His shirt was open and his pants were lowered like he was taking them off. His belt was unfastened. His arms were muscular like a weight lifter and there was a tattoo on his left arm, a bird of some kind.

"Get out of here, kid," he said to me in a deep, gruff voice.

But I ran straight at him, throwing my shoulder into his midsection as though I were going to tackle him.

He swatted me away like a fly.

I fell to the ground and rolled. I screamed, "Leave her alone!" I gathered myself and ran toward him again hitting him as hard as I could.

He staggered back just a bit and pushed me aside once again.

Suze stood behind him and grabbed him around the neck. "Help!" she screamed. "Help us! Someone, please, help us!"

The man turned and pushed Suze to the ground, but as he did this the knife swept across her throat.

She grabbed her throat with both hands and fell to her knees.

I ran at the man again, hitting him lower this time and causing him to stumble. He stood with the knife in his hands, looked at me one last time, then turned and ran out of the garden.

I went to Suze.

She was holding both of her hands over the base of her throat. Blood was pulsing through her fingers. She looked at me with wild eyes. She was scared.

I ripped my shirt off, folded it and put it on her neck wound. I held it as tightly as I could.

She slid to the ground and lay on her back.

I held her head in my lap. "Help!" I screamed. "Help!" I applied pressure to the wound like I had been taught at Boy Scouts.

She looked into my eyes. Tears streamed down the sides of her face. She put her right hand on both of my hands and pressed as much as she could. "Thank you, Brad," she whispered.

~~~

The next thing I remember was my mother standing beside my bed at Darden Memorial Hospital. She told me that the doctors had given me something to calm me and that I had been sleeping. When I was ready, the policemen wanted to speak to me about what happened at the Abbey. The college girl I had tried to save was dead.

Part I

Losing Erin

Chapter 1

I T WAS NOT GOING WELL with Erin and me. Married just four years, we had hit a speed bump. No question about it. She was still in Falls Church, Virginia. I was in an extended stay motel in Charlotte, North Carolina. I was sitting on a balcony looking up as the late afternoon sun filtered through tall buildings in what locals called uptown. It was six o'clock and I was making my obligatory daily call.

"So, how was your day?" I said as I enjoyed the sweet taste of a cold beer, my feet up on a low table, the uptown traffic sounds growing quieter.

"Let's not talk about that tonight," she said. Her voice had an edge.

"Okay. What do you want to talk about?"

"Us. Where we are? Where we're going?"

"We've been through this a dozen times. I am halfway through the school. I have an opportunity to do something that interests me. I am training for a new job, maybe a new career. It's closer to what I had been doing the twelve years before I accepted the job at Bechtel." I took a long drink of my beer and tried to slow my breathing and my pulse. I desperately wanted to reassure her that I had made a good decision. "The next phase in the training will go pretty fast, then we can move down here.

I spoke with the chief and he has no problem with us living in Darden County."

I thought I heard a light sob as she said, "But you have said nothing about what I want. You do recall that I am pregnant. I'm not sure I want to move Claire, my new baby and me to a small southern community."

"Our baby." My voice rose and I fought it. "Our family," I said more softly. "You, Claire, the baby and me. We are a family. And I know that I can be a better husband and father if I am doing something that I like. I'm not cut out for the corporate world. And it was highly probable that my job would have been eliminated anyway. I'm sorry."

She started to speak, but stopped.

"Look," I said, perhaps a little too sharply. I softened my voice. "Please, honey, listen to me, I love you. Don't you know that? Don't you know that you and Claire are everything to me? I want you to be with me no matter where I am. I promise if you will just give it a chance, you'll see that it's not a lot different here than in northern Virginia. The people here aren't all ignorant. I grew up here. This is home to me."

"Home to you, but not to me," she said, now in full control of her emotions and showing her anger. "I love our home and neighborhood here. I love Claire's school. I have friends here. I don't want to move around. I'm used to being in one place."

"But you were an Army brat. You never spent more than three years anywhere and usually shorter than that."

"Exactly. But I've been here fifteen years, eleven years before we were married and now four more years. I don't want to do to my children what my parents did to me, moving me every two or three years, different schools, losing good friends, starting over all of the time."

"I'm sure this can be permanent." There were some things I could not tell her and it was eating at my gut. "My sister," I swallowed the words.

"My sister," she said immediately, "lives in Richmond, less than two hours south of where we now live. I'll be seven hours away from her in Darden."

"Look. Dad and I are going in together on a new SR-22. I can get you to Richmond in an hour anytime you want to go." As soon as I said this I knew I should not have mentioned it.

"Isn't that a $750,000 airplane? Are you out of your mind? How are you going in with your father on a $750,000 airplane when you will be earning an entry level policeman's salary? You're going from nearly $110,000 per year to $36,000 per year. I don't understand this, Brad, any of it. It's just plain crazy."

I knew that it would be no problem, as far as the money was concerned, but I had made a pledge not to get into the details.

"Well, it's something we want to do if we can. We have the Cessna already, so let's say an hour and forty-five minutes, maximum. Anytime you want to go to Richmond, I'll fly you up. I know your sister is just as important to you as mine is to me. I promise we will visit often, as often as now."

I thought I heard her crying again. "You said the other night that if we, I assume you meant either of us, are unhappy in a couple of years, we can maybe work toward moving back here."

"Yes. I promise." Now we were going over the same issues as the prior evening. "Look, let's just take it one step at a time. I have a great job, something that I really want to do. I know the pay is not so high, but it will be fine. I promise. Let's not try to plan out our whole lives right now." I was tired of talking about it, but I certainly would not say that to her.

She was silent for a minute. "Claire wants to speak with you," she finally said.

"Hey, Daddy," Claire said in her tiny voice.

"Hey, Bunny Rabbit," I said. "What did you do today?"

"Come home tonight."

I swallowed hard. "Not tonight, honey. I'll be there on Friday. I'm flying home in Poppy's airplane. You and Mommy will pick me up at the airport."

"Is Friday tomorrow?"

"No, Friday is in two days. I'll see you in two days. I miss you."

"Please come home, Daddy."

I heard Erin sob audibly in the background. It sounded like she took the phone from Claire.

"Brad," she finally said. "I guess we'll see you Friday."

"Yes," I said. "I love you."

The phone went dead.

~~~

I heard the bell on the microwave signaling that my ready-made food was now too hot to eat. I took a long swallow of my beer and let the dinner cool. My brain was spinning. It all started three months prior when my boss at Bechtel told me that the company was offering a buyout. He thought my job was safe, but with the defense industry cutbacks, there was no guarantee, so he said I should look at it. Six months' pay to walk away from a $110,000 annual salary with top benefits was a hard pill to swallow. But I took it. There were other matters that factored into the decision, not all of which I had disclosed to Erin.

A rapid knock on metal meant my dinner companion had arrived. I walked to and opened the door.

"Hope you have at least two more of those Coronas," Quentin Davis said.

"Eight more if I counted correctly."

"We better stop at two. We have to do that run in the morning." He walked to the refrigerator and got his first beer. He peered into the microwave. "Looks like dinner is ready."

"Yeah. Chicken and broccoli. That's mine. Yours is on the counter. Takes three minutes." I pulled the warm dish out of the microwave oven, filling the kitchen with a pleasant smell, and slid another dish in. "Did you call home?"

"Oh, yeah. Got the usual. You?"

"Yes. The usual."

He tipped his beer toward mine and said, "I guess it doesn't get any better than this."

"You think?" I said as I took a long swallow.

Quentin was a big man, maybe six feet, eight inches tall, which made him about four inches taller than me. His dark skin was course, the color of used oil draining from an engine after too many miles between oil changes. It may have been a matter of genetics or his skin may have been darkened further from multiple deployments to the Gulf and other god-forsaken places around the world. Probably both. He had recently retired from the Army with twenty-two years of active service and the rank of first sergeant. We shared a lot in common. I did twelve years in the Army, including one tour in Iraq and two in Afghanistan. I got out a sergeant first class. Quentin had four children, ages fifteen to eight. I had a three-year old daughter and another child, a boy, on the way. We were, by a pretty wide margin, the oldest cadets in the Charlotte-Mecklenburg police academy training program. The average cadet was twenty-three. I was pushing forty and Quentin was just on the other side of that mark. We were halfway through the formal training which would be followed by fifteen weeks with a field training officer. Then we would be rookie cops, but I would be a rookie with a twist.

I slid my plate onto the table and scooped the food onto it from the microwave container while we waited for Quentin's food to stop cooking.

"I think I've found a place for us in the mid-town area. It's a nice rental. They call it Dilworth," Quentin said, as he stood by the microwave. "I know Kia will like it. It's very artsy, with old style homes like the area in Atlanta where we both grew up. Multiple coffee shops. Lots of young women jogging behind baby carriages, so there are some perks for me, too." He laughed.

"Sure," I said. "Dilworth is real nice. But the schools are a challenge in Charlotte. You can't tell where your kids are going to school based on where you live. That's what I like about Darden County just west of Charlotte. The schools are more community based."

"I understand. Believe me, Kia is all over that and we'll probably do a combination of public and private schools with the four kids. Our two boys have been in Catholic schools. Seems like the girls do pretty well in public schools, but not the boys. Those nuns are tough. Amazes me how a four foot tall woman in a black dress can bring a six foot teenage boy to his knees just by looking at him."

I laughed. "Will Kia work outside of the home?"

"Oh, yeah. She likes to work for non-profits like United Way or something like that. You can usually get part-time hours in those organizations where they don't have to pay for benefits. We don't need the health insurance and other benefits due to my Army retirement." He sat down beside me, arranged his plate, and we both began eating our civilian version of meals ready to eat. "How about Erin? Will she get a job after you move?"

"I doubt it. Claire is just three and the new baby is three months away. She might work when the kids are in school like yours, but I'm thinking not until then."

"She was Army like us when you got married?" he asked between bites.

I laughed. "She was Army, but not like us. You and I were grunts in the trenches. She was a major, soon to be lieutenant colonel, but was working as an officer in Department of Homeland Security when we got married. She's a West Point grad."

"Really? You never told me that. So you married up?"

I laughed again. "Yeah, I guess I married up. She got wounded in the line of duty and, well, it's a long story. Anyway, we met and clicked and one thing led to another. We got married four years ago. I got out of the Army and got a job with a defense contractor near DC. We bought a house and started a family."

"But here you are trying to become a rookie cop in your old age?" He smiled and took a long drink of beer.

"Not as old as you, my friend. We'll see who finishes that three-mile run first in the morning." I punched him on an oversized arm, hoping he would not hit back. He was a big man. But he was a gentle giant. He just smiled.

"I just want to finish in less than thirty minutes. Slow and steady will do it for me," he said. "I don't think the chief expects us to compete with the twenty year olds on the three-mile run."

"Speak for yourself," I said. "I'm going for the gold."

~~~

It was raining when my alarm clock dragged me from a deep sleep at 5:30 a.m. the next morning. Quentin and I rode to the academy building together, a steady rain pelting the roof of the rental. We pulled into the parking lot at 5:55 a.m. still sipping large cups of hot coffee and chewing on sausage biscuits.

Fifteen men gathered in the men's locker room and changed into the uniform of the day, in this case, running shoes, shorts and tee-shirts. We met ten female cadets on the training grounds. We were a mix of men and women, Caucasian, African American, Hispanic, and two Asians, with an age range in the class from twenty-one to forty-two. All but three were college graduates. Two, including me, had masters degrees. The masters was one of the reasons I was here.

Not long after taking the job at Bechtel, I realized that I did not like working for a large corporation. I took advantage of my GI bill credits and enrolled in a graduate degree program in criminology at George Washington University. My thesis topic was Solving Cold Cases the Old Fashioned Way. One of Erin's cul-de-sac friends was a literary agent. She suggested that I try to convert the thesis into a book and she made a successful pitch to a small publishing company. The book, Finding Old Killers, was not a best seller, not even close, but it caught the attention of the new police chief at the Charlotte-Mecklenburg police department. The chief wrote me and said to give him a call if I ever wanted to change jobs. When the time came, I made that call.

Sergeant Pete Denton, the training officer in charge of our class, pulled the trainees together and reminded us of the rules for the mandatory three-mile run. Any cadet who did not finish the run in thirty minutes would be remanded to an extra hour of daily physical training for one week and then given another opportunity to pass the test. Failing a second time meant you were washed out of the program.

Twenty-five rookies with stop watches were assigned, one to each of us, to record our time. We started the run in a long staggered formation in a light rain.

I was not worried about it. After I left the Army four years prior I continued the military discipline of rigorous daily physical training. Erin was a runner and in excellent physical condition also. We ran together when childcare permitted until her pregnancy got in the way. I usually got in twenty or thirty miles every week. I was an early riser. My normal routine was to do pushups, sit-ups, and pull-ups every morning, rain or shine, regardless of how I felt, and to run four or five miles. I supplemented this daily running and exercise routine with two or three trips to the gym to lift weights. I was in excellent physical condition and completely confident that I could pass any physical exercise test of any kind at any time.

I gave Quentin a thumbs-up and took off around the oval track, my rookie cop staring intently at his stop watch. I checked my wristwatch, which had a timer, and saw that I had finished the first quarter mile in about seventy-five seconds, a pace I might not be able to sustain, so I slowed just slightly. My goal was to do the three miles in eighteen minutes, meaning I would average six-minute miles and I figured that would be good enough to put me in the top five of the twenty-five cadets taking the test.

It was. I finished third, caught my breath and tried to find Quentin in the group of remaining runners.

Given his size, finding Quentin was no challenge. I located the rookie who was clocking him. He told me he was cutting it pretty close. I ran up beside him on the inside of the track. His head was down and he was sucking wind. "You gotta pick it up, big man," I said.

He looked to the side at me and smiled, his big teeth white in the drizzling rain and early morning light. He did not say anything, but nodded. I thought he quickened his pace slightly.

I went back to the timer. "How is he doing?" I said.

"Better," the rookie answered, looking hard at his watch.

"Come on, Quentin," I said as he neared me on the turn. "Pick it up! Pick it up!" He nodded, smiled, and ran just a little faster.

I went back to the rookie and checked his time. It was better, but still close. I ran up beside him and started running alongside on the inside of the track and singing, *"Bo Diddley, Bo Diddley, have you heard? I'm gonna jump from a big iron bird."*

He smiled and started singing with me. *"C-130 going down the strip, airborne daddy gonna take a little trip,"* we sang together. *"Stand up, buckle up, shuffle to the door,"* some of the other cadets who had been in the Army picked up the tune with us, *"chutes gonna open on the count of four."*

Quentin was running well now and singing every word.

"If that chute don't open wide, I got another one by my side. If that chute don't open too, dress me up in my dress blues. Pin my wings upon my chest. Tell my girl I did my best. Go Bo Diddley. Go Bo Diddley go."

Quentin finished next to last, but it was twenty-nine minutes and thirty seconds. Just one cadet was remanded to remedial physical training.

~~~

Two months later we were in the last week of training. Erin and I were on a little bit of an upswing. She was less than a month away from delivering the baby. She seemed happy on our last call. I had found an acceptable place to rent while we built our new house on some land that my father had given us. We had talked about floor plans and Erin's talk with my sister about doctors and schools for Claire. Claire could have a dog and maybe, someday soon, a horse. She was packing and I would go up after graduation from the Charlotte-Mecklenburg police academy. We would drive together from northern Virginia to our new home just west of Charlotte.

~~~

I had just completed the final written tests at the academy and was on my way out of the front door when I nearly ran over Chief Nelson. The chief was a fireplug of a man, just five feet eight inches tall, but thick and muscular. His name was Norman Nelson which did not fit him very well. In a national search for a new chief a few years back, with just three candidates remaining, it was not clear that Chief Nelson would be selected. An exceptionally well-qualified candidate from Arizona seemed destined for the job. Tall and handsome, smooth and articulate, the Arizona candidate had a well-deserved national reputation. The current number two man in the department was also a strong candidate for the open job at that time. Chief Nelson was the only African American candidate among the finalists. When he got the job, there were whispers in the force and in the community that race had been the key factor. That may have been true to some degree, but no one who had any involvement with the chief since would think anything of the sort. No police chief anywhere in the country had ever worked harder or more effectively for his community than Chief Nelson. He was not just respected by every cop on the force, he was idolized. When he spoke in his quiet, authoritative voice, whether one-on-one or to a large group, he got the full attention and respect of his audience. His officers loved him and he reciprocated fully. He was the consummate professional. I was proud to call him my boss.

"Brad," he said.

"Yes, sir," I said, straightening as in a military attention.

"Son," he said, "sit here with me for a minute." Actually he was just a few years older than me, but I looked on him as a senior statesman.

There was a bench nearby and we sat together, side-by-side.

He was quiet for a few seconds. "Brad, I have some very bad news for you." Tears formed in his eyes. "Brad, your wife, Erin." He caught his breath. "I just got word that your wife has been killed."

I sat stunned for a few seconds. "Killed?"

"Yes," he said. He put his hand on my shoulder. "Murdered in your home last night. I'm taking you to the airport. The FBI will pick you up at Reagan National and take you to your home."

"Claire?" I said, catching my breath.

"Claire was not harmed physically as far as they can tell. She is with a neighbor, a pediatrician I think, in your neighborhood, and a social worker."

"Mary," I said, "the neighbor. I can't believe this." I tried to stand, but my legs were wobbly. I slid back onto the bench.

The chief helped me to my feet and we walked together to his waiting car.

I sat beside him in the back seat, completely dazed.

"I have asked Dr. Thornton to ride up with you and help you meet up with the FBI."

I didn't respond. Then I said, "The baby?"

"Brad," he said as softly as he could. "The baby is missing. That's why the FBI is involved."